BLESS 'EM ALL

BLESS 'EM ALL

Allen Saddler

PETER OWEN PUBLISHERS
LONDON AND CHESTER SPRINGS, PA, USA

F SADD

PETER OWEN PUBLISHERS
73 Kenway Road, London SW5 0RE

Peter Owen books are distributed in the USA by
Dufour Editions Inc., Chester Springs, PA 19425-0007

First published in Great Britain 2007 by
Peter Owen Publishers

ISBN 0 7206 1282 9

Printed and bound in Great Britain by
Windsor Print Production Ltd

For Doris,
with love and thanks

I

M RS Melrose's eyes provided a running commentary on what she was thinking – or maybe what she thought you were thinking. You couldn't help reacting to this signposted information, especially when the eyes were signalling that your desires had been registered and approved. Mrs Melrose, Bunty, was totally deaf and dumb and presented herself as a dumb blonde straight out of Busby Berkeley, but she was always ahead of you. Mrs Melrose had accepted her role as a glamour stereotype. She always managed to give the impression that she was lying around in a harem waiting to be ravished and was looking forward to the experience.

As well as the outrageous eyes there was the mouth: bright red and shiny, the mouth made exaggerated movements like a silent film star speeded up, registering anger, joy, ecstasy, fear. But, however much the mouth moved, however carefully each vowel was given its due, each consonant a spitting excess, no sound emerged. It was a graphic performance and conveyed such nuances of feelings that you might have wondered whether words and speech were strictly necessary.

Bunty was married to Tim. Tim worked for the water board. It was Tim's job to traverse the district on an official bicycle with a turnkey fixed on the bars to switch off the water when any leaks were reported and back on when the leaks were repaired.

You could see that Tim had a problem. He was a short, stumpy man, naturally surly, and married to this delicious confection, a creamy French sponge smelling of Turkish delight, a man magnet, a woman who was not only expecting trouble but inviting it. Tim had the job of fighting off the entire male population of London. If he shouted at her she couldn't hear. Her eyes would turn tragic. Her mouth would frame 'Sorry?', although it was clear that she didn't know why or for what she was apologizing, and Tim, realizing it was hopeless, would allow himself to be folded into her capacious breasts and comforted like a baby.

'That jumper is too tight,' Tim would mumble and point, and Bunty, thinking he was paying her a compliment, would turn and preen in profile, smiling knowingly.

Most afternoons, when Tim Melrose was riding around his patch, turning water on or off, Bunty Melrose was getting herself ready for a public appearance. Smart-looking men in hand-made suits would arrive in smart cars and sound a horn for Bunty, who, knowing that she wouldn't hear the signal, would be watching from the second-floor window. Bunty would come down, looking as though she was off for an audition for *42nd Street*, and climb into the car, the eyes working with flirtatious zeal, sitting beside the driver with an air of entitlement.

'She's off again,' said Mrs Bennet with some resentment mixed with admiration and envy. 'There'll be trouble when he finds out.'

It had always been a mystery how Bunty managed to be so well dressed and fashionable. Turnkey was an official job, and Tim had a tunic and peaked cap to prove it, but it wasn't in the fur-coat league. Bunty had bottles of perfume that didn't smell like they were from Boots the Chemist and an endless supply of bright-red lipstick and hair dye. Where did she go on these afternoon jaunts?

You had to admit that Bunty was a jolly good sort. Generous, outgoing, always fizzing off like champagne. Mrs Bennet, who tended to see the worst in everyone, warmed to Bunty.

'She's playing a dangerous game,' she said.

But was she? Surely Tim knew that his wages didn't stretch to the sort of black skirts and creamy blouses she wore. His glamorous wife had drawers of silk stockings and lacy underwear; she was at the hairdressers twice a week; she had so many shoes that she was able to share some with Mrs Bennet and other residents of the building, including young Mrs May, not long married, who blushed at the sight of silk stockings.

South London was full of such houses. Built at the time of Victorian prosperity, and occupied at the time by wealthy City businessmen who travelled to town by the Southern Railway, leaving their wives at home to cope with umpteen children, to bully the maid and send tradesmen around to the back. The houses were built three storeys high, with rough stairs leading down to a basement. They were a scaled-down version of the grand town house.

The ground floor contained the living-room, with the kitchen at the back; the second floor the bedrooms and the top tiny attic rooms for the live-in maid. The basement might be let to an odd-job man at a concessionary rate but included the proviso that he do all the odd jobs around the house when required.

The prosperous citizens had always regarded their stay in one of the houses as temporary. There would always be the chance of a rise to a higher level, a promotion from office to board. Now run-down and in disrepair, these houses had acquired a seedy sheen. None of the houses was occupied by a single family any longer; all were divided up into flats and floors, with disputed landings, sometimes with up to a dozen people living in the various sections.

Number seventy-seven was in the middle of a terrace. The owner-landlord was never seen, all the rents were collected by an agency. Occasionally, when a tenant got hopelessly behind, a small market barrow would be piled high with all somebody owned and wheeled away, with the owner following, as though owner and effects were on their way to the crematorium.

Bunty and Tim had the middle flat. It was favoured because the bathroom and toilet were on the same level. The other residents had to endure the inconvenience of banging on the door of the toilet or bathroom when Bunty was inside, knowing that she couldn't hear. The only way to obtain relief was by poking a piece of paper under the door. Of course there was always the chance of seeing Bunty in her open dressing-gown scuttling away to the bedroom.

In the basement, below ground level, were the Penroses. Bert Penrose, a wiry music-hall figure with Charlie Chaplin moustache and rakish bowler, did something mysterious in the West End. He carried an air of a daring man about town, and he would burst into a suggestive dance without warning, the climax always involving two fingers poked into the air in a triumphant gesture of lewd glee. Bert was a comic figure with slipping false teeth but thought he was irresistible to women. Bert's confidence was beyond all logic and reason. His wife, Edie, was plain and resigned. She regarded her husband's daring pursuit of the blonde Bunty as inevitable. The fact that Bunty was stone deaf released Bert's tongue:

'Lovely bit of crackling, aren't you? Yes, I could slip you a length.

Any time you like . . .' and Bert would lick his lips as though he was savouring a succulent piece of fillet steak. Bunty, without hearing the words but getting the gist of the sly smile that accompanied them, would smile uneasily and look anxiously around for the protection of her husband, who was never there at the time.

If you could have taken a side view of number seventy-seven, opened out like a dolls' house, you would have seen four levels of seething activity. There was young Mrs May on the top floor, with the one tiny maid's room, which was half filled by a bed, and an even smaller kitchen. Mrs May spent most of the day lying on the bed, daydreaming. Mr May – Stephen, never Steve – worked in a local department store. He always looked immaculate in shirts lovingly ironed by Mrs May, drifting on a cloud of romantic love as seen in the latest release in the cinema. Stephen got cast in all the romantic leads, ancient and modern. Mr May was often out late. He said that various departmental managers invited him for drinks, and that he had to go as to refuse would seal his fate in his present position. It might even endanger it. Mrs May wanted him to get on, didn't she? There had to be sacrifices at this early stage.

The middle was Bunty and Tim, and the ground floor was Mrs Bennet, a widow, who hardly ever went out. In some mysterious way Mrs Bennet seemed to have control over the building and its occupants. She was the tenant who had been there longest and seemed to have a special relationship with the agency that collected the rents. If any of the tenants needed a repair to a blocked sink or a stuck window, Mrs Bennet would take the matter in hand, and in due course, which was usually a month, a repair would be effected.

From time to time Bunty's mother would call. She was stony-faced, but her eyes had a twinkle, especially when relishing the exploits of her daughter, which Bunty explained with expressive hand gestures and facial contortions. Bunty read her mother's reactions through her expressions. Bunty had never learnt to lip-read. She didn't need to.

The inevitable slip-up occurred one afternoon when Tim spun around the corner on his bike and saw Bunty getting out of a smart car and entering the house. Tim parked his bike and went up the stairs carrying his turnkey in his hand. There was shouting and scuffling, and Mrs Bennet, knowing that Bunty could not scream out if she was hurt, went up to see fair play. There was Tim, red-flushed with rage, and Bunty flashing frightened eyes, with the heavy indentation of the turnkey on a cushion beside her.

Mrs Bennet fumbled in her handbag for a small bottle of smelling salts.

'You'll have to stop this. This is a respectable house.'

'You don't know what she's been doing,' he shouted.

'Don't you shout at me,' said Mrs Bennet, puffing herself up into a formidable figure. 'I don't care what she's done. Poor thing, she doesn't know what you're saying.'

'She knows.'

The fact was that Tim did know what Bunty was up to and hoped that he wouldn't have to deal with the situation, but, having seen what he saw, felt that he had to register his disapproval. Bunty picked up the telephone and dialled her mother's number. The mother knew that if the telephone rang and, on answering, she could only hear stifled gulps, Bunty was in trouble.

By the time parental support had arrived Tim had calmed down.

'What do you expect her to do? Sit here on her own all day? She's entitled to a bit of life.'

'Where does she go then? Drinking clubs with dirty old men?'

'They appreciate her more than you do.'

'She's a dirty cow.'

Bunty's mother smiled. She couldn't help it. Bunty's face, just behind Tim's indignant features, was registering mock indignation. Bunty wasn't taking any of this seriously. It was just a game. Tim would have to take her as he found her.

Mrs May's troubled young face appeared at the door.

'Is everything all right?'

Having gone through his ritual explosion Tim was prepared to simmer. 'Sure. I lost my temper. You've no idea how hard it is to get through to her.'

'She likes to get out,' said Bunty's mother.

'Of course,' said young Mrs May.

'How would it be if, er . . . What's your name?'

'May. Mrs.'

'How would it be if Mrs – here – went with her?'

Young Mrs May blushed down as far as anyone could see. 'Oh. I don't know about that.'

'It's nothing. Just dancing, that's all.'

'I could ask my husband.'

'That's up to you. No harm in it. Anyway, you wouldn't be involved. Just company for Bunty.'

Tim, brooding in a corner, suddenly looked at Mrs May. 'What your name?'

'Mrs –'

'No. Your name.'

'Betty.'

'Betty and Bunty. Bloody hell.'

'Very nice,' said Bunty's mother. 'Very appropriate.'

The seed was sown. It burst open in the imagination of the young Mrs May and in the scheming mind of Mrs Melrose, who knew how to make it flower into reality. The next day Bunty and Betty were as close as rabbits. Bunty, with hand beckoning and beseeching eyes, brought Betty into the flat and brought out drawers of fine clothes, the sight of which made Betty May feel as though she had committed a mortal sin. There were brassières and camisoles, silk slips and knickers and silk stockings by the yard. With daring eyes and gestures Bunty indicated that Betty should try some on, and Betty, red-faced with embarrassment, took off her plain sweater and skirt and allowed the creamy silk to ripple against her flesh. Getting bolder, Betty tried on daring garments and felt transformed from Cinderella to film-star glory. These were not young girls playing at dressing up; these were grown women bringing about a transformation, a change that would have a permanent effect on the outlook and personality of the younger woman.

'Dancing clubs,' said Bunty's mother. 'Afternoons. You get taken and brought back.'

Betty May felt a surge of excitement. 'But what do you have to do?'

'Just dance.'

'With?'

'With men who want to dance. You partner up.'

'And then?'

'Well, if they're pleased with you they might give you a present.'

Betty was puzzled. 'Just for dancing with them?'

'Yes. That's all. It's up to you what you do after.'

Bunty's mother was getting impatient. Wouldn't the stupid girl ever catch on? Did she want a map or something?

'Look. Go along with Bunty. See if you like it.'

'But does Bunty like it?'

'She does,' said Bunty's mother firmly. 'She certainly does.'

That night Betty May thought about telling Stephen of the invitation, but somehow she didn't get around to it. After all, there was no harm in dancing with a partner in a place that was designated for such a purpose. She didn't know anything about the place yet. Wouldn't it be better to try it out before bothering Stephen? She may not like the place and never go again. In which case it would be making a fuss about nothing.

One afternoon Bunty dyed Betty's brown mousy hair blonde. Lipstick and makeup were applied, and when the two women, side by side, looked into the mirror, they looked like sisters. The only difference was in the eyes: one pair was slow and knowing, the other bright and excited.

Stephen was enchanted with his wife's new hair. It aroused something embedded in his mind. Blondes were fast and willing. This new Betty was a temptation – and, what's more, she wasn't a film fantasy. She was available. She was his.

When Betty and Bunty went out together it was watched with considerable interest by all the other occupants of the house. Bert was home, and he peered over the top of his dug-out with wonder and want. Mrs Bennet's expression showed that Bunty had already taken the fatal step to perdition and was now encouraging Betty down the same primrose path. Betty was trembling. She didn't know whether it was with excitement or fear. Dancing with someone didn't seem a crime. She used to go a lot with Stephen when they first met. She became quite good at it and delighted at the feeling of being swept around on a cloud in waltz time. When she came out of the dance hall she always felt lighter and somehow happier. She knew it was all illusion, but that didn't matter at the time.

The granite-faced man who drove the car showed no sign or feeling. It was just a job. Pick up two women and deposit them as instructed.

2

Maurice Green was a grey man. Not only his hair but his face, too, and his hands seemed like they had been powdered with grey dust. He gave the impression of a man who was enduring an existence rather than living a life. Every day was a fresh burden to be borne with a resigned boredom. He was fed up with the modern world, with its fads and fancies. Most of the time he was fed up with his family and his wife, too. He was fifty now, and he wasn't looking forward to the rest of his life or to his retirement.

Maurice was tall and heavy, with a serious churchwarden's face. He was a director of a wholesale booksellers. It was an old-established firm, which he controlled with his brother Bernard and his sister Bella. Their father, who had started the business before the turn of the century, bequeathed the firm to them. When old George died the trio found that they had equal shares in the business. Maurice wanted to keep the concern ticking over, Bernard wanted to expand and Bella wanted to sell, a situation that set up a lifelong dispute between the three, as they all had to agree on a course of action before it could be taken.

Maurice loved the business how it was, the warehouse with its rows of bookshelves, all categorized by subject and author. He looked along the narrow corridors between the shelves with pride and reverence. The books were to be respected. Who knew how many hours had gone into the creation of just one book? There were the bestsellers – *The Arches of the Years*, *The Bridge Over San Luis Ray*, *Gone With the Wind*, *Anthony Adverse* – the up-and-coming Cronin with his new one, *The Citadel*, and the latest bleat from Wells and blast from Shaw. There was the entire output of the Everyman Library, which covered every corner of history and knowledge as well as a comprehensive selection of the greatest novels ever written and now approached one thousand noted volumes. There was the religious section – H.V. Morton and Hall Caine – and there were even browning leaves of novels by Marie

Corelli, whole sets of Dickens, Hardy and Trollope. Then there were the current detective and crime novels, which were having a vogue – Freeman Wills Croft, Oppenheim, Sydney Horler, Anthony Berkeley, Agatha Christie, John Buchan, 'Sapper', with his slapdash tales of Bulldog Drummond and foreign spies and murky plotting, smart-arsed Peter Cheyney with his sardonic private eye Lemmy Caution, Leslie Charteris's Saint – all best-sellers when they first came out but soon replaced by the next novel by the same writer. Writers seemed to turn out a book every year – Dornford Yates and P.G. Wodehouse might even go faster than that, although Edgar Wallace probably still held the record.

In the biography section were names associated with politics, sport, maybe, and memoirs of anybody who had ever been a headline in public life. For some reason Maurice thought that he was responsible for the good standing of all these people. There was Freud, Adler and Jung, Marx and Plato. One didn't have to agree with the views advanced by any of these persuaders, but they had earned their place.

When war was declared Maurice didn't think it would last long. The cost of waging war was enormous. England's economy was hardly stable, and Germany had never recovered from the 1914–18 bash. The war wouldn't last long for the simple fact that nobody could afford it.

Green's had taken on new staff: Jimmy, a sixteen-year-old post boy, and Miss Tcherny, an invoice clerk. The Tchernys – father, mother and daughter – were from Austria. They were Jews who had become frightened at their treatment in their homeland, and had decided to flee well in advance of trouble. News leaking out of Europe showed that their fears had been justified: Jews, if you could believe the reports, were being locked up, persecuted and insulted. Maurice knew that it could be propaganda, maybe to persuade wealthy British Jews to give financial support to the war effort.

Miss Tcherny was plump and pretty, with dark eyes and slightly frizzy black hair. She wore tight jumpers, crimson lips and blue eye-shadow. Despite the fact that she had lived in Britain since her early teens she still had traces of an accent and could say some disconcerting things – 'I don't look very good in a bathing costume, but I look quite good without it' – that caused young Jimmy to splutter, red-faced, into his tea mug.

When Maurice received an order he took the list along the shelves, picking out the books requested, lifting them out, shaking off the dust, sometimes cleaning up the jacket with an India rubber, making a neat pile for packing and post for Harry the packer. Maurice knew that expansion, particularly the kind that Bernard had in mind, would lead to a downgrading of the business, to mass orders of the latest sensations, such as *No Orchids for Miss Blandish* and the latest American crime trash. The firm had standards, a position in the trade. Small booksellers in all parts of the country relied on Green's by-return service. They knew that, however obscure, however out of the way the request, that Green's would supply. If they hadn't got it in stock they would send somebody out to the publishers with an order that would be fetched back in a collector's canvas sack the same day. They knew that Green's stocked up on books that were going out of print, hoarding them like precious manuscripts. It had taken years to build up the stock. And they knew that Maurice was dedicated to this service.

It was Bernard who had started to supply dubious bookshops in Soho with the type of book that Maurice thought let the firm down. The 'Leicester Square Run' stock had a special flavour: books about prostitution and the 'white-slave' trade, *The Road to Buenos Aries*, *The Awful Disclosures of Maria Monk*, *Brother and Sister*, the published books of D.H. Lawrence, soft paperbacks by Paul Renin – translated from the original French – and what Maurice thought were pseudo-scientific volumes about sex by Havelock Ellis, practical help from Marie Stopes and all kinds of horrors about sadism and masochism, along with what were called 'studies of the photographic art', which turned out to be photographs of naked women. What would you think of a firm that supplied a book called *Psychopathia Sexualis*?

It was a quick turnover, and these books sold in dozens, not ones and twos. It was, as Bernard frequently pointed out, 'money for jam', but Maurice was unhappy with the connection. After all, he was still a Sunday-school teacher in the local Baptist church. If the Soho connection was made with his church activities he could soon find himself pilloried in the *News of the World* or the *People*.

Bernard, with his raffish ties and hound's-tooth jackets, was a constant source of annoyance, but the formidable Bella, with her imposing bosom and countersunk eyes, was a different proposition. While Maurice used gentle and, ultimately, good-humoured persuasion, Bella's method was scorn: 'messing about with bits of paper', she called the order business; 'fiddling with pennies' was how she described the small discount the firm got from the publishers to handle their wares. It was true that the margin on orders was of the order of 3 per cent, but it was the volume of business that made it worth while. For Maurice, providing a service – to the publishers, to the authors, to the bookshops and to the pubic – was all the justification he needed.

It was strange how different from one another the two brothers were. You could see the family resemblance in their faces, but any similarity ended there. Maurice's dark suit, stiff collar and neatly knotted tie, his expression of resigned disdain, his eyes seeing nothing they liked, enduring the modern world with pain and distaste, contrasted with Bernard's sly grin and clockwork wink, his eyes full of merriment and anticipation of roguery to come. Bernard was open to everything life had to offer. He loved his canvassing of the bookshops on his Soho patch, swapping stories, leaving a trail of sniggering females in his wake. The war had brought with it a loosening of morals. London was a garrison town, with thousands of servicemen on short-leave passes, trying to grab a weekend of fun before returning to a life of drab meaningless drilling, unnecessary guarding and pointless discipline. There might be a time when they would have to face up to the Germans, when, as likely as not, they would be killed. With that prospect in view, who could blame their desperate search for pleasure?

There were many for whom the war had opened out new horizons, new positions of authority, new outlets for previously unrecognized organizational abilities; people who had missed their place in life, who had spent decades looking for the right niche. Maurice's wife, Clare, had suddenly become a figure of authority in the WVS. She knew that she had been born to boom over lesser creatures. Maurice and Clare lived together but only at a distance. They shared the same house, ate meals together, took holidays in harness, slept in the same bed, but the separation was deep. Clare soon realized that she had married a stick-in-the-mud. She couldn't bear the adolescent Bernard, but he was, at least, a person with whom you could tangle, whereas Maurice seemed almost removed from the world. He lived with thousands of books, not with her. When he was at home she knew that he would much prefer to be in his warehouse. After the early perfunctory love-making Clare and Maurice tailed off into a comfortable celibacy. It was clear that Maurice couldn't be bothered, and Clare wasn't going to beg. So they had not had children, and now it was too late.

One wintry afternoon, when the warehouse lights had been on all day, Maurice was enjoyably engaged in stocktaking. He turned a corner between the shelves and came across Miss Tcherny reading Rider Haggard's *She*.

'You like adventure stories?' he said.

'I don't know,' said Miss Tcherny. 'I've never read any. I thought this was about . . . a woman.'

'It is,' said Maurice. 'It is.'

He squeezed by Miss Tcherny's bulging frame. He was close to her, but she was looking away. He could smell the warmth emanating from her body, see her glistening lips close up. Maurice's face showed no expression of any kind, and yet he was quite moved by the encounter. Miss Tcherny looked undisturbed, as though a man squeezing against her was all in a day's work. After all, she came to work in the Tube.

A little later Bernard was packing his bag of samples.

'On your rounds again?' said Maurice.

'It's the only thing that keeps this place going,' replied Bernard belligerently.

Maurice thought that Bernard's appearance resembled that of a door-to-door salesman. Green's had never canvassed for business. Maurice knew that Bernard's excursions brought in the money, but they could have managed without it. After all, the three of them owned the business outright. There were no shareholders demanding results. The business was free of debt. There were no bank loans to cause sleepless nights.

'You know it wouldn't do you any harm to come out on my round,' said Bernard. 'See how the real world lives. The way business is done.'

'Somebody has to look after the shop,' said Maurice lightly.

'You mean you want to keep your hands clean. You don't mind taking the money, as long as you don't have anything to do with the getting of it. You make me sick.' This was strong, even for Bernard. Mostly Bernard showed his amiable side, but Maurice was aware of the vicious side beneath. 'Do you think the troops want to read Shakespeare? Do you?' Bernard had a nasty glint in his eye. He didn't mind doing all the footwork, quite enjoyed it in fact, but he didn't see why he should be looked down upon for doing it. 'Censorship. That's what you want. Telling people what they can read and what they can't.'

The two brothers had always been at loggerheads. They had been to the same private school, Maurice two forms higher than Bernard. Maurice's schoolwork had been exemplary, while Bernard's was dubbed 'slapdash'. As the elder, Maurice had been favoured by their parents. He always had the knack of looking presentable, while Bernard always looked as if he could do with a good wash and tidy. The situation of the joint ownership had only increased the tension between them.

Maurice was about to retort to his brother's challenge when he saw the telltale signs of mouse droppings. The staff at Green's fought a ceaseless battle with the mice. The little creatures were numerous and destructive, and many a book was found to have holes gnawed through its pages. Just a slight trail of dust could lead to another chewed volume. And the mice always seemed to go for the most expensive books. Maurice had tried to insure against them, but no company would take the risk. He had set traps and brought cats into the premises, although the smell they created had made the exercise counter-productive. This time he actually saw a grey furry ball shoot under a heap of packing paper.

'Under there,' he shouted, and Bernard grabbed a huge dictionary and stood guard as Maurice raked the paper with a packing stick.

'Come on,' Bernard called, and soon young Jimmy and Miss Tcherny were lined up with heavy tomes to drop on the mouse as it made its escape. It did, of course, skittering deftly between the crashing books, neatly disappearing under the floorboards.

'Bugger,' said Bernard, looking crestfallen. Maurice looked at his brother and suddenly felt some compassion. Bernard had carved out a niche for himself. He wasn't any good in the warehouse. His sloppy methods only caused mistakes and refunds. Maurice knew that Bernard was better employed away from the business as much as possible. In the circumstances, Bernard had done something on his own initiative that suited Maurice fine.

It may have been the disturbance of the brief encounter with Miss Tcherny, or the feeling of compassion for his brother, or the exhilaration brought on by the mouse hunt. It may have been the situation of the war in which nobody knew what was going to happen. It may have been the realization that he was safely in his middle age and would soon start to go down the other side of the hill. Who knows what groundwork forms a decision that is quite out of character? 'Come on,' he said to the astonished Bernard. 'I'll come with you.'

The two brothers left the premises with a light step. Both thought they were on some sort of a spree. Maurice felt unaccountably light-hearted. He was indulging his younger brother in his fantasy. Bernard thought he was going to introduce his staid, bookish brother to a slice of real life.

They walked down Ludgate Hill, passing Cassell's publishing office in La Belle Sauvage Yard, crossed the circus into Fleet Street, where intricate courts and uneven paved-stone lanes snaked behind the imposing buildings of Fleet Street. These housed a number of small publishing houses: Foulshams, with their famous *Old Moore's Almanack*; Watts, with their vest-pocket-sized Thinker's Library, each book a classic of speculative theories, Logical Positivism or economic propositions, all under the umbrella of the Rationalist Press. Just up Farringdon Road was Mills and Boon, with their shop-girl romances, and on the left, behind New Bridge Street, was the home of the Collins empire and its Crime Club imprint, with at least a dozen top crime writers on the books. In among these thin winding courts was Whittaker's, the Almanac people, and several other small concerns with specialist stocks.

The two brothers debated whether to hail a taxi but decided that, as it was dry and bright, to continue their stroll to the Strand. Fleet Street wasn't very long. As soon as you passed the stern grandeur of the *Telegraph* and the ebony-and-glass box of the *Daily Express* – christened by some wag as 'King Kong's lavatory' because of the huge rolls of newsprint often seen being unloaded into the print-shop bay – you were at Chancery Lane and up to the Law Courts. At this point Bernard was able to signal to a taxi from the Bush House rank. He muttered something to the driver that the driver seemed to recognize, and they set off along the Strand. At Trafalgar Square the taxi went around into Charing Cross Road. The two brothers got out at Cambridge Circus and started walking up the side of the Palace Theatre into Soho.

It was a district that Maurice had scarcely visited. He knew its reputation: the haunt of prostitutes and queers, foreign restaurants – Chinese, Italian, Jewish – raffish pubs with their Bohemian clientele, the catering-trade wholesalers, Wardour Street, home of the film industry. On the outskirts – bordered by Leicester Square and Shaftesbury Avenue, Charing Cross Road and Oxford Street – there were scruffy but enticing bookshops with a furtive air that gave the impression that there was more inside than could be seen in the window.

As they visited shop after shop Maurice felt that he had made the wrong decision in accompanying Bernard. There was something rather sordid about the whole business. The people who ran these shops were not bookish types. Many of them were plainly foreigners who communicated by gestures and flashing eyes. Bernard seemed to understand them. They were sharp salesmen, but often women, who looked as though they had never read a book in their lives. Books, to these people, were a commodity to be turned over as quickly as possible. They didn't know or care anything about writing, about literature. It was a wonder that they didn't weigh the books on a scale and sell them by the pound.

Bernard laid out the new titles like a conjuror producing grubby deformed rabbits from a hat. He wasn't aware that he was being devalued by even mixing with these people. The women, brass- or copper-haired and fur-coated, smelling of whisky and foreign cigarettes, were the worst. After a particularly unsavoury encounter Maurice felt that he had seen enough. This was Bernard's world and he was welcome to it.

'I think I'd better get back,' he said.

'Nearly finished,' said Bernard. 'Tell you what. Let's go for a drink, and then we'll call it a day.'

Maurice was aware that the pubs closed at two o'clock and didn't officially open again until six, so he thought that Bernard was suggesting tea or coffee.

'All right,' he said. 'Where shall we go?'

They weren't far from Lyons' Corner House in Coventry Street. Maurice liked the atmosphere in these places, the smart interiors, like Eastern palaces, the courteous service, but Bernard went deeper into the heart of Soho and found a house at the end of an alley that didn't look like a café or anything resembling one.

'We'll go in here,' he said.

Maurice accepted that Bernard must know his way around his patch and, despite the unlikeness of the exterior, accepted that this must be some kind of small hotel or guest-house that Bernard had got to know. Inside, there was a small vestibule for coats, from which a bored middle-aged woman in a black dress and lots of hanging jewellery was issuing cloakroom tickets. Somewhere in the background a pianist was playing softly, and there was the swish of drum brushes. Bernard made for the door and indicated that Maurice should follow.

As the door opened Maurice could hear voices and the music got louder. Maurice went in.

It was only a small room, dimly lit by wall lights. There were small tables with chairs for four people at each, and there was a clear square of floor space in the middle. At the top end of the room a languid pianist and an automatic drummer tinkled and scraped away as though the pair of them were locked in a trance. The pianist was black, the drummer big and swarthy. In the space in the middle, couples were slowly dancing: some very pretty girls and a collection of older men.

'What is this place?' Maurice asked.

'The Hostess Club,' said his brother. 'If you fancy a dance you just help yourself.'

They sat down and a waitress appeared.

'Two gin and tonics,' Bernard said. 'And put some in.'

'Just for you,' she said, and smiled a gap-toothed smile.

Maurice was surprised. Drinks in the middle of the afternoon? 'Are you a member?'

'I am,' said Bernard with an air of satisfaction. Bernard, with his halo of light hair encircling his bald crown, was like a schoolboy out to shock his elders.

Just opposite their table were two blonde women. One looked hard faced and confident, the other seemed a bit nervous. Bernard beckoned to the hard-faced one, and she got up, beaming, joining the two brothers at the table.

'Bring your friend,' said Bernard loudly, and gestured in the direction of the other woman. The first woman turned back, and her companion, younger and prettier, shuffled with embarrassment. 'Come on,' said Bernard, and she blushed and looked worried.

'This is Bunty,' said Bernard, by way of introduction. Bunty smiled a toothpaste smile and pulled down the top of her blouse, preening herself in a frank and obvious manner. 'Who's your friend?' said Bernard, looking over at the younger woman. Bunty pouted as though she was a trifle put out at Bernard's interest in her companion. She patted the seat of the empty chair, and the other woman got shyly to her feet and came over.

'What's your name, love?' Bernard asked, and the embarrassed woman muttered something that no one could hear. 'Speak up,' said Bernard. 'We all want to know.'

'It's Betty,' said the woman, obviously wishing that she were at home scrubbing the floor or peeling spuds – anywhere but here.

'Good,' said Bernard, smiling a wolfish smile. 'This is my brother, Maurice.' Bunty flashed Maurice a bright smile, but the one called Betty looked down at the floor.

'Would you like to dance?' Bernard said, standing up, and Bunty, thinking that this was her cue, stood up and held out her arms. Bernard, aware that he had drawn the short straw, good-naturedly grasped Bunty around the waist and set off. There wasn't much room for dancing, so the couples stayed close together, swaying as one, but hardly moving from the spot where they had started. Maurice, left with the clearly unhappy Betty, thought that something in the way of gallantry was required of him. He cleared his throat.

'Er, um. Would *you* like to dance?' Betty stood up, still looking at the floor. Bernard took her hands, holding her stiffly at a distance, as if they were at some strict and formal aristocratic ball. Once on her feet Betty relaxed: this was what she had come for, to dance. This Maurice might be a bit on the ancient side, but he was undoubtedly a gentleman. He hadn't pressed himself against her, which was how all the other women in the room were being treated. He wasn't much of a dancer; he was too stiff and jerky. She looked up at him. He seemed nice enough. The couple kept on around the tiny dance floor, twice as fast as any of the other couples, and when the pianist stopped playing Maurice gravely escorted Betty back to her seat.

'Thank you, dear,' he said. 'Very pleasant.'

'Yes,' said Betty desperately. 'I enjoyed it.' She looked around for Bunty, who seemed to have disappeared along with Bernard.

'Would you like a drink?' Maurice asked politely. After all it wasn't the poor girl's fault they were trapped in this awkward situation.

'Thank you,' said Betty. 'Could I have a small sherry?' A small sherry was a polite drink. Not enough to do any harm but just enough to show that she wasn't stand-offish.

'Have you been here before?' Maurice asked.

'No. Never.' Betty shook her head. 'I don't think I should have come. I thought it would be a big place – you know, with a band and lots of people.'

Maurice called the waitress. 'A small sherry. I'll have a whisky.'

'I can't stay long,' Betty said, looking anxious.

'No. Nor can I. I wonder what happened to Bernard.'

'He'll be down in a minute,' said the waitress, sidling up with the drinks.

'Bit of a dim place,' said Maurice. 'Not my idea of fun.'

Betty sipped her drink. 'Are you, er, in business?' She didn't really care whether Maurice was an international tycoon or a dustman. She just thought that she ought to contribute something in exchange for the small sherry.

'Yes,' said Maurice, slightly surprised at the girl's interest. 'The book trade.'

'Oh,' said Betty. 'That sounds interesting,'

'Yes. It is. Do you do much reading?'

'Not lately. I used to.'

'Oh, really?' said Maurice. 'And what kind of thing did you like?' Betty desperately raked her memory for books glimpsed in her schooldays.

'*Little Women*,' she replied.

'Ah,' said Maurice. 'An old favourite.'

'What kinds of books do you have?'

'All kinds,' said Maurice, in a matter-of-fact way. There was no need to boast. 'A whole big warehouse, full of books of all kinds. We fill orders for the bookshops. We have a massive stock. Taken years to build up.' Maurice was sure he was boring the poor girl into a coma, and yet she seemed impressed. 'Do you want to dance again?'

'No, I don't think so,' said Betty. 'I'd much rather hear about your old books.' So Maurice explained about the service he supplied. How he thought he was doing something worth while. And then he saw Bernard, looking flushed, with the other woman called Bunty, her eyes bright and knowing. Bernard slumped down in the chair next to Maurice. Maurice noticed that Bernard was sweating.

'It's all laid on, if you want it,' he said heavily. 'I'd taken a shine to yours, but I couldn't shake Bunty off.'

Maurice frowned. 'What the . . . Good Lord, Bernard. Is this a knocking shop?'

Bernard looked at his brother with a quizzical grin. 'If it isn't I don't know what we're doing here. I don't like dancing, and this is washing-up sherry – and they're not giving it away.'

Maurice looked at Betty. Was she aware of the kind of place she was at and what was expected of her?

'Oh go on,' said Bernard. 'A couple of quid will cover it.'

After years of loveless nights with Clare, Maurice's sense of sexual adventure had practically died from lack of use. He doubted whether he could ever be aroused again. He stood up, and Betty, thinking she was being asked to dance again, got up and stood ready to whirl off. But Maurice grabbed her by the arm and made for the door, pulling the startled girl with him. In the street he linked arms with her and strode away quickly from the building, with Betty clattering along beside him, breathless from trying to keep up.

'What's the matter?' Betty gulped.

'That place. Do you know what it was?'

'A club. A club for dancing.'

'No. It was more than that.' Maurice slowed down. 'Where do you live?'

'It's all right. I can get the bus.'

Maurice stopped and looked down. The girl was clearly puzzled, out of her depth. She almost looked like a child, playing at dressing up in her mother's clothes.

'Come on,' he said. 'We'll have a cup of tea somewhere.'

Tea at the Corner House was hardly racy, but the odd pair found the pseudo-posh atmosphere more to their liking.

'Why did you go there with that woman?'

'She's Bunty. She lives downstairs. She's a good sort.'

'Maybe, but she's a tart, isn't she?'

'I don't know. She's a poor thing. She's deaf and dumb.'

'I wouldn't count on that,' said Maurice. 'Tell me, what do you do all day?'

'I'm married,' said Betty. 'Stephen works, but I stay home. I make the tea, but I never really know when he's coming in.'

The girl seemed lost. She had got married at eighteen in Liverpool, her home town. Then her husband, who was a floor-walker with British Home Stores, got a London posting. She didn't know anyone in London, so, when her husband went off to work, she was alone all day in her tiny flat. She seemed to be entirely without thought or personal ambition. He mind was a blank canvas, and yet she was pleasant enough, eager to please and too well aware of her shortcomings.

'Would you like a job?' he said, on the spur of the moment.

'What, with all them books?'

'You could do worse,' Maurice said. 'Just being there is an education in itself.'

They dawdled over cream cakes, and Maurice began to feel very confident and relaxed. After all, the girl was young enough to be his daughter. He enjoyed the fatherly role, *in loco parentis*, as it were, to instruct and inform this almost entirely virgin intellect. She wasn't sure about coming to work for him. He gave her one of his business cards, which seemed to delight her no end.

'My,' she said. 'You've got your name all printed out.'

He grinned. It was like being out with a child. 'It's just for business.'

The one area where she had some expertise was in the latest films. Betty and her husband went on Wednesdays, which was half-day closing for the shop. She liked love stories and musicals, but not westerns. 'I hate westerns,' she said. 'All that riding and shooting. What do you hate most in all the world?'

Maurice didn't need to think. 'Mice,' he said. 'Mice.'

3

Y OUNG Jimmy Fosset stopped outside an eating-house in
Carter Lane. It was under a railway arch. All the dishes were in
the window, kept warm on hotplates from a gas burner. There were
metal trays of sizzling sausages, fried onions, pease pudding,
faggots and saveloys, sliced slivers of ham and beef and pork with
crackling. The shop was full of standing diners – there were no seats
– with their plates on a shelf running along three walls that were
dripping with condensation. Jimmy pressed his nose to the window,
but he couldn't smell anything. He opened the door and went in,
and the smell, warm and oily, assaulted his nostrils. It was predom-
inately of burnt onions, but there were traces of hot beef dripping
and an occasional sniff of boiled ham. Jimmy hovered behind a
group of men at the counter, piping up when he saw a clearing.

'Two sausages and a penn'orth of pease.'

'Please.'

'I said pease, didn't I?'

'Oho. Clever stuff, eh? Onions?'

'No onions. Gravy.'

'You get gravy. Thruppence.'

Jimmy took the warm plate to the shelf by the wall. There was
just room for him to squeeze in between two burly diners, scoffing
quickly, like pigs in a trough. Globules of condensation dripped
from the ceiling, sometimes plopping on to their plates. He soon
ate the warm swill, dousing the pease pudding in the gravy and
chasing it on to a slice of bread. It was warm and quick and left him
with enough for a penny bar of Cadbury's to eat on his round.

On this side of Ludgate Hill was T. Werner Laurie, who
published some of the books that Bernard dealt with – *The
Cautious Amorist* came from there. Also, in Carter Lane itself, was
Hutchinson's, who published a string of crime writers, including the
prolific Dennis Wheatley with his novelty Crime Dossiers – loose-
leaf folios with maps, plans of houses where a crime had been
committed and little envelopes containing lipsticked cigarette ends,

fingerprints, hairs and dust and fragments of letters to help solve the crime. Hutchinson's also published biographies of the stars of stage and screen. Further along were Routledge and Kegan Paul, which was all serious stuff about something called psychology. Sometimes Routledge's stuff was heavy, although not as heavy as Dean's Rag Books, the indestructible books for very young children, and Jimmy would go back to empty his sack on the other side of the hill, where all the publishing houses were gathered in the shade of St Paul's.

It was Paternoster Row and Warwick Square where the bulk of Jimmy's collecting took place: Nelson's on the corner, then Longman's, then Sweet and Maxwell. Along Paternoster Row every building seemed to house a publishing office, and they all had trade counters where Jimmy would sit on a polished wooden bench waiting his turn. In Warwick Square he could spend a comfortable ten minutes with the young girl at Hodder and Stoughton – staring at her until she became embarrassed and blushed – which was conveniently situated alongside the Oxford University Press.

You could walk around the bulk of British publishers in ten minutes. There were some out-of-the-way firms in the West End – Constable, Michael Joseph, Fabers – others, like Warne and Dent, near to Covent Garden, and even one awkward one in the City, John Murray, but most of them were within easy reach of Green's.

Jimmy had got used to his round, and was able to cut corners to give him time to dawdle outside the Old Bailey and sometimes pop into the public gallery to see the theatrical trial of some murderer or financial swindler. It was the lighting that enhanced the effect of the drama. The judges and barristers looked like they had makeup on their faces. The people on trial were usually pitiful figures, staring blankly around as though they didn't know where they were or how they had got there.

Jimmy's Uncle Mick, a sailor, had been reported missing. He wasn't in the Royal Navy, just a merchant seaman. He was a big cheerful man with tattoos and biceps like Popeye, who rolled around amiably drunk whenever he was home. But there had been an explosion, and Uncle Mick's ship had been lost in the North Sea and nobody knew what had happened to the crew. This was the first time that the war had registered on Jimmy's consciousness. It was there in the background. The silly man with his moustache and the fat man who looked as though he might explode in any minute. There was some talk of getting an Anderson shelter put in the garden, but it would be a job as the whole area was concreted over.

Jimmy hadn't any special feelings about being in the book trade. He had answered an advertisement for 'Smart Boy Wanted' in the *Telegraph*. Now he had been there six months he knew that he had landed a doddle. If he worked his round right he could be two hours just wandering around. As long as he got back in time to catch the post nobody questioned the time it took him to do they job. Sometimes, if he had to go to Long Acre or Covent Garden for Gollancz he could be out for over three hours. He liked just wandering around and exploring London, seeing the sights, looking outside theatres at the photographs of what was on at the time, meandering into the National Portrait Gallery, examining the foreign stamps at Stanley Gibbons in the Strand, delighting in the joke shop in the arcade in Trafalgar Square, watching people coming and going at the Savoy. It was only a waiting period until he could follow his father into 'the print'. He could get a junior card at eighteen and the Greens could stuff it. As a proud member of the NUPBPW, membership of which could only be conferred on sons of existing members, he would be one of the swaggering élite, leaving home at six in the evening and back home before midnight after a session in the pub.

There was another stratum of life that was way beyond fish and chips and saveloys and faggots. He saw them. Toffs and posh women, getting out of cars as though they were in a film or something. They wore smart clothes, big hats. They never noticed Jimmy Fosset, but Jimmy noticed them. There were more officers about nowadays, looking as though they had something important and urgent to do. There were some women in uniforms, too, who looked self-conscious and out of place. Jimmy's dad had nothing but scorn for these people. 'Stuck-up bastards' was his verdict. 'Parasites,' said Jimmy's father with a venomous snarl.

When Jimmy got back he could see that old Maurice was in a tizzy. There were piles of books to pack, and they had to be at the post office in New Bridge Street before six o'clock. Maurice himself was helping Jack with the packing, and Miss Tcherny was making out invoices as fast as she could go.

'Ah, Jimmy,' said Maurice. 'Start getting this stuff down-stairs and load them on to the trolley.' Jimmy groaned. He knew that there were going to be too many parcels for him to carry, and taking the trolley meant that he had to wheel the bloody thing back before he could go home.

The afternoon's escapade had put Maurice behind. He hadn't got back until half-past four. He didn't like doing things in a rush. That way you made mistakes, sent the wrong goods to the wrong people. He always checked everything over twice, and this time he would have to trust that he had it right the first time. Although his mind was engaged, there was still time for it to wander back to the curious meeting with the young woman he had met at Bernard's dive. If he hadn't just happened to be there the innocent girl might have landed in all sorts of trouble. In fact, he was probably the only male in the disgusting place who wouldn't have taken advantage of her. He did not really expect her to take up his offer of a job. He did not really need any extra staff. It would just be a gesture made in charity.

'All right,' said Maurice suddenly. 'That'll do for tonight.' He had noticed how Miss Tcherny had kept glancing at her watch. 'Off you go, Jimmy. You'll have to run.'

Jimmy dashed down the stairs with the last remaining parcels and met a delivery man with two huge rolls of corrugated paper on the way up. When he got downstairs he found that the trolley was piled so high that he couldn't go fast over the cobbles or the whole bloody lot would fall off. On the other hand, if he arrived too late to get them in at the post office he would have to bring the whole bloody lot back. As it was, one parcel fell off in Ludgate Circus, and he kicked it away across the pavement. That one would have to find its own way.

Experience had given Jimmy an instinct with the traffic. He knew when it was safe to cross the road. He could calculate whether a car or a lorry or even a bus had time to stop before mowing him down. He got hooted for his daring, but it was a game he enjoyed. This time he got half-way across New Bridge Street when the air-raid siren went off. Bloody hell, he thought. In the bloody daylight. In the bloody rush hour.

The siren had a peculiar effect on people who were out when

it started wailing. The first reaction was to stop dead in their tracks and stand frozen for a few seconds, and then to set off as if they had been wound up like clockwork. So it was in the sudden freeze, when everybody was standing still, that Jimmy took advantage of the general paralysis and pushed to the other side of the road, trying to hold the tower of parcels in place, only to see it collapse and spread books all over the pavement and the gutter. Jimmy bent down to pick up the parcels but got bowled over by the rush of people who now seemed to be on a panic mission to get off the street and into a building, any building, in case something falling from the sky would prove to be fatal to their continued well-being. Furthermore, if any of Jimmy's parcels got in the way they got kicked aside. Then a policeman came along.

'What's this? We can't have you cluttering up the public footpath.' By this time Jimmy had got the trolley on its back and had stacked most of the parcels on it.

'I've got to get them to the post office.'

'They'll be closed, son. The air-raid warning has gone off.'

Tell me something I don't know, thought Jimmy. The problem was that it was nearly six o'clock and that the post office might not reopen. That meant that he was stuck with all the parcels.

Eventually, he got them to his destination, which was closed, and stacked the parcels against the outside wall. He looked around. There was nobody in the street. All the traffic had stopped. It was like a ghost town. Why should he be taking the risk? If a bloody great landmine landed on his head no one would say a prayer for Jimmy Fosset. Old Maurice and Miss Tcherny and everyone would be down the cellar that old Maurice called the 'air-raid shelter'. Sitting there, all snug, getting cups of tea from a flask, while he was out on his own, confronting the enemy. It was at this point that Jimmy gave up. He left the pile of parcels and the trolley and strolled towards the river.

It began to rain, hard. The parcels would get wet, the rain would seep through the outer brown paper, turn the corrugated paper into mush, and the books would be ruined. Probably a couple of hundreds'-worth of books turned into papier mâché.

Somehow, in his illogical and juvenile mind, Jimmy was glad. It served them right.

4

'BUT what sort of a job?' Stephen May looked earnestly at his wife's perfectly oval face, the face he first saw in a draper's shop in Bootle as she carefully measured and cut a yard of blue ribbon. He hadn't wanted the ribbon; he just wanted to get close to this girl who reminded him of Cathy, the part played by Merle Oberon in the film *Wuthering Heights*. He wanted to capture this delicate creature and to have her for his own. He was enthralled by her beauty and by her dark eyes, which seemed honest and trusting. Long before Maurice, Stephen had been bewitched by the idea of a virgin, untrammelled mind. Betty was dark-skinned; perhaps there was a touch of the tar-brush in her ancestry – in Liverpool, who knew? The dark skin was now enhanced by the new blonde hair, which made her seem more exotic than ever.

Stephen, a proud but shallow young man, was shocked by the idea that his wife was not entirely contented just in being his wife. 'What can you do? You can't do shorthand, typing.'

'You have girls working in the shop, don't you?'

'They're shop girls.'

'I used to work in a shop.'

'That was before we were married.'

Betty frowned. This wasn't going to be easy. Should she tell him the truth? That she had got the offer of a job? A job were she had to go on a bus or on the Underground to get there? 'It's a bit of money. Not much, I expect, but we might be able to get out of here and get a place of our own.'

'It's the best we can manage at the moment,' said Stephen, frowning. 'It won't always be like this. I'll get promotion. I'll be a manager, a buyer or something.'

Stephen was shocked at the idea of his wife going out to work. His mother had never gone to work. She had been content to run the home and look after Stephen and his sister Lucy while their father went down the docks. He didn't always get work, sometimes he was down there all day without getting any work at all,

33

but he went there to get it. Of course, they always had two lodgers in the house, and Stephen's mother supplied their breakfast and an evening meal, and she always had some knitting on the go – asbestos gloves that were needed for an iron foundry – but she never went out to work. That was unthinkable. That was the deal, the wife's role. Young girls went to work when they left school, but that was only until they got married and began to have children. Stephen had always been careful to use a French letter, but now he wondered whether he ought to have got Betty pregnant. That would have given her something to think about. But having a baby in the tiny flat would have been ridiculous. That was for later, when they had got on a bit and were better settled.

'I thought I might do something with books,' Betty said, in a surly, semi-defiant way.

'Books? You don't know anything about books.'

'I can read.'

'You were taught to read at school, but that's just stuff for children. Books – I mean real books, that have long words – you wouldn't understand them. You never read anything but the *Family Circle*. You're not even a member of the public library.'

'I could learn,' she said, sulkily.

Betty looked at her husband's hurt and puzzled face. Should she tell him of her adventure? She shouldn't have secrets from her husband, but he was taking the idea of her having a job so badly. He hadn't got the room to pace up and down, but he kept turning around, like he was locked in somewhere and couldn't find the door.

'I thought you were all right. It's early days,' he said, casting around for an argument. For God's sake, if a man couldn't afford to keep his wife he shouldn't have got married. Only maiden aunts, spinsters and rough women who did cleaning had jobs.

'Look. Just see how it goes. I might get a raise.'

Betty decided to brave it out.

'I met this man, Maurice, and he offered me a job. Something to do with books.'

'What? He must be mad. You're a lovely girl, but . . . you're not educated, are you?'

'I can learn.'

'People don't pay you to learn. They expect you to be able to do something. Who is this man? Where did you meet him?'

Now for it, Betty thought. But then I haven't done anything wrong. Why should I be afraid? 'I went with Bunty. She introduced me.'

Stephen's head begun to spin. 'You did what? With Bunty? Do you know what that woman is?'

'She's been very nice.'

'I bet she has.' Stephen – who had been told that he resembled Robert Taylor and had tried to let the ends of his hair curl up in the same way as the handsome film star while trying to affect the cultured elegance of Ronald Colman – ruffled his hair with exasperation. 'I can't be here all day looking after you. I trusted you.'

'But what is wrong? He's a perfectly respectable gentleman who happens to deal in books.'

'Bunty doesn't know any respectable gentlemen.'

'Well this – Maurice – is very nice.'

Stephen felt as though his head would explode. 'For God's sake, Bet. You don't know what some men are like.' Betty fished into her handbag and found Maurice's business card. 'Green's Wholesale Booksellers. That could mean anything. I mean, what would you be doing there?'

'I don't know until I start, do I?'

Stephen sulked all over the weekend. They went for a walk on Clapham Common, and Stephen strode along as though he was deep in thought while Betty pattered along by his side trying to keep up. They went around the bandstand three times, and then Stephen suddenly stopped at the pond and glared at the ducks as though they had personally offended him. 'If I let you go – just for an interview mind – will you tell me everything that goes on? I mean everything.'

'Yes. I will,' said Betty, submissively.

'Then we'll make up our minds what to do.'

After this was settled Stephen cheered up. He felt that he had held on to a thread of authority. Betty would only go to work if he allowed her to. It wasn't a rebellion. She had accepted that there would be conditions, and she wasn't going out of necessity. And he had made her promise that she wouldn't go out with Bunty any more.

So they rambled over the common, watched a scrappy game of football and stared at the motionless chess players outside the Windmill pub, who seemed as though they were sculptures carved out of stone. Stephen had a glass of beer and Betty had a lemonade.

'You see, it has to be a respectable place,' Stephen said, as if explaining a tricky point to a child. 'It's easy to slip down the scale. Let yourself down.' Betty only had a vague idea of what Stephen was driving at. Were Bunty and Tim down the scale? Probably Mrs Bennet was, and certainly the Penroses let everyone down. It was how you felt about people. But Maurice was quite obviously up the scale and would never let anyone down.

On the Monday morning, as soon as Stephen went off to work, Betty left the house for the telephone box in the high street.

'Hello. Green's.'

Betty pressed the button that allowed her two penny coins to clank into the tin box.

'Hello. I'd like to speak to Mr Maurice Green, please.'

'Hold on.' It was a young man's voice, and then:

'Hello. Maurice Green.'

'Ah, Maurice. It's Betty.'

'Sorry. Who?' Oh dear. He'd forgotten her. He's probably dealt with hundreds of people since their meeting.

'Betty. We met at –'

'Oh yes,' Maurice said hurriedly. 'How are you?'

'I'm all right. I've asked Stephen.'

'Stephen?'

'My husband. About taking a job. You remember?' Oh my God, Maurice thought. The silly young thing had taken him seriously. 'You do remember?'

'Yes, of course.'

'Well, then. Should I come up?'

'Eh? Well, I don't know. We are rather busy.'

'Oh.' Betty felt tears sparking in her eyes. It was all a swizz.

She'd been silly to think that someone like Maurice, with all his education and knowledge of the world, would give her a job. Stephen was right. What could she do to justify her employment? 'It's all right,' she said, with a catch in her voice. 'If you're busy . . .'

Maurice felt awful. The girl was so vulnerable. It was so easy to hurt her, to make her feel unworthy, to give her fragile confidence a blow from which it might never recover. But *Little Women*, for God's sake. Of course, the Christian thing to do would be to try to help her in some way, not to push her down. It had probably taken some courage for her to make this call. Could he just leave her with the option of the sordid Soho knocking shop?

'Look,' he said. 'We'll meet and talk about it. Do you know the Milk Bar in Fleet Street?'

'I can find it, I expect.'

'We'll meet there. At one o'clock.'

Betty was going to thank him, but the telephone started buzzing and she was cut off before she could press another two pennies into the slot.

It seemed odd. A meeting in a milk bar. If she were going to work for a book firm she would expect to be shown around the place, shown the ropes, as it were. Besides, she wasn't sure how to get to Fleet Street. She could get on a Number 88 bus and ask the conductor. The 88 didn't go to Fleet Street. The nearest it went to the famous street of newspapers was Trafalgar Square.

'Get another bus in the Strand, love. On this side, opposite the Strand Corner House.'

Betty was familiar with Oxford Street and Regent Street from window-shopping trips, but this area of London was new to her. There were shops but not clothes shops. You wouldn't come here to buy a new outfit. There was an HMV record shop, a shop that sold bicycles, pianos and prams, stationery shops, shops that sold wireless sets and gramophones and everything to do with them, and lots of poky cafés that smelt of strong coffee. The Milk Bar was quite a new idea. She hadn't been in one before.

She thought that she shouldn't go in on her own. It wasn't the same as a pub, but all the same . . . She was about fifteen minutes early, so she spent some time looking at the display windows in the newspaper offices, looking at photographs of the King and Queen at some posh party and footballers who had scored a winning goal. There were pictures of Winston Churchill, looking like a prize bulldog, chatting with Army generals who looked so serious and proud. They were winning the war in France, although they weren't even there at the moment, so they were bound to look pleased with themselves. She crossed the road back to the Milk Bar and saw Maurice approaching. My, he was a gentleman. He had a long, dark-grey overcoat and a bowler hat, polished shoes and a furled umbrella neatly by his side. He stopped and looked down at her, smiling like a kindly old uncle.

'Hello,' he said gently. 'I hope I haven't kept you waiting.'

Of course, Stephen was a gentleman, but Maurice was a kind of super-gentleman. Stephen was young; Maurice was older and more practised in the art of courtesy and consideration.

For his part, Maurice was overwhelmed by the girl's attractiveness. She looked even better in the daylight than she had in the smoky and flattering dim light of the sordid dive where they had met. There was something rather prim and yet pleasant. The girl didn't have any idea of how attractive she was. It wasn't artlessness, for she was entirely without pretension. She had on a two-piece suit in a sky-blue shade, which she probably kept pressed all the time, with a cream blouse that snuggled around her neck and a small hat with a fur trim. The whole outfit was probably a cheap version of one sketched on a fashion page of a Sunday newspaper. You wouldn't have taken her for a lady – not in the class sense – because the outfit was not first class, rather more of a cheap out-of-town department store, more Arding and Hobbs than Aquascutum. If you saw her on the street you might judge her to be a parlour maid on her day off.

'Come on,' said Maurice, suddenly feeling the hell of a dog. 'I've always wanted to try this place.' They went into the shining super-hygienic environment. Betty found it exciting. You would have expected some exotic cocktail rather than a drink that, whatever its fancy description and flavour, was, essentially, a glass of milk. Everything was white and shiny, and the staff wore white suits and caps. It was more like an operating-theatre in a hospital than a café.

'What shall we have?' Maurice asked, as though the whole operation was a larkish dare. There was a list of various flavours that could be injected into the milk. 'Banana, strawberry, blackcurrant. What d'you fancy?'

'I'll have strawberry,' Betty said, feeling like a young girl out on a treat. It came in a tall glass, very fluffed up, but with a straw. It all seemed very daring and modern. Maurice suddenly felt ten years younger. He knew he looked out of place in this razzmatazz environment, all chrome and bakelite, but had the consolation that he was with the prettiest woman in the place.

'You see it's like this,' he said. 'We employ experienced staff.' Betty, crestfallen, and feeling more than a bit foolish, blew down the straw into the milkshake and the frothy mixture frothed up over the top of the glass.

'Oh dear. What a mess.'

'It's all right,' said Maurice, producing a crisp snow-white handkerchief and starting to mop up the surplus milk. 'We have to be careful about mistakes, you see.' It was all sounding a bit limp. He was trying to let her down gently, but there were tears in her eyes already. It was too humiliating for the girl.

'It doesn't mean that we can't use you. It's just that you need a bit of experience first.' What was he getting himself into? This was bosh. People could pick it up as they went along. There was no training or certificate that allowed someone to work in the book trade. The wages were not good enough for employers to be particular.

Betty was puzzled. 'But how? How can I get this . . . experience?'

'Well,' Maurice floundered. 'You could serve a sort of apprenticeship. I could give you something to read and see how you get on with it.'

'I see,' said Betty. But she didn't. Surely an apprenticeship was something that men did, to be a carpenter or a plumber?

'Of course, I should pay you something while you're training, and then, if all goes well, we could see about taking you into the business.' Maurice, who had fashioned this bizarre scheme entirely off the top of his head, was, in the end, quite pleased with the idea. If he employed Betty at Green's there was a danger of her not being able to cope and making mistakes and probably bursting into tears. It was already apparent that, in Betty's case, brains did not go with beauty. The employment of an additional pair of hands that were not needed would, as likely as not, lead to trouble with the other staff. So, employing this girl, in any capacity, would be an act of charity. This way he could continue to see her and, in some way, fashion her education. The more he thought about it the more he liked the idea. If it was an indulgence it was nothing against the liberties taken by brother Bernard.

But the girl seemed puzzled. 'You want me to read books?'

'Yes. But that's not all. I want you to tell me about them.'

She shook her head. She was extraordinarily pretty. She could have been his daughter, his granddaughter even. He had never considered the joys of fatherhood because, with Clare, there was no chance of such a thing occurring – but then, if he had had a daughter, he would have been fearful of her falling into the hands of a man like Bernard, as this poor girl nearly did.

'I can pay you fifty shillings a week.'

Fifty shillings? Two pounds ten shillings? It was more than she expected. You could buy a suit for that at the Fifty-Shilling Tailors: jacket, trousers and waistcoat, all measured and fitted.

'How many?' she said.

'How many what?'

'How many books would I have to read?'

'Oh, lots,' Maurice said vaguely. 'I'll make sure you have plenty to do.'

So this was how the twice-weekly tryst was set up. They met in different places: in Lyons' tea shops, in the Aerated Bread Company – or ABC – in Express Dairies, in St Paul's Church-yard, in Lincoln's Inn Fields, in Gamages and in Foyle's, where Betty was dazzled by the sheer number of books on display and of Maurice's knowledge of published works. He certainly knew his business.

He started her on *The Wind in the Willows*.

'Was it written for children?'

'Yes, I suppose so, but adults can enjoy it.'

'But they're all animals.'

'They are in the book, but there's people about who are very like Toad and the Badger. I mean they have the same characteristics.'

'Yes.' She sounded doubtful. Maurice had soon reached the barrier. The girl took everything literally. She had no room for whimsy, and she thought that humour was a childish game.

He tried to get her to see the fun in P.G. Wodehouse.

'He puts things in a funny way. And they're all such snobs.'

The Stars Look Down was 'too depressing' and *How Green Was My Valley* was 'too muddly'. It was literary criticism from the ground floor. She liked *The Grapes of Wrath* because she had seen the film and the American expressions were no barrier as she was familiar with them, but she found *Gone with the Wind* formidable. 'It'd take months to read all that. It's a four-hour film.'

Maurice sighed. Was this a wild-goose chase, trying to make a mark on such a blank unyielding canvas? The poor girl was fulfilling her side of the bargain – she must have spent the whole week reading – and yet nothing she read made an impression. Nothing excited her. He still had to find the way to unlock her perception of life, of people, of her position in the world. What would be her eureka moment?

'What does your husband think of your new job?'

'He can't understand it,' said Betty. 'And to be honest, neither can I.'

5

Rosa Tcherny was working herself up to it. She had been on the point when the bloody siren sounded and they all had to go down to the cellar again. At first these sudden excursions produced a flush of excitement, but now it was just boring. All you could do was sit and smile if you caught someone's eye. You could try to read something. The trouble was that these little *frissons* didn't lead to anything. You just waited until the all-clear came through and all trooped back upstairs again.

She knew that she ought to have been given a raise. She had worked for Green's for six months; she could do the job with her eyes closed. Most of the work was dead easy. Harry the packer sometimes said something saucy, which she liked, but then there was that acned youth Jimmy, who stared at her as though he was imagining all kinds of forbidden lusts with her as the principal lead. As for Mr Maurice, he had the expression of an undertaker and a demeanour to match. He patted the books into order like he was conducting a mass and they were all sinners. She didn't much like it when Bernard came in, with his wolfish eyes that took snapshots, no doubt to refer to later. Bella, the other person on the notepaper, she had never seen.

After all, she needed to build up some capital. When the war was over her family intended to return to Vienna and resume their old life. There was always that feeling of not quite fitting in here. It wasn't because she was foreign, it was because she was a Jew. Her boyfriend Charlie was keen enough to get up to his antics in empty air-raid shelters and in the back row of the Odeon, but he had never even approached the subject of marriage. The English seemed to be embarrassed about the Jews. Before the war there were street battles between the Jews and the fascists, just as there were in Germany. It was clear that a large proportion of the population thought that Jews were sly and not to be trusted. They wouldn't have gone so far as to consign them to camps, but, nevertheless, they weren't easy with them about. However,

Hitler's treatment of the German Jews had made the position of those in Britain a little more secure.

On her way to Holborn Underground station Rosa liked to window-shop. In comparison with Vienna the shops looked drab and untempting. These English, they had no style. Everything was square and durable, even more so now they had been told to 'make do and mend'. There was hardly anything on which it was worth spending a single clothing coupon.

It was all right for Charlie. Tall and gangling, with a prominent Adam's apple that seemed to swallow harder when he was working himself up into a sexual frenzy – which he did with tedious frequency – awkward and backward as he was in the art of communication, he was a member of the élite. He had served an apprenticeship as a 'comp'. His strong union went in for rises *en masse*. At Green's you had the embarrassment of asking. She thought she had an opportunity when Mr Maurice pressed against her between the shelves. But his expression had given nothing away. He was married of course, but he never mentioned his wife, and Rosa had the impression that it wasn't a very close union.

Mr Maurice had started taking long lunch hours, more like two. This meant that she had to work like fireworks when he returned to get everything ready for the post. Not that it was a strain. In fact, it was a change from the leisurely pace of most of the day. She wondered where he went for his lunch. Maybe some hotel along the Strand. When he came back he always seemed reinvigorated, and yet, he never smelt of alcohol. Rosa went to Joe Lyons'. A roll and butter and a small wedge of cheese and a cup of tea gave change out of sixpence, in a fairly civilized atmosphere.

'Mr Maurice?'

'Yes, what is it?'

'Er . . .' she said hesitantly.

'Spit it out. We've got a lot to do before we can send Jimmy off.'

'I was thinking . . .' She stared at the side of his face. His expression was like armour.

'Yes?' he said.

'I was thinking about a rise . . .' It came out in a rush. She felt herself going red and then assumed a defiant expression of

43

justified insubordination. Maurice did not register any emotion at this challenge.

'I've been here six months,' she said, beginning to pout like a naughty child.

'Yes, yes,' he said testily. 'We'll think about it.' Rosa was annoyed. This meant that she would have to bring the matter up again. Another period of steeling herself to broach the subject and the embarrassment of asking again. She flicked her invoice pad with an irritated finger.

Rosa couldn't help it. She spent the rest of the day in a sulk. Little Jimmy, staring at her in his customary fantasy, got the full brunt of her fury.

'Didn't anyone tell you that it's rude to stare? What are you looking at anyway?'

Jimmy, caught with his guard down, blushed and stammered.

'Nothing, miss. Didn't . . . didn't mean anything.'

'Nothing he can tell you,' said Harry the packer out of the side of his mouth.

Rosa marched away. She had a bar of Cadbury's chocolate in her locker. She felt she needed it.

For the rest of the day she barely communicated with the rest of the staff. Maurice handed her a pile of books for invoicing and she took them without even glancing at him. Quickly and efficiently she entered them in the books, tore off the counterfoils and stood mute, awaiting further instructions as if the whole operation was beneath her contempt. As the work came to her, she dispatched it immediately. Soon there was a pile for Harry the packer.

'Hold on,' said Harry. 'I shan't get this lot off tonight.' Jimmy's eyes widened as he saw his haul growing to trolley proportions. Jimmy was still on probation after the incident when he left a pile of parcels out in the rain. The post office people phoned up, and Mr Maurice had to go over and straighten things up.

That night she reported the whole incident to Charlie.

'Give in your notice,' he said. 'You can easily get something else, if you've got a head for figures.'

Rosa didn't want to leave Green's. All those books. She had been able to satisfy her curiosity about Hitler, Freud, Israel, birth control and various other subjects. Everything she wanted to know was there. And Rosa's mother urged caution. The time in Austria when brown-shirted louts had shouted at her in the street had done something permanent to her confidence. You had a job, you kept your mouth shut. Everybody was always looking for an excuse to sack a Jew. Rosa's father was not so meek, although he always expected the worst and seemed to take some sardonic pleasure when he was proved right.

'These English, they don't say anything, but you can see them looking, see them thinking. The Germans just brought it out in the open, but it's here – everywhere.' He said it as though it was fact, not just opinion.

Rosa took due warning from her parents and said no more about getting a raise. So she was surprised when her pay packet showed an increase of ten shillings at the end of the week. Nobody said anything. Money wasn't a subject to dwell on. Maurice regarded the work of running the warehouse almost as a higher calling.

Later, just before they were closing he said, tight-lipped: 'Everything all right?'

'Yes,' she said. 'All right, thank you.'

When she got home and told her mother she was greeted with: 'Well, they must be pleased with you – but don't go too far.'

That night Charlie took her to the cinema. It was a Betty Grable film – it always seemed to be a back-stage musical. On the way home Charlie pushed her into the small front garden of a house and grabbed her breasts urgently. There was a smell of dog turd and earth soaked in cat's pee. She felt as though she was being mauled without even the tenderness of a kiss and a few loving words. Then he put his hand between her legs and she gasped at the cheek of it all and pushed him away.

'For Christ's sake,' he said. 'We've been going out for weeks now.'

'It doesn't mean that you can jump on me like that.'

A cat slithered out from a privet hedge.

'You're just like an animal.'

'I am,' he said miserably. 'I am. The fact is, I've got me calling-up papers.'

'Oh . . . When?'

'In a few weeks.'

'I'm sorry. I didn't know.'

Charlie had slumped into a slough of self-pity.

'What do you care? You'll soon find someone else.'

Rosa was puzzled. 'You never said anything.'

'What d'you want? A ring?'

'Well,' she said primly. 'It would be good to know where I stand.'

Charlie walked out of the front garden, and Rosa followed. It was a mess. Charlie wanted a token, something to take with him, a promise, an understanding. He had been so clumsy, so tongue-tied and so awkward, and yet he wasn't a bad man. He might go away and never return. Should she send him on his way with a night to remember? Was it so much of a sacrifice?

Charlie stood on the pavement, a picture of dejection, all elbows and knees, just as he was when they first met at the Locarno, when he was pushed out from a gaggle of leering lads, pushed in front of a phalanx of eager, excited girls.

'It's all right for you,' he said.

'How? How is it all right for me?'

'You don't have to go.'

She felt sorry for him. He was only a boy. 'What about when you come back?'

'I'd marry you like a shot,' he said, as though he was bravely owning up to his responsibility in the affair.

'But you haven't asked me,' she said. 'Just took it for granted.'

Charlie shuffled with embarrassment. 'Thought you knew,' he said.

It was dark so she couldn't see his face, but she knew he would be looking like a sulky schoolboy apprehended in some juvenile misdemeanour. 'Well come on then,' she said.

'What?'

'What you're going to ask me.'

'Bloody hell! You will? Will you really?'

He seized her around her waist and pressed his body against hers.

'Wait a minute,' she said. 'You still haven't asked me.'

His excitement was infectious.

'Marry me. Will you? Please. It'll be good. It'll be . . . Rosa, I want you so much. I can't go away without knowing . . . any-thing.'

'All right,' she said. 'But not here. Not up against a wall in a stinking side street.'

He seemed jubilant. He jumped up and down, his loose limbs at awkward angles. He kissed her on the mouth, so hard that it left her breathless. He loosened his tie and flapped his arms. He spun around. He came up behind her and squeezed her breasts, burying his face in the hair at the back of her neck.

'Rosa,' he breathed in a thrilling throttle. 'My Rosa.'

They made arrangements to meet the following evening, when Charlie would try to arrange for a hotel room. Somewhere they could be together, quiet and warm. Or maybe his sister's place: she was broad-minded, and her husband was working nights at Hawker's, the aircraft factory.

'But what about your parents? I haven't even met them. They may not like me.'

'They're not marrying you,' he said earnestly. 'I am.'

The next day at home, working through the Saturday tasks, washing and ironing, was spent in a daydream. She was going to be married; maybe not soon, but eventually, married to a man with a good job with prospects who was, after all, a Gentile. She didn't know how her parents would take to the idea, but she didn't have to tell them just yet.

The next evening was spent watching Errol Flynn charming his way through Hollywood, outrageously winning the demure Olivia de Havilland. Errol Flynn was a man's idea of a man that women found irresistible. Confident, brash and yet courtly, always knowing that he would get his way in the end; flash good looks and a god's physique, he was manliness personified.

When they left the cinema Errol's overconfidence seemed to carry over to Charlie. He put his arm around her and stepped out, as if carried on from the dream detailed in the film. He pressed her up against an unlit lamp-post. He acted like he wanted to plant a year's kisses in one night. She levered herself away.

'What?' he said. 'What's the matter?'

'Have you told your parents?'

'What? About what?'

'About us getting married.'

'I'll tell them,' he said.

'You can come to tea on Sunday.'

'What? At your place?'

'Yes.'

'But why?' He was like a child: he wanted something, he grabbed it, put it in his mouth and sucked it dry. He had no thought of the consequences. No idea of civilized behaviour.

'They have to see you. Get to know you. I want to meet your parents, too.'

He seemed stunned. 'Do we have to do all this? There's only you and me. That's all.'

They went into a pub. There were pictures of the King and Queen and Union Jacks hastily pinned on to the walls. There were lugubrious old men and rackety old women sipping beer as though it was the last wake. The war had begun to press on the general consciousness. It had started. There were identity cards, ration books, shortages, conscription, barrage balloons, Mr Chad, Winston Churchill, Spitfires and Messerschmitts, Anderson shelters and 'We're Going to Hang Out the Washing on the Siegfried Line' and 'Roll Me Over'. People on the loose exhibited a kind of enforced gaiety, a near-sighted optimism, falsely buoying up spirits against a hollow fear just beneath the surface. They took every chance to assert their Britishness as though it was an invisible shield that protected them from all harm. They sang a lot. It was the party to end all parties. The war had been a disappointment up to now, but they knew it was coming, and they were ready for it. Some already had formed underground communities, sleeping all night on Tube station platforms. They had transferred their bank holiday picnic from Hampstead Heath to an underground location, complete with sandwiches, jam tarts, flasks, oranges and bananas, and piano accordions.

On the Sunday Charlie came to tea in a clean shirt and a carefully knotted tie, looking like he thought he was up before the firing squad. Rosa introduced him to her mother and father who eyed him with suspicion. It may be that he had professed undying love to their daughter, that he was presenting himself as a respectable suitor, but they knew better. He was being called up, wasn't he? And what did he want before he went? He wanted to screw their daughter. There was no engagement ring, no contract of any kind. The boy wanted to be taken on trust, and they didn't trust him. Not a bit. He wasn't one of them, not that a Jew would have been more trustworthy, but there was a family that you could get a hold on if something went wrong. With these Gentiles they had no such understanding. They would think that Rosa would be lucky to have been impregnated and left to suffer for it. After all, she shouldn't get above herself.

So it was a cautious meal, with polite scrapings of conversation, without warmth or humour, with the two principals aware that the attempt to form a bond was pushing them further apart.

'A compositor,' said Mr Tcherny, in a tone that suggested he could hardly believe that this shambling, tongue-tied youth could even spell his own name.

'Yes,' said Charlie, trying to swallow a gherkin that was having a scrambling fight with his Adam's apple. 'My dad was, so –'

'So you inherited the job,' said Mr Tcherny.

'Eh?' said Charlie. 'No. He, sort of, spoke for me. It's an apprenticeship. I got out two weeks ago.'

'So now you are qualified?' said Rosa's mother.

'Well, I got me card.'

The next step was for Rosa to meet Charlie's parents.

'They're all right,' Charlie said. 'They won't bother.'

'You don't want me to meet them. Is that it? Why?'

'My dad goes out most nights.'

'Well tell him to stay in. You don't want to do this, do you?'

Charlie groaned. 'It's such a fuss. My sister said it would be all right.'

Rosa was stung. It was as everyone said. Men were only after one thing.

'No,' she said. 'I think we'd better forget it. You don't really want to marry me. You just want –'

'No,' he said. 'I do. I do. But . . . I didn't think it'd be so cut and dried.'

They went into a big pub with a big bar. It was rowdy and yet they were isolated in their gloom. Suddenly people started singing and dancing the hokey-cokey, swinging along in lines, singing as though their lives depended on it. Life was to be grabbed for the moment. There was the ever-present threat of invasion, of bombing, of relatives being sent away and never seen again. The anxiety produced an excess of emotion, crying and laughing.

'Come on,' shouted a wild young woman with sparkling eyes. She grabbed Charlie's hand and dragged him into the mob of dancers. Rosa watched him, out of his depth, as usual, with no idea how to deal with the situation, just carried along, without really knowing whether it was against his will or not. Was this the man she was going to marry? This wet week, this natural chump, this prime candidate for the awkward squad?

She got up and extricated him from the row of dancers and dragged him into the street. He was dishevelled, with his shirt spilling out of his trousers, his hair lank with sweat.

'All right,' she said. 'You can fix it up with your sister. And that's it. We'll see what happens when you come back.'

6

A BOMB had dropped in Wimbledon. Why Wimbledon? Tim went out on his bike to see the wreckage. It was just an ordinary terrace-house in an ordinary street. Was it an accident? Did some German plane just unload it as surplus to requirements? There hadn't been an air raid as such. Just one stray bomb, unloaded in this mindless way. Was it a warning of what was to come? Was it a threat to the civilian population? You thought the war was overseas, but here it was on your doorstep. Were the Germans trying to induce panic? There was nothing special about Wimbledon. There was Hawker's aircraft factory at Kingston, which was near enough. Was it intended for there? Fortunately the bomb had fallen during the day when everybody was out, so no one had been injured. It was odd. Not quite real. There was a war on, of course, but you didn't expect it to show up in Wimbledon.

The bomb fell on a Friday. On Sunday afternoon the street was full of sightseers, who looked at the gap in the row of houses, shivered as though someone had walked over their grave and bought an ice cream from a man on a tricycle and ice box that proclaimed 'Stop Me and Buy One'. The people who lived in the street stood outside their houses looking puzzled. Why them? Were the Germans trying to hit the railway? Not exactly a major route, just a suburban line.

There were two policemen outside the house. There didn't seem much point in guarding a house that wasn't there any more. The sightseers looked glumly at the ruins, annoyed rather than frightened. It was a shock; uncivilized behaviour. It was, in the phrase, 'not cricket'. Foreigners – all of them – hadn't got the British sense of fair play. Well, if they thought they were going to undermine the British backbone with underhand bowling they had another think coming. There was quiet determination in the British. They weren't going to be pushed around.

Maurice read about the incident in the *Telegraph*. Jimmy

couldn't understand it at all. Bombs in London? These bloody Germans were getting above themselves. Somebody would soon put a stop to that. Mrs Bennet's reaction was to turn all the electricity off. She still didn't trust electricity. She swore she got a shock every time she touched a switch. Only Miss Tcherny seemed to regard the bomb as within the realm of everyday life. She knew that this was just an overture – not even that, just a tuning up. Bunty Melrose never even heard about it.

Bunty was on one of her jaunts into the West End when she saw a newspaper placard that proclaimed in large letters 'Bomb Falls on London'. It worried her. She wanted to ask someone about it. She didn't feel so secure any longer in her silent world.

She pulled down her dress. The car was getting near to the club where, bomb or not, she had to be pleasant and accommodating.

She was sorry that Betty wasn't with her. She only came the one time, but she had got off with a rich gentleman straight away and never needed to come again. Bunty didn't want anything serious to happen. She wanted to stay with Tim. He wasn't much, but she had got used to him. He didn't ask for much, and although he knew what she was up to he was prepared to turn a blind eye as long as she didn't rub his nose in it.

Bunty knew that she only had one chance in life. She was born deaf and dumb, so she had learnt a vocabulary of eye contacts, shrugs and pouts that seemed to get her through. The gentlemen at the club often rattled on at her, and she just smiled and they were happy enough. They didn't want her to talk, and most of them didn't know that she couldn't. She danced with them and they pressed themselves against her as though they were trying to make a waxwork impression. Then it was upstairs where they watched her strip off and then banged away on top of her, going red-faced, pop-eyed and breathless, gradually subsiding into a dead weight. Bunty reckoned that she earned her money. She was concerned occasionally that the gentleman may have overdone it. Sometimes they looked strained and white afterwards, and often had to have a large brandy to get them on their feet again.

But after they'd performed they were so pleased. You'd have thought they'd done something grand and been honoured by the king. That they had climbed a mountain, won a race or the world heavyweight championship. They were all silly, like young boys boasting, squaring up and drawing attention to their puny muscles. They were invariably fat and pretty ugly, but they were so courteous, so worried that they might have hurt her, which was a joke, because most of them couldn't summon up the strength to swat a fly. She played along, making them feel strong and powerful. The better they felt the bigger the tip. Bunty didn't have set fees. She just took what was given. If the gift were paltry, that gentleman wouldn't be seeing her again. She felt that three or four was enough in any one day. She didn't want to get sore again.

That Bernard was there again. There was something about Bernard that Bunty didn't like. The way his eyes darted about the room, taking in everything and everyone. If a new girl arrived at the club Bernard thought it was his right to try her out first. She had been with him so many times that he had begun to take liberties. He wasn't polite like the other men. He was brutal in the act and seemed to enjoy hurting her, and he didn't give much at the end.

That day Bernard was in a foul temper. He had been after a contract to supply books for the troops overseas, but a crafty bastard upstart with a tuppenny-ha'penny firm had underbid him. As it was a government contract they had to be sealed bids. Bernard wanted to develop his side of the business so he would overtake Maurice. He wanted to increase his turnover, so it would increase his position and power in the business. He wanted to bring his toffee-nosed brother down to his level. Already his Leicester Square run underpinned the general supply side, but Maurice wouldn't recognize it.

Bernard stared around the clubroom. The same dreary collection. All worn-out, raddled old whores. The only sign of new talent was when he had brought Maurice in and Maurice had snaffled her from right under his nose. She hadn't been since. He asked Bunty about her, but the silly cow just smiled and batted her eyes at him as if he had suggested something particularly outrageous. There was something wrong with her, but he couldn't be sure what it was. She was a bit loopy, he thought, although that didn't matter when he got her upstairs. She was all right for all that, never complained, took what she was given.

The bomb worried Betty May. Things were getting serious. She had never thought of anything disturbing her blissful existence with Stephen, but there was talk of conscription, men being called up for service in the Army, whether they wanted to go or not. She couldn't bear the thought of that. What would she do, on her own, in a strange city? Would she have enough to live on? She would have to go back to Liverpool. At least she knew people there. But she didn't want to go back to Liverpool. Of course, she would have to find a job. Not the joke job she had been doing for Maurice Green. Mind you, he had been as good as his word, had met her twice a week and was usually on time. He still said that when she had got enough background knowledge he would take her into his firm.

She had begun to enjoy these little jaunts, always setting off early so she had time to saunter. She was getting to know the little cobbled alleyways behind Fleet Street, the tiny squares and tiny gardens. She heard the roar and hum of the printing presses, watched men in sports coats and rakish trilbys pushing urgently through glass doors, as though they had some earth-shattering news to impart. If you looked up Farringdon Road you could see Holborn Viaduct, with traffic going across, while traffic went underneath in the opposite direction.

Then there was High Holborn, a long, wide street with all kinds of specialist shops. There was one that only sold umbrellas, another that sold jokes that you could buy and 'startle your friends'. There were shops that sold foreign newspapers, one that only sold pipes and tobacco. There was a shop that sold fishing tackle, one that sold bibles and religious books, one that sold lost property, and His Majesty's Stationery Office, which seemed very stern. If you went right to the end you came to Gamages, a ragbag of a department store that sold an extraordinary range of ill-matched goods. There you could buy all kinds of rough clothing suitable for all kinds of jobs: overalls, dust coats, heavy-duty jackets and oilskin trousers, giant wellington boots, tyres for motor cars and cans of oil, tar, paint, bushy gloves, warm hats that came down over the ears, and yet conjuring tricks, a ventriloquist's dummy, boxes of fireworks, books of pictures and very unfashionable ladies' underwear, frocks and coats. Nothing flighty about Gamages.

She had discovered this area when she had had to meet Maurice Green in Lincoln's Inn Fields; a square park, populated, it seemed, by smart men and women eating sandwiches that they brought in briefcases or large handbags. It seemed that the most important thing to do in Lincoln's Inn Fields was not to notice that there was anyone else there, even if they were sitting next to you on the same bench. Everyone surrounded himself or herself in isolation. Those that came alone sat glumly munching, stern or sad-faced, as though only necessity had forced them to be in proximity to all the riff-raff around them. Of course, if they had come in pairs they never stopped talking, and the people near by couldn't help but listen to the high-pitched stream of invective directed at some other member of the firm where they worked. When it was wet most of them went into the Express Dairy or the ABC.

To get to Lincoln's Inn Fields she had to pass the Holborn Empire, a variety theatre, which always had photographs outside showing who was performing that week. The photographs were often faded mementoes of past glories: a brass-faced comedian leering from between a line of leggy chorus girls; a singer looking like she had been transported to a heavenly cloud.

There were all kinds of life in this strange corner of the city. There was life here, after dark. It didn't close down when the shops stopped trading. Betty longed to be part of this world. It was exciting, different, like nothing she had encountered elsewhere. There were all kinds here, from the ultra-smart to the downright drab: women in furs, with sleek hair; men who looked like business tycoons, in belted overcoats, bowlers or trilbys. No Liverpool-style cloth caps here. There were many foreign people, in the shops, in the offices. Holborn was not the City or the West End, but it had its own flavour and its own cosmopolitan charm.

It didn't care whether it wasn't the centre of the metropolis. It was what it was, unpretentious.

Bunty didn't want to go with Bernard. He glared at her, and she tried, vainly, to get another partner. But Bernard was insistent, jerking her out of her seat and pushing her towards the door. She was fearful and beseeched with her eyes, but no one was watching. She got to the bottom of the stairs and turned into the vestibule, but Bernard pulled her back, gripping her arm in a vice-like grip. If only she could have cried out. She was being bullied, forced into something for which she had no inclination, and she couldn't even cry for help.

At the same time Betty May was sitting in St Paul's Churchyard, waiting for Maurice. When they met in the churchyard it meant that Maurice was short of time. He arrived looking a bit flustered.

'Sorry if I'm late,' he said.

She noticed that he kept looking out across Ludgate Hill. He hadn't told her where the warehouse was, but she guessed it wasn't far away, and he was concerned that someone from the firm might see him on this odd, secret tryst. Whatever would he say? 'I meet this young woman, she's a married woman, and we talk about books'? She had to admit that even Stephen had begun to get suspicious. 'But where will it all lead to? What is the point of it all?' And she had been hard put to find an answer. That is why she had resolved to put that exact point to Maurice this very day. Fifty shillings a week was very nice. It had practically doubled their weekly budget. They had been able to go into the best seats at the cinema and afford a box of chocolates, too.

'It's all right,' she said. 'I'm here anyway. And you're paying me to be here.'

He gave her a strange look. 'Yes,' he said. 'But I hope that's not the only consideration. I mean, I quite enjoy our little meetings.'

'Yes, but is it going anywhere?' she said, echoing her husband.

'What do you mean?' he said, slightly put out.

'I mean, am I going to get a proper job? I like to give good value, to feel I'm earning the money – somehow. I mean, I've never seen the place where you work.'

He seemed surprised. 'You want to see the warehouse?' he said. 'Well, that can soon be arranged.' He threw a handful of nuts down in front of him, and a flock of pigeons descended on them.

Betty shivered. 'It's cold,' she said.

'We could go inside,' said Maurice.

'No,' she said, with a force that surprised her. She was beginning to feel uneasy about these meetings. It was all right at the start when they talked about books, but things had got beyond that. After all, Maurice was a married man. Would his wife ever believe that they met just to talk? And that she was paid for it? Maurice had never suggested anything more. And yet, she had met him in what was clearly a pick-up place. Was it just that he was taking a long time to get around to it?

'When can I come to your place?' she asked.

'Well,' he said. 'We're doing stocktaking this week, but soon.'

Maurice wondered whether he had been right to take up this girl, this piece of literary clay. What was he trying to prove? The girl was young with a kind of innocent freshness that aroused a kind of protective gallantry. It was a long time since Maurice had been out with a pretty woman. He enjoyed her ignorance. It made him feel as if he had absorbed so much through his work that to her he was some kind of oracle. She confided in him, about her mundane ambitions for herself and her shop-walker husband. He liked to feel wise and responsible. There was no value in his exchanges with Clare, with his brother and sister. They all thought of him as a dull old stick. What if they could see him now with this young woman, as pretty as paint, who hung on his every word? He would have liked to have had children. It would have been this kind of relationship. Him looking out for them, helping them to avoid the pitfalls, getting them on their feet. Did he want anything more intimate from Betty? It wasn't in the front of his mind, but it could be in there somewhere. But it would be ridiculous. He was more than twice her age, and she was married to a man she obviously adored.

Maurice took out his pocket book and gave Betty one of the firm's brochures. She seemed pleased.

'I'll show Stephen,' she said. Then she looked troubled. 'Do you think that Stephen will get called up? For the Army, I mean.'

'It's possible,' said Maurice. 'But it won't be for long.'

'No,' she said. 'I suppose not.'

'Nobody really wants the war. That's why there hasn't been much fighting. Just sparring. Sooner or later the politicians are going to come to their senses. I shouldn't worry about it.'

'There was a bomb in Wimbledon.'

'Just a stray. There's always going to be accidents.'

Suddenly, as they were sitting in the peaceful and safe ambience of the churchyard, there was the sudden wail of the air-raid siren. Surely they were safe where they were? Nobody would bomb St Paul's.

Maurice stood up. 'I'd better get back. Why don't you go into the crypt until the all-clear goes? You'll be perfectly safe there. I'll have to go to organize the fire watch. In fact, I believe it's my turn.'

In the street there was an unnatural hush. Buses and cars, lorries and vans, stood deserted by passengers and drivers. The brewer's dray, with two patient horses, was standing awkward, half on the pavement and half in the road, with the dray man holding the reins, murmuring to the horses a kind of comforting lullaby.

Betty went into the cathedral. There was a sea of anxious faces. She didn't want to go into the crypt. It was cold and spooky down there. She decided to risk it and try to get home, but outside on the steps a policeman and ARP men had formed a chain to keep people in. Suddenly there was a humming in the sky and the sharp rat-tat-tat of machine-gun fire. Oh God. It was really happening. She needed to find a toilet, she felt faint and her mouth was dry. She wanted to get home. It was only one tiny room, but she felt safe there. There was a muffled thump from somewhere behind the cathedral and the very structure of the ancient building seemed to shake to its foundations, and then the sound of fire-engine bells, clanging out an urgent warning. She got to the top of the steps, but a sudden surge of the crowd drew her into the building. She looked up and saw the inside of the dome. What if all that came crashing down?

There was a sort of angry rumble from the crowd, and then another thump, which sounded nearer. People began to get down on the stone floor, some struggling to get under the pews. White, contorted faces registered fear and panic. A toothless old man standing next to her, with a row of medals pinned to his tatty overcoat, said, 'Miles away. I was in the last lot', by way of explanation. 'The one that hits you, you don't hear it.' There was anxiety in every eye. These people couldn't believe what was happening. They had come out for a stroll or just popped in to see the interior of the famous old building, and they had suddenly found themselves trapped inside while bombs rained down around it. It wasn't real. It was like something from the films. A woman grabbed her two children and enveloped them in her arms as though to ward off any damage. The children, feeling that something was wrong, started to cry. There was a group of people kneeling down, silently praying. Dark-frocked ushers were trying to get people to sit down, clearing the aisles. Betty tried to get back to the door but was swept away into another aisle. It was like she had no control over her movements. She sat down at the end of a pew and, irrationally, opened a prayer book. Was this how it was going to be? Everything out of control, just pushed around like an object in the game of pass the parcel? She found herself praying. Praying was something she hadn't done since she was at school. Dear God, let me get home safely. And don't let anything happen to Stephen, who has never done any-thing wrong. She must have remained in the pew for half an hour, full of dread thoughts, stiff from cold and fright. The other people all seemed preoccupied with their own thoughts. Nobody looked at anyone else, as if avoiding the fear in another pair of eyes, knowing that would mirror their own.

Betty felt that the world had stood still though these nerve-wracking minutes. Something was happening that was out of the usual order, something strange, frightening, barbaric. Anyone who was in the cathedral at this time would remember the way they restrained the feelings of cold terror. At odd moments in their life they would suddenly think of this time, this awful void in time, when they were trapped with a couple of hundred strangers, waiting to be blown sky high.

Then there was the sound of the all-clear, a doleful, mourning sound, but not alarming. People around her started to relax. You could almost hear the sound of muscles and nerves stretching, breathing, escaping from the restrictions of fear. Expressions assumed a haughty disdain. Why were all these people such cowards, crying before they had been hit? Each human component of the trapped congregation separated itself from the rest. They shuffled out in some sort of order, with polite gestures, winking to reassure themselves.

They had all known, of course, that God would protect St Paul's.

7

M ISS Tcherny was in the warehouse when the bombs started to fall. She was surprised that bombs were actually falling in broad daylight. She thought that these attacks were scheduled for stealth of the night, when the bombs were released into a black void, and the people in the air would have no knowledge of what, or who, might be underneath.

Night bombing was somehow more acceptable. At least she would have had a chance to get home. God knows what would happen when the rush-hour started. Tube stations might be closed, buses erratic. If she was home she would at least be with her family or maybe with Charlie. As it was she was likely to perish with spotty Jimmy, Harry the packer, and dry-as-dust Maurice Green. They had made many trips to the cellar recently, but they had all proved to be false alarms. The trapdoor opened directly on to the street, so they could hear the destructive activity and see pairs of feet scurrying by in an indecisive frenzy.

She heard the thumps and saw the lower half of a fire engine skidding by. Maurice had elected to stand on the roof. What good he was doing up there she couldn't imagine. Did he think that the sight of an angry Maurice Green on the roof would scare the pilots away? And what was the point in spotting where a bomb had fallen after it had hit something and exploded? These British seemed to think that they were somehow impervious to harm, that a show of righteous indignation would scare people off. They were children in this game of war. Her parents had seen these Nazis at work, had been terrified by attacks on their dress shop, packed everything they owned and left, leaving their life savings, which they had been unable to reclaim, in an Austrian bank. Hitler, it was said, was an Austrian, which made their situation worse. When they first came to Britain they were able to make contacts with relatives and business friends, but it all dried up. She had never told Charlie about the family history. It was best to let it lie. What he didn't know couldn't upset him.

She had promised him that she would stay a night with him in his sister's house. It seemed a tremendous event at the time she agreed, but, with air raids and bombs, going on a seduction seemed a minor matter. She wasn't keen anyway, it was a sacrifice, but if it sent him away happy was it a contribution to the war effort?

She looked across the cellar at Jimmy. His young face was anxious. He was white and his Adam's apple kept going up and down. He was sitting bolt upright, as though sitting to attention, his whole body stiff with strain.

'Come and sit near me,' she said, in a sudden fit of compassion, and he turned towards her, near to tears.

'Why are they doing it, miss?' he whispered.

'Because they're just stupid,' she said. 'Crazy.'

'Are they all crazy? The Germans?'

'It's orders,' she said. That seemed to satisfy Jimmy, although why she couldn't understand.

Harry had brought a flask of tea, which he poured out carefully, offering the stewed brew to the others. 'What's the time?' he asked, yet again.

'Four o'clock,' Rosa said.

'Time for tea,' Harry said, without humour.

The boy Jimmy had somehow got his head in her lap. He was gulping back tears.

'It's all right,' she said. 'You're all right down here.'

'Yes, miss,' he choked. The bravado of the cheeky youth seemed to have left him.

It was nearly five o'clock before the all-clear came through. Young Jimmy had sobbed a bit and dribbled a bit down her blouse. After the all-clear he suddenly sat up and gave her a wink, and somehow managed to get his nose between her breasts. She pushed him away. How early did these boys start feeling for their oats? In a few years' time this little runt would be uncontrollable.

Maurice Green came down from the battlements as though he'd warded off a panzer attack single-handedly. They were still playing a game. They didn't realize how serious it was. They were so secure in their Britishness. They won the Great War, didn't they? It cost them a few hundred thousand lives, but they won in the end. The British were special. There was something in their blood, their history.

Maurice had seen two ugly machines going over towards the docks. He had been close enough to see the markings on their underbellies. There was an arrogance about their appearance in the sky right over the capital. It was an invasion of the peaceful haze over London. They were, in every way, foreign bodies, out of place, flaunting their daring, attacking the heart of Britain. It was something that made the blood rush to the head. Then he heard the thumps. They sounded near, but the smoke that rose afterwards was miles away. The warehouse was almost in the shadow of St Paul's, but Maurice knew that that holy place, with its history and all it stood for, was sacrosanct. Not even the Nazis would dare to attack St Paul's.

He hadn't seen Bernard all day, and now, at five o'clock, he could do with an extra pair of hands to tackle the post. Harry came upstairs.

'What you going to do, guv'nor?'

Maurice stared. 'We're going to get the orders off, of course.'

Harry looked down at the floor.

'It's five o'clock,' he said.

'Well, we're working till six.'

Harry sort of shuffled his feet. 'Don't know what it'll be like getting home. The wife'll be worrying.'

Miss Tcherny and Jimmy came up, and stood, forming a sullen rebellious trio.

'We ought to get off,' said Miss Tcherny. 'It's going to be murder on the Tube.'

Maurice suddenly felt angry. 'You're letting them win. Letting them disrupt our routine. We always get the post off at this time.'

Nobody argued with him. They just stood together in silent disagreement.

'There's a war on,' said Harry. 'The customers know that.'

'The post office will be closed,' said Jimmy. 'They were the last time.'

'You're paid until six,' said Maurice weakly. 'All right. But sharp in the morning.'

They tumbled down the stairs, and Maurice picked up an order pad and started to look out the titles, walking between the shelves, picking the requested books, sorting them into neat piles for packing and invoicing. He'd make sure that they caught up tomorrow. If he let go the place could descend into a shambles. The customers relied on a prompt service. 'By return' had always been Green's boast, and they were going to keep to it.

Bunty was sure that Bernard had done her an injury. Her arm felt twisted and her thighs felt sore and burning. She was glad when the car came, but then, half-way home, the driver stopped and indicated that she should get out and get into an Underground shelter on the edge of a park. It was crowded down there and smelly. There was a fat woman playing an accordion, and people were singing as though their lives depended on it. She lost sight of the driver.

A huge woman in a stretched-to-bursting dress said something to her and pushed a small boy to his feet to make room. The boy, who may have been eight or nine, stood sucking his thumb. Bunty sat down beside the woman. She felt lost. What was happening? Why had she been shoved into this concrete cave with all these people? She looked all around for the driver. The boy was staring at her and he tried to sit on her lap.

'Get up, you horrible Herbert,' said the large woman. 'Mind your manners.'

Right opposite Bunty an old man took out his false teeth, sucked the crevices with his tongue and put them back in again. A youth sat steadily picking his nose while he stared at her. A fat man with staring eyes patted her thigh reassuringly. A baby was being fed, surreptitiously, by a flushed-faced young woman.

Bunty got up. She wasn't doing any good here. She pushed past people until she got to the entrance. There was a policeman on the door.

'I shouldn't go out just now,' the policeman said.

Bunty just smiled and stepped out into the street. There was no one about, and the street was like a vast car park, but with cars parked randomly rather than in rows, left in a hurry by drivers rushing to find shelter. She didn't know where she was. Kennington? Wandsworth? Ah, there was a bus, but it wasn't moving. If she started to walk she wouldn't know if she was going the right way and she couldn't ask anyone. Suddenly she saw the car. It was parked next to a telephone box. She could ring her mother. Then Bunty realized that even if she were able to reach her mother she wouldn't be able to tell her where she was. She didn't know where she was. It was hopeless. She had a sudden feeling of panic. She knew that things were somehow different. People pursed their lips and opened them wide, as if they were saying something of immense significance. Everybody did it, and they always looked solemn or scared, so it must have been something important. Bunty's mother wrote it down for her – WAR – and pointed up at the sky. Bunty had seen pictures of soldiers sloshing about in mud in the last war, and she knew it wasn't up in the sky.

She stood by the car. Surely the driver would come back. Why had he left it in such a hurry? And not only her driver. All the cars were stopped and no drivers to be seen. A policeman was beckoning her. What did he want? She started to go over and then, quite suddenly, the policeman relaxed and stopped his entreaty, and people started filtering out of the dark cellar where she had been, blinking in the daylight. The driver appeared, looking worried. He gestured to her to get into the car. Why had everything returned to normal so suddenly? Something was happening that she did not understand. She could write it down and ask Tim.

When she got back Tim was standing outside the house looking worried. She smiled at him and he shouted at her, 'Where the hell have you been?' And she smiled as though he had paid her a compliment, which seemed to annoy him. He pushed her up the steps and up the stairs into their flat. She felt better. Here was Tim, angry as usual, but she was home, safe.

'Who was that man?' Tim shouted.

She nodded in agreement with whatever it was he had said. But Tim was worked up about something. He took her by the shoulders and shook her, shouting all the while like a madman. His eyes were angry. What was wrong? Surely he ought to be glad to see her after all that had happened?

She put on her 'sorry' face, but Tim would not be placated. She was aching to go to the bathroom. She pointed, and Tim let her go.

When she came back Tim was looking out of the window. He seemed calmer. He gestured that she should sit down on the settee. He was saying something, very seriously, very earnestly. She composed her face to deal with this new phase. Tim was clearly worried. It was her job to comfort him. She snuggled herself into his arms and held him tight. Tim was a poor sod. He couldn't really cope with life, and he couldn't cope with her. She was very fond of Tim, in a sisterly, even motherly, sort of way. He had these little tantrums. He lost his temper, but it was soon over and she knew how to deal with him. She started to open his flies and Tim became like a lump of putty in her skilled hands. She drew his penis out and felt it stiffen in her hand. His eyes shut and he lay there like a puppy waiting to have its tummy tickled.

Then she began to undress, taking off her blouse and then her brassière, and Tim was staring at her, not like a bewitched male, but pointing to her shoulder. He got up and dragged her before the wardrobe mirror. She could see a big blue bruise. Tim was pointing and shouting, looking angrier than ever. He jerked the blouse off and pulled down her skirt and knickers, but not in the nice, saucy, loving way they were used to but in an angry way, looking at her as though he were examining her for imperfections. He pointed to her thighs that were red with a scratch on the inside of the left one. He was shouting again: that pursing of the lips and wide open mouth. Everything seemed to start with this facial contortion. Tim was clearly in a high old temper. He kept pointing at her scratches and bruises, and pointing them out to her in the mirror. Did he think she'd done them herself? He was a funny boy was Tim. She put on her nightdress and got into bed. Tim was staring out of the window. He lit a cigarette. He was trying to steady himself, control his nerves. Bunty waved at him, but he turned away.

The next day when Bunty's mother came Tim insisted on Bunty showing her the bruises and scratches. Bunty's mother wasn't impressed. 'They'll heal up. I'll put some iodine on if you like.'

'But where has she got them from?'

'Only she knows that, and she's not telling.'

'Somebody has been knocking her about,' Tim said with heat.

'You don't know that. She could have fallen down somewhere.'

'When I got back from work she wasn't here.'

'I expect she went down a shelter or something. There was a warning. Maybe she fell or got knocked down in the rush.'

These off-the-cuff explanations did not serve to mollify Tim. 'It's these blokes she goes with. Bloody animals.'

'Why should anyone want to knock her about? She's done nothing. Poor thing.'

'How do you know what she's been up to?' Tim shouted wildly.

'All right,' said Bunty's mother. 'There's no need to inform the whole house.' Bunty's mother always came out on top in these exchanges. She knew that Tim had realized what was going on, but he just hadn't got the will-power to put a stop to it. He was allowed his little rant and rave. Nothing could come of it. The fact was that Tim couldn't really afford someone like Bunty. He was lucky was Tim. If it wasn't for the speech difficulties and not being able to hear, Bunty would have been on the stage, or even the films. Bunty was, after all, a beauty, and Tim couldn't expect her to be waiting behind the door for him all day long.

After this incident Tim became sulky. He knew that he didn't have any control over his wife. She may not be bright, but she was very headstrong, determined to go her own way, whether he liked it or not.

Bert Penrose was in the basement of the Claridge's Hotel when the warning came through. He didn't hear it, but he knew because the basement where he was engaged in interminable washing up suddenly filled up with other members of staff. They wouldn't come down there otherwise. Bert resented these periods of alarm. All the others – porters, page boys, maids, waiters and maintenance people – stood around, smoking and chatting, while he continued to slop around the dishes in slimy water. He didn't mind working, but he didn't like all these people watching him. The head waiter often peered over his shoulder, wiping a finger over a plate. 'Look at that,' he would say. 'Disgusting.' And later, the manager would come down and give Bert a ticking-off.

Bert hated working in the underground slop house. When he left home he always tried to dress up a bit, to give the impression he was going to some important job in an important firm. When he got to Claridge's he undressed and put on floppy overalls that, even when just back from the laundry, smelt like they had been boiled in carbolic.

Nevertheless, he knew he was lucky to have the job at all. He had been an imposing hall porter, with brown-and-gold livery, and would have been still if that cow hadn't reported him for busting into her room while she was getting dressed. True, he hadn't knocked, but he had been too busy with the cases to notice her in her scanties. In any case, there wasn't much of her, the skinny cow. Lady Alexandra Something, and a right little snob she was, had demanded that he was dismissed, and the management had made a show of giving him the sack but had, in fact, hidden him in the basement as a dish-washer. It was either that or out on his ear, without notice and without a reference. If he weren't too old he would have volunteered for the Army or the bloody Navy.

This alert went on longer than usual and all his old mates seemed to enjoy watching him. He stood back, dried his hands and lit a fag. He would have to get out of this place. If he did this stinking job for a few weeks they would have to give him a reference. Wouldn't be so bad if the missus would do something. She seemed to think she was above going to work. But why not? Women were doing all sorts of things: clippies on the buses, some in the ATS, all sorts of things that women had never done before. It was about time Edie got her finger out.

It was his time for a break. He only got ten minutes, during which he usually went out into the daylight to breathe some real air, but while this blasted alert was on he was stuck down this hole.

Then there was a slight movement, and the employees of Claridge's, reluctantly, began to leave.

'Good night, Bert,' one of them called. 'Happy dreams.' Fat

chance, Bert thought. He'd only just got through the lunch, there was tea and dinner to cope with yet. If he got away before ten o'clock he'd be lucky.

Mrs Bennet heard the siren and immediately switched off all the electricity and started filling kettles, bowls and saucepans with water. She could manage without electricity. In fact, she felt safer with it off, but she couldn't manage without water. She got a tin bath from the scullery and started to fill it from a hand basin. Some of it splashed on to the carpet, which, after a few trips, became sodden. She wondered if there was anybody in upstairs. If so, they would have been down by now. No. She was in the place on her own. If anything happened she would either be blown up or buried alive. She warmed to her task, filling every receptacle she could lay her hands on. Then she stood back and reviewed her handiwork. Everything was full to the brim. She sat down. It was deathly quiet. She peered out of the window. The street was deserted.

They had been promised an Anderson shelter, but there was some difficulty about getting one big enough for everybody who lived in the house. They all seemed to be about the same size. Six people stuffed in like sardines. Mrs Bennet thought she would much sooner die in her bed. She remembered the fairgrounds, where there was a sideshow called 'Tipping a Woman Out of Bed', where some young tart would be in bed in her nightshirt and men would pay to throw balls to see if they could upset the bed enough to tip her out. That was what it would be like: tipped out of bed while the roof fell in on top of her.

She knew she had a drop of whisky somewhere. Was it in the kitchen cabinet? It could be in the bathroom, if you thought of it as being medicinal. She rummaged around in the kitchen and found it. It was only a small bottle, but it had never been opened. It was there for an emergency. As she moved the bottle from its hiding place a little brown mouse skidded out. They were all over the house. The floors and walls were riddled with them. When the last cat died the mice must have had a party and started to breed twice as fast.

She drank the whisky straight from the bottle. If her Tom were still around he would have been shocked. A life-long teetotaller, Mrs Bennet's deceased husband had been very strict about drink. He despised people who got drunk, thought that pubs were evil places, swore that he'd never touched a drop all his life. Well, a fat lot of good it did him. He was dead before he was fifty.

She wondered if she should pray. She used to go to church. That was where she met Norman. In the Band of Hope. He had a big, round, shining face. They used to go on rambles, to Box Hill and around that way and Oxshott. He kissed her one day in a wood, and then apologized as if he had committed a mortal sin.

Oh God. She'd wet herself again.

8

YOUNG Jimmy had a secret weakness for pork dripping. You could get it from the ham and beef shop. You could get beef dripping as well and fish paste, all glistening in huge mounds. You bought it loose. You just said 'a quarter', and they scooped it off with a butter pat on to greaseproof paper, and you took it home and spread it thick on nice fresh bread. He could get some and get home before his mum came in, and get through five or six slices before she got back to cook his tea. The smell of it made him drool. They sold everything in ham and beef shops: faggots, saveloys, pease pudding, silverside in gravy. For that sort of stuff you took two plates and ran home with it while it was hot. But not pork dripping; it was meant to be cold and flecked with little bits of brown jelly stuff.

But the last time he went for pork dripping it wasn't there. The succulent mountains of his favourite savoury treat had been rationed. It was a swizz! It wasn't butter, was it, or even margarine? It was the fat they got when they cooked a pig to make cold pork. But you couldn't get it any more. The same thing had happened to bacon, which was also on the meat ration. Jimmy's mum had his ration book, so he couldn't even choose what he wanted. It took three ration books to produce a small piece of meat. You could get offal – liver, hearts, lights and brains but not kidneys (it seemed as though sheep and pigs didn't have kidneys any more) – but he didn't like that stuff anyway. One of the main pleasures of his existence had been taken away from him. Did the Army get it all?

Jimmy liked the time when his dad had just gone to work and his mother was still out at the laundry. It was quiet and he could read his *Gem* and *Magnet* comics and see what the Famous Five had been up to, old Mr Quelch and the bounder from the Remove. These long stories, which filled an entire magazine, were like escaping to another world. The boys at St Jim's and Greyfriars were cheeky enough, but they had a code of behaviour. One or two had been unprincipled at times, but these were quickly cast as 'outsiders' to whom nobody spoke. They were, as a whole, good chaps. Would they all go into the Army or the Air Force or get blown up at sea by a submarine, or some underhand trick? Had old Maurice been to St Jim's?

Jimmy, who had tried to attend to what he was taught at his elementary school, knew that there were large gaps in his education. At Greyfriars they had Latin and equations, whatever they were. They played a lot of cricket, which was hardly feasible on a concrete playground. They had tripos and a tuck-shop and they wore stiff collars over their jackets. They didn't have mothers and fathers, they had maters and paters. Young Maulverer was already a lord while he was still at school and Gussie was an aristocrat. Of course there were plain ordinary boys – Johnny Bull and Tom Merry, for example – that were very steady and honourable.

It was clear that there was this other life, somewhere out in the country, where boys had probably never heard of pork dripping. They seemed to eat a lot of porridge. Jimmy had persuaded his mother to get some, but he didn't like it. Maybe she didn't do it right.

He went out into the backyard, a small area of concrete where his father kept the birds. He called it an 'aviary', but it was just a wooden shed, full of birdcages. There were canaries and budgies mostly, with a few more unusual birds, sometimes a parrot. His father spent most of his free time out there. He had tried to breed them, thinking that when he retired he might be able to set up a business supplying shops, but the breeding hadn't worked out. Sometimes the birds caught something that raised ugly bumps on their throats, like boils, and then they died. As he opened the door there was a rustle all around the shed. The birds all seemed agitated. Did they know there was a war on? They didn't do much. They sat on their perches and fell asleep. What did his dad do in there for hours on end? He cleaned out the cages. Did he enjoy that? Cleaning up bird mess? Mum said it was his hobby, as though she was glad it wasn't something worse.

Jimmy knew that his dad didn't like anybody going into the aviary while he was out, but he didn't lock it up. The birds seemed to be watching him; dozens of little eyes wondering what was coming next. Would they like to be free, flying around in trees, finding their own food? His dad said they were 'cage birds', which meant that they didn't know any life outside a cage. If they were let out, street birds, such as sparrows and rooks, would attack and kill them. No, they were better in the shed, although it didn't seem much of a life, just sitting and scratching.

It had been all right in Miss Tcherny's lap. She was all soft and woolly and she smelt nice. He could feel her bumps a bit. She was a bit of all right was Miss Tcherny. She knew what he was thinking, and he enjoyed the fact that she knew. There would be a rush on in the morning. Old Maurice seemed to think that they should work all night if the air raid held them up.

He would go to the pictures on Saturday. There was a Popeye on and a Laurel and Hardy and Jack Payne's Band on stage. He would get in at twelve o'clock and stay in all afternoon. That way you could see the shorts twice.

When Jimmy's mum came in she looked tired. She had two shopping bags, one in each hand. She gasped a bit as she lifted them on to the table.

'Has that fire gone out? Couldn't you put a shovel of coal on?'

'I've been reading.'

'Reading what?'

'The *Gem* and *Magnet*.'

'Show me. Give it here.' He showed her the magazines. 'They'll do,' she said, shoving them into the grate.

'No,' he shouted. 'They're mine.' But it was too late. His mother had put a match to them and piled some kindling wood on top.

'That's rotten,' he said.

His mother was unimpressed by his show of fury. 'Get some coal,' she said flatly.

He sulked a bit. 'What's for tea? I'm starving.'

'Kippers, but I can't do them on a cold stove.'

He fetched a shovelful of coal, and his mother tipped the coal on to the smoking wood.

'Open the window,' she said. 'It needs a draught.'

'Thought you said it was cold.' His mother ignored little jibes like this. She just patiently attended to the fire and the stove.

'Did you hear the air raid?' Jimmy asked.

'Yes, I heard it.'

'Did you go downstairs?'

'No, we didn't. Too much to do. They don't pay us for sitting in a cellar.'

Nothing seemed to excite his mother. If King Kong had poked his face through the window she would have told him to go and wash his hands. She didn't register surprise or joy. Her face was a blank mask. She just plodded on with the task in hand – washing, cooking, ironing, cleaning, shopping. She did all these chores adequately but with no sense of achievement or pride. She seemed to have given up any sense of satisfaction. Life was just a dreary experience. She never laughed or even smiled. Jimmy's father was the same when he was in the house, although he could break out a bit if he'd had a drink. Why were his parents so miserable? Were all parents the same? Some of his uncles and aunties seemed more jolly, but that was only when he was visiting. When he'd gone they probably settled back into their own morose selves.

There was usually a gathering at Christmas, when all the aunties would get together and plan and budget for the Christmas dinner and tea like it was a military operation. The uncles were all sent out to the pub, which they did with humorous sighs of regret. Then they would all meet up in one house and one of the aunts would hesitantly play the piano from sheet music and the rest of them would stand at the back of her and sing the words. Jimmy would be left to play with his cousins, who were all younger than him and still at school, and Greyfriars seemed a million miles away.

Jimmy's dad wouldn't have an Anderson shelter because it would have meant taking the aviary out. Most of the relations had Anderson or Morrison shelters, but they filled up with water. People had special clothes to wear in them called siren-suits. There was a current joke about a young woman wanting a siren-suit to go down into the Anderson: 'It's not a siren-suit you want, it's a bloody diving-suit.' The bloody war seemed to have spoilt everything. Bloody sirens, bloody bombs, bloody sandbags, stirrup pumps and hoses, buckets with long shovels for putting out incendiary bombs, bloody old Churchill, who seemed to be enjoying the chance of everybody being blown to buggery.

That night when he went to bed, Jimmy heard the drone of planes flying overhead. He got up when his dad came in.

'All right?'

'Got a lift in one of the vans,' his dad said.

'There's a lot of aeroplanes,' said Jimmy.

'Over the docks. They're catching it.'

His mother got up, looking grim. 'Why aren't you in bed?'

'Leave him alone,' said his dad. 'The poor little bugger is frightened.'

'I'm not,' said Jimmy.

'Well you ought to be,' said his dad heavily.

'How long is this going on, keeping people up all night?' demanded his mother indignantly, as though they ought to report it to someone.

'Gawd knows. Let's get to bed.'

'I should think so,' said his mother crossly. 'I've got work in the morning.'

'And so have I,' said Jimmy, feeling left out. As he went up the stairs he caught a glimpse of a red glow in the sky.

'Dad! Dad, what's that?'

'Fires,' said his dad. 'It's in the papers already. I saw them before I left.'

Jimmy went to bed wondering what was it all about, this war? Why had these foreigners turned so nasty? Something had happened. There had been a war before, but that was years ago. They had a Poppy Day at school when everyone wore a poppy for wounded soldiers. That was what the war was for. It was for soldiers, not for people in their beds.

He had nearly got off to sleep when there was a fluttering, hissing noise, like a small box of fireworks had caught fire by accident. Then there was a light outside the window. He heard his father shout 'Christ!' and rush downstairs, followed by his mother's angry cry of 'Now what?' Jimmy went downstairs in his pyjamas. There was a bright flame in the backyard. Little bundles of fire were spitting away in fiery clumps all over the yard. The roof of the aviary was burning, and his dad, in his vest and long underpants, was running from the kitchen with bowls of water, which he flung on to the aviary, but the fire spat and then roared back with increasing fury.

'Get the stirrup pump,' his mother yelled from the first-floor window. But his dad was in a panic, running around like a circus clown, spilling water over himself. There was an awful fluttery sound coming from the aviary.

'My birds,' his father shouted. 'My bloody birds!'

The roof was blazing, bright orange with a blue centre, and there was a smell of frying and cracks as the wood split.

A face appeared over the wall. 'Ain't you got a hosepipe? Have you called the fire brigade?'

Jimmy's dad was too panicked to take notice of any practical instructions. He forced open the door of the aviary and the birds swept out, some black, some with their feathers singed, some fluttering a bit then falling to the ground; some perched on the washing-line, swaying, until they fell off. Somebody chucked a sandbag over the wall, which split on impact. Jimmy's mum, hair streaming, with an overcoat over her nightdress and no shoes, bent down and picked up handfuls of sand, which she flung, wildly, in the direction of the fire.

'By God, Lucy,' Jimmy's dad shouted. 'I'll kill the bastards. What had they done, eh? Bloody helpless birds.'

Jimmy's mum continued to paddle, barefooted, in the sand, scooping up handfuls that dripped through her fingers. Then there was a roar, and the structure of the aviary collapsed; a cloud of smoke and dust blew up and engulfed them. Jimmy's dad was crying. His black-faced mum stood, helpless, her hands still full of sand.

The neighbour scrambled over the wall. 'All right?' he said. 'Fit to fight another day, eh? Bloody incendiaries. Cause more trouble than they're worth.'

Jimmy looked at the dead birds, lying in various strictures of shock, some with their beaks open as though they were struck down as they were crying for help, some twisted in agony, their charred bodies trailed all over the yard. Should he pick them up and bury them? It didn't seem right just to sweep them up and put them in the dustbin.

Jimmy's mother was temporarily stirred out of her placid stupor. She put her hand around her husband's shoulder.

'Come inside, George. Don't want the neighbours to see you like that.' Jimmy's dad stared at the dead birds. He didn't care who saw him without his trousers and shirt, soaking wet, crying. 'You can get some more birds.'

His body shook with a huge sigh. 'No. It's all over,' he said. He allowed himself to be led inside, where he sat staring at the stove while Jimmy's mum busied herself making tea. But as soon as she'd made it her husband got up and went up to the bathroom.

'Go to bed,' said the distraught woman. 'He'll get over it.'

'Can't I have anything to eat?'

'Eat?' Jimmy's mother let out a fearsome scream. 'Eat? Ain't you got no feelings?' And she slapped Jimmy's face with the back of her hand, sending him reeling against the coal scuttle.

'It's not my fault,' Jimmy whimpered. 'Don't take it out on me.'

His mother regained her composure. It was only a momentary lapse, but Jimmy understood. It was all too much. Things were happening outside the normal experience, things that interfered with their lives and over which they had no control.

His dad was silent for days afterwards. He came and went, ate and slept like he was under sentence of death. He cleared up the remains of the shed and burnt it. Then he swept the concrete, getting up every speck of dust and charred wood, and slopped it over with buckets of water. Then he rang the town hall and ordered an Anderson shelter. There was a waiting list. It would take six weeks before they could send one.

'We could all be dead,' said Jimmy's mother.

She had gone to work the next day as though nothing had happened. After all, it was only a few old birds. They wouldn't appear on the casualty list.

When Jimmy got into work the day after, old Maurice told everybody off. Jimmy didn't understand why. They only went off a bit early because of the air raid. You would have thought they'd deserted from the Army or something.

'We have to keep things running as normal,' Maurice said.

'Otherwise the enemy is winning.' Jimmy couldn't see how him getting off a bit early was going to effect the course of the war. Anyway, what was old Maurice going to do about it? Report him to Churchill? 'This country', continued Maurice, 'has got its back against the wall. We have lost the battle in France so we can't lose the battle in England. It's up to us to keep things going.'

The battle in France? That must have been when all those soldiers set out in rowing boats across the Channel. He'd seen it on the newsreels. All dirty, wet soldiers grinning and giving the V-for-victory sign with two fingers. His dad said that his paper had run an extra edition. He did an extra shift and got paid so much that he took him and his mother to a Corner House brasserie, where they ate a joyless meal – that Mum said she could have done at home for much less money – while a troupe of gypsies played violins and things. Was that when they lost the battle of France? France, he knew, wasn't far away. They said that you could see France from Dover – or was it Clacton?

The newsreels were full of soldiers anyway. They were always doing something – running, firing guns, marching, singing, painting their faces to look like trees. It was a grown-up game. There were people down his street who had had people called up. They all got drunk the night before they went. One reappeared in a light-blue suit, with one of his legs missing. He wasn't giving the V-sign; he was holding on to his crutches. Did the people who wrote the *Gem* and the *Magnet* know there was a war on? They never mentioned it. There were other things like *War Stories* and *Battlefield*, but they were boring. Who wanted to read about the war?

He went on his round, collecting books: Longman's, Nelson's, Charles Letts for diaries, SPCK, Hodder's. Everyone was talking about the bombs. Apparently there had been a right packet in the East End. Houses had been blown up and factories and warehouses set on fire. A place where they kept brandy and whisky had burnt down, and much of the gear was taken, unofficially, into the. safe keeping of peoples' homes. Bottles were exchanging hands all over. He saw one collector put a bottle in his sack.

At Hodder's he indulged in his embarrassment of the girl at

the trade counter, once again staring at her until she blushed. She had pale copper-coloured hair and a pale face and, that particular morning, red eyes, and she reacted angrily to his obvious scrutiny. 'Who are you glinting at?'

'Glinting?' he said. 'Glinting?' This came from working in a publishers. They pick up these strange words.

'It's rude,' the girl said.

'You been crying?'

'I've haven't,' she said.

He looked at her eyes. They were blue, but the rims were red. 'You have,' he said.

The girl looked down. 'My dog ran away.'

'Don't worry,' he said gently, warming to this show of vulnerability. 'He'll come back.'

'He ran off when he heard the bombs. They weren't far away. He was frightened.'

'So he should have been,' said Jimmy, echoing his father. 'My dad's birds all got burnt. With an incendiary.'

'What birds?'

'Cage birds. Canaries and budgies. He kept them, in a shed in the garden.'

'That's terrible.'

'Yeah. They were all burnt up.'

The girl looked up and gave him a cool appraisal. 'You come here a lot, don't you?'

He wanted to say, 'Yes, I come in to see you', but he didn't feel that sure yet. 'Where do you go dinner time?' he asked.

This time the girl didn't blush but just looked at him with her own cool stare.

'What's your name?' he asked, pressing on.

'Helen,' she said.

'Helen,' he echoed, as though he was sampling a new sweet. 'Helen.'

'You don't have to keep saying it,' she said crossly.

He grinned. 'No. I like it. Helen. What do you do dinner time, Helen?'

This time she did blush. 'ABC,' she said.

'I'll meet you. One o'clock.'

He had got to know the other collectors from other firms. They all went into a bookshop in Blackfriars Road for bread and dripping: big doorsteps of beef dripping, never pork, which they would eat with a pint mug of tea. Most of the collectors were older men. Old Maurice knew what he was doing making him do it. If he had a man he would have to pay them a man's money. Old Maurice was a skinflint and no mistake.

Jimmy dawdled until half past twelve. Then he rushed into the warehouse and unloaded his sack. Old Maurice was at the other end of a row of shelves. He beckoned him, but Jimmy pretended not to notice. He shouted 'Jimmy', but Jimmy cocked a deaf 'un and scooted down the stairs in quick time. He had an important assignment, to meet Helen at the ABC at one o'clock, and a whole army of Maurices weren't going to stop him.

He waited outside the tea house – the Aerated Bread Company was a sort of sub-Joe Lyons', not quite as posh and a bit cheaper – for ten minutes. A workman was piling sandbags outside the shop, and the windows had been stuck over with tape.

He wasn't sure that she would come. His heart gave a leap when he saw her coming along. She was wearing a smart outdoor coat, dark blue, with fur trimming around the lapels. Her hair wasn't what you might call ginger, but it was light-copper colour and straight, falling neatly and evenly from a centre parting. He thought she might have applied a bit of makeup to that pale face, but he couldn't be sure. Surely those lips couldn't be such a luscious shade of red all by themselves? She was so neat, with neat, short steps. The whole effect of her appearance was like a bunch of ripe cherries, a knickerbocker glory, a fresh cream cake; to Jimmy, she was good enough to eat.

'Hello,' he said. 'Do you always come here?'

'Mostly,' she said. 'Roll and butter and cheese. Cup of tea. Sixpence.'

'Would you like to go somewhere else for a change?'

'I don't mind,' she said.

Walking down Fleet Street with this fabulous girl by his side was like being in the films, the finale of a musical, when after a series of misunderstandings the girl and boy come together and, walking on air, smile brilliantly until 'The End' comes up. He was exultant, full of himself. Of course, they shouldn't be in these dusty streets, they should be down at Brighton or somewhere, eating a plate of cockles together, sitting on the sea wall, sucking ice cream. He would be wearing a blazer and grey flannels like they did in the *Magnet*, and she would be wearing a nice print dress with flowers on it and smiling at him, like he was the only boy she's ever wanted to be with. Sod the dog, bugger the birds, bugger the war and bleeding old Churchill. Piss on old Maurice and Green's. This was the life, with Helen, all neatly packaged, by his side.

They weaved along until he saw the Milk Bar. That was it. Something new, something smart. He'd never been in before, but he wasn't going to tell her that.

'Shall we try this place?' he said, trying to sound casual.

'I don't know. What's it like?'

'It's milk, you know. Different flavours,' he said, after rapidly scanning the menu. They went in and sat on the high stools, like the bar of a Hollywood soda fountain they had often seen in American college films, with hot-eyed girls and brash boys acting the fool.

'What you going to have?' he said, in a worldly way. 'Banana, raspberry, blackcurrant?'

'What? Milk?' she said, seemingly a bit bewildered at the turn of events.

'We can go somewhere else,' he said quickly.

'No,' she said. 'This is all right.'

The whole place was made of chrome and glass. You could see people walking by, peering in. It was like being in a shop window. It wasn't what he'd wanted. He wanted a dark alcove, not this exposure.

'Come on,' he said. 'Let's go somewhere else.' So they left, but not before Jimmy had seen old Maurice in a big glass mirror at the back of the counter talking to a young woman Jimmy had never seen before. She was looking at old Maurice as if he was something marvellous, and the silly old sod seemed to be enjoying himself. Christ, that was something: old Maurice smiling. Enough to cause a crack in the ceiling.

Jimmy led Helen through a maze of winding courts until he

found a small teashop. It was quiet and had a dark interior. They sat down. The tea was in little teapots that you poured out yourself. There were buns and biscuits. They settled in and began to talk.

'Do you go to the pictures?' Jimmy asked.

'Sometimes,' the girl said. 'Depends what's on.'

'There's a Laurel and Hardy on this week,' he said. 'I reckon I'll go on Saturday.'

'They're just silly,' Helen said, disparagingly. Jimmy felt a numbing feeling. She was wonderful to look at, but was it possible that she had no sense of humour? Laurel and Hardy were wonderful, but maybe girls couldn't see that they were acting.

'What do you like?' he said.

Helen stirred her tea, pouting a little with those delicious lips. 'Well, I like a good story. Something that could really happen.' This was feet-on-the-ground stuff. What about fantasy, larking around and romance?

'Who's your favourite film star?'

'I like Norma Shearer,' said Helen. 'She's sensible.'

'She is,' Jimmy agreed, but his heart was sinking. Who wanted to be sensible? 'What about men?'

'Robert Taylor.'

Ah. That was better. The baby-faced, good-looking Taylor was nearly in the realms of fantasy and certainly in the realms of romance.

'You want to come with me Saturday?' Helen looked down. Had he rushed it a bit? Too quick? 'Doesn't matter about Saturday. Friday will do.' Now she was blushing again. It didn't take much to get her going. He hadn't said anything. Was it the way he said it? Was it because he had said Friday, which meant going in the evening, whereas Saturday was a daytime meet? Was it because she knew what he was thinking, imagining her small scarcely formed body quite naked, with the little bumps culminating in pips, and the mysterious triangle of hair between the thighs as he had seen in some of the books at Green's, catalogued as Medical, and even more graphically in books that Mr Bernard took out called Studies in Art or some such cover-up title? He didn't mean anything. He was just curious. Was she a mind-reader? What was she thinking?

'I don't know,' she said finally. 'I'll have to see.'

She had been to Clark's College for shorthand and typing. She still went in the evening. She wasn't good enough yet to do it at work. She wanted to be a secretary. This was bad news for Jimmy, who knew that a secretary would be out of his range. She liked working at Hodder's, especially when some of the authors came in. 'It must be wonderful,' she said, 'being an author.'

'I'm going into the print,' he said. 'My dad's getting me in.'

On the way back he took her arm, and she didn't seem to mind. 'See you on Saturday.' She looked up at him, and he felt somehow powerful. She needed looking after, and he was there to do it. He would gladly accept the responsibility.

'I live miles away from you,' she said.

He brushed objections aside with his King Arthur sword. 'I'll come over,' he said, 'or we can meet half-way.' She was looking at him intently. She seemed to be searching his face for some truth, something to trust. 'Tell you what,' he said. 'We'll meet again tomorrow, and then you can tell me how you feel about Saturday.'

He watched her go into Hodder's and then walked around Warwick Square, grinning. He was delirious with delight. He'd pulled it off. He'd clicked.

Maurice wasn't at all pleased to see his young collector in the Milk Bar. What was the little fool doing in there and with a young girl as well? (There was no denying that Jimmy had the kind of urchin cheek and charm that Maurice had never had and even now envied.) On the other hand, what was he, Maurice, doing in the Milk Bar with a young girl? At least Jimmy was with someone his own age, whereas he was there with a woman young enough to be his daughter. It was all wrong. How had he got into this mess? The fact was that these short meetings with Betty had become of an overriding importance to him, the only time he felt alive. He had rescued her from prostitution, and yet, in a way, she was still in the business. She was being paid for her time. He hired her by the hour. She didn't see it that way. She was naïve and easily led. That was how she must have got into that ghastly club with that hard-faced bitch. Betty was a girl who could easily be taken advantage of. Is that what he was doing? Would she ever be of use in the business? That was doubtful. It wasn't just her lack of education, but her general lack of awareness. She was like a child, full of pretensions, dreams and petty snobberies. She obviously thought of him as a respectable escort, but why didn't her husband intervene? Why was he willing to risk his wife's well-being and safety to a man he had never seen? Was it just the money? She could hardly earn fifty shillings a week so easily else-where. He was treating her generously, so why did he feel so guilty? She was good-looking, no doubt of that. There was quite an intense pleasure in just looking at the girl: her perfect oval face, her perfect little ears, her teeth with slight smudges of lip-stick on them, her eyes, so innocent and trusting. A girl like Betty ought not to be out on her own – and yet she had no idea that her very presence was a provocation. Perhaps he ought to bring the arrangement to an end. Where was it going after all?

'There was a fire in the next street,' she said. 'Incendiary bomb.'

'Did it do much damage?'

'No, I don't think so.' Even her small talk was shallow: no depth in anything she said. She was very good at listening, how-ever. When he held forth about books her eyes shone as though he was a wizard, imparting some secret formula.

'Have you finished the stocktaking?' she asked, innocently. He knew what she meant. The mythical stocktaking was the reason why he hadn't been able to take her to the warehouse.

'Not quite,' he said uneasily. He was lying, and it didn't sit easily on his conscience. Why didn't he want to show her the ware-house? He didn't want to because there were other people there. Not the staff so much, they could mind their own business, but Bernard, who dropped in at all different times. He might see her and know where she came from and so draw his own conclusions. Bernard wouldn't tell Clare – well, Bernard hardly ever saw Clare – but it would give Bernard a hold over him, give him a naughty secret that would affect his position in the business.

And Maurice couldn't have that, not at any price.

9

BUNTY was all of a tizz. Tim had told her mother – who had conveyed the message by way of hand signs and looks – that Bunty was not to go out any more.

When the message got through she stuck her tongue out at Tim and patted his face, lightly, in the way that someone might reprove a slightly fractious but not particularly naughty child.

'You're making her a prisoner,' said Bunty's mother.

'I know,' said Tim grimly. 'I'm doing it for her own good.' He had been brooding about the situation for a week or more. It wasn't to do with jealousy; it was to do with injured pride. Somebody had been knocking his wife about. If anyone was going to set about Bunty it would be him. Christ, she gave him enough reason. Always showing herself off, giving blokes the eye. He knew she couldn't help it. He knew, in some dim recess of his mind, that desirability and availability were the props that kept her going, her way of fighting back from her disability. She may not be able to contribute to a conversation, she couldn't keep up with the news on the wireless, but in the vital matter of life she was supreme. Men fancied her, they lusted after her, she was important in an important way. And Tim knew this, and, although he didn't like the position it put him in, he could see that Bunty had a point. Nevertheless, he wasn't prepared to be made a fool of. He had his pride.

But Tim couldn't be around all day. He had his job to see to. He was having special training about linking up fire-brigade hosepipes so that water could be transported right across London, from the pond on Clapham Common to Westminster and maybe the City. It was called Operation Linkage, and it was important that he understood what to do. In fact, there was little ordinary work to do, as all connections, faults and leaks had taken a back seat to the overriding importance of Operation Linkage. The truth was that there weren't enough water supplies in the City to deal with fires, and, if they occurred, there would quickly be a shortage. Tim quite liked his new role. He might never get called up, but he was doing something. At the same time he couldn't have these blokes making free with his wife. Maybe her affliction had sent her a bit loopy, but he felt he ought to exercise some control.

All that morning he contrived to organize a route that would lead him past the house or at least to the corner of the road, where he could take a long view of the comings and goings at number 77. He cycled around, making sure he was at least in the area. He knew that the time Bunty went out was around lunchtime. From half-past twelve to two o'clock he was sitting on his bike at the end of the road like a sentry waiting for an attack.

Eventually, he saw a car pull up. Nobody got out to knock at the door, but Bunty came out, as if to a prearranged signal, and got in. The car drove off, and Tim found himself following on his bike. It was all right in the side street, where he could follow at a safe distance, but when the car turned into the main road it sped away from him, and, even pedalling furiously, he lost sight of it in a maze of traffic. If the lights hadn't turned red he would have lost it. He weaved his way between the stationary vehicles until he saw the car, a big grey affair, a Humber, set off as the lights changed. Then it was speeding away from him. Top speed on his heavy service-bike was about twelve miles an hour, so he soon got left behind again.

He sat there, sweating. He was never going to track the car to its destination. But one thing was clear: Bunty had defied him, had taken not a blind bit of notice of his orders. If that was the way she wanted it she was in for a shock.

At lunchtime he found himself eating his sandwiches, sitting on his bike, at the corner of the street. He decided to go back into the flat. There might be some clue as to where she had gone.

He parked his bike against the railings and went in. In the hallway he met Mrs Bennet, looking white and frail and puzzled. She looked at him as though she had never seen him before. 'What time is it?' she demanded, as though someone had been interfering with the clocks.

'Half-past two,' he shouted, as he was bounding up the stairs.

'She's gone out,' she mumbled.

'I know,' he said defensively, as though he knew all about Bunty's movements, which had his full approval. He wasn't having that raving old bat poking her nose into his affairs.

The flat was strewn with clothes. Obviously Bunty had been trying things on and discarding them as she went. He'd never seen the place so untidy. She must have a good tidy-up before he came home. He sat down and held his head in his hands. He was baffled, impotent in the face of her defiance.

'For crying out loud,' he said. He stared at himself in the mirror. He wasn't no Errol Flynn, that was for sure, but he was all right. Stocky, fit – of course, from all the cycling – but no athlete, light fair hair, a certain jut of the jaw, nice blue eyes and an air of determination: this was a man of conviction, fair-minded, of course, but honest and resolute. Was he good enough for Bunty? Could he expect someone with her outstanding charms to be faithful to such a run-of-the-mill bloke as him? But, whatever the rights and wrongs of the situation, he had to deal with it. He couldn't let her go on making a fool of him. One day someone would see her when she was out. People in the street must already know about the afternoon jaunts. They must think that he allowed her to go out in some bloke's posh car, dressed up to the nines. They might think that he was involved, a – what was it? – a pimp?

In the afternoon he was engaged on Operation Linkage. The local chief fire officer was keen on running through the drill until everybody could do it blindfolded. As he explained, the chances were that they would have to do it in the dark anyway. After the sixth run-through it became tedious, and Tim was tired.

What the devil was he going to do about Bunty? Did he really care what she was up to? Her life of silence needed some compensation. If she could only communicate by touch you had to reckon with that. She had always been good with him, any time he wanted, and the full works every time. What if he got her up the spout? That would stop her little gallop. He could make out that he had forgotten to get some skins and get her on the crest of a wave. Although Bunty had always been particular about skins and had devised a little ballet when she put them on him. And he would have to see off that bloody mother of hers. She encouraged Bunty, the scheming old witch, and where did she come into it? Did Bunty give her some money, some clothes? There was no telling what went on between the mother and daughter. They had learnt, over the years, to communicate without language.

That night when he came home the place was spick and span. She'd got haddock for his tea and some sort of jelly stuff to follow. She always contrived to put something appetizing before him. In these days of rationing it was a miracle what she came up with. But how did she get it? Were there butchers at this place that she went to? Fishmongers, perhaps? He knew that her idea was to give him nothing to complain about. If he had nothing to complain about that gave her licence to go about her own business.

'You went out,' he said. And Bunty smiled, as she usually did, and gave him an arch look. Was this her response to any item of conversation? He pointed at the door, and she gave him a puzzled look. What was he on about now, for Christ's sake?

'I said you weren't to go.' He knew that she couldn't hear him, but she was very good at reading expressions.

She shrugged her shoulders. Whatever it was hadn't got through to her so she dismissed it as unimportant. He scowled heavily and began to undo his belt. As he was releasing the notches she pushed him over, on to the sofa and then fell on top of him. He pushed her away, and she made a mock pout of disappointment. He felt his temper rising. He felt hot. He got up and lit a fag. If he started on her he didn't know where it might end.

'I think you'd better go to your mother's,' he said. As he had his back to her she had no idea he had said anything. He turned around. She looked at him with immense compassion and understanding. She held out her arms. He felt helpless, like a small boy trying to grapple with an adult world. He couldn't control her. Bunty, with her immense disability, was still the stronger. She liked him, he knew that, but not in a passionate, loving way; rather more like an older sister. She understood how he felt, but he couldn't lock her up. She would not be dominated by him. He began to cry, not out of misery but out of frustration. He couldn't deal with the situation. Big racking sobs came, and

Bunty put her arms around him and held him tight. He would be all right. He would have to settle for it.

Rosa Tcherny felt awkward. She was sitting in Charlie's sister's house, having tea and a jaw-breaking home-made cake, talking about nothing in particular. It was clear that the sister, Renee, knew what Rosa had come for, and her accusing eyes never left Rosa's face. Renee had scratty brown hair, and she kept drawing in her cheeks and then blowing them out again, her expression indicating the thought, Well, what about this, eh? Charlie was awkward as well, sort of hopping from one foot to the other, as if he couldn't make up his mind whether he ought to go the toilet.

'You're in the book trade?' said Renee, as though it might be a crime, a vice at least.

'That's right. Wholesale.'

'Must be interesting,' said Renee, as though she couldn't think of a subject more boring.

'Yes, it is,' said Rosa.

Charlie hopped about a bit more. 'What time you going out, Reen?'

'Oh, in a bit.' Renee didn't want to go out. She was enjoying embarrassing this hoity-toity bitch. They all knew why she was there. It was a goodbye present for Charlie. It was blatant, and Renee wasn't sure that she approved. This Rosa had airs and graces, working with books and all that, her smart clothes and hair all done up nice. About three guineas' worth, Renee reckoned, but, underneath, she was just a common tart.

Renee lit a fag. 'Do you smoke?'

'No . . . and I couldn't at work, of course.'

'I should think not,' Renee laughed, 'with all those books.'

There was another awkward silence. Renee was making no effort to leave, Charlie was beginning to sweat and Rosa was sunk into the depths of misery. This wasn't how it should be. They should be in a nice hotel with deferential and tactful staff or on a beach or in a wood carpeted with bluebells or primroses, not in this tiny house. Here everybody was on top of one another, the three-piece suite crammed into the parlour so that there was no room to move, the sight of dirty dishes in the kitchen, where the single window offered a glimpse of the outside yard, with its looped washing-line, trusty mangle, a galvanized bath hanging on the wall, the Anderson shelter decked with Union Jack on top like it had just been captured from the fuzzy-wuzzies.

'Oh well,' said Renee, suddenly tiring of the sport. 'I'll only be next door if you want anything. Can't go far, can you? Don't know what might happen. He was over last night. Jerry, I mean. Just incendiaries, but that's bad enough.' Renee took her time packing her handbag with all the items she considered necessary for a visit next door, which included a hairnet, a *Picturegoer*, a packet of Senior Service, a tube of wine gums and a writing pad and envelopes, a pencil and a sharpener.

'Oh well,' she said again, 'don't do anything I wouldn't do', and stopped, smiled a knowing smile and left.

'I never thought she was going,' said Rosa.

'She's all right,' said Charlie. 'She knows what it's all about.'

'She made that very clear,' said Rosa. 'I thought she wanted to stay and watch.'

Charlie looked miserable. It was all going wrong. He had wanted things to be more light-hearted than this. He turned the wireless on, and there was a faint buzz from Grosvenor House. Sydney Lipton, was it? Or Ambrose? 'Oh! They're Tough, Mighty Tough in the West', but the soft crooning voice belied the sentiment. Why didn't they sing something sentimental? Something appropriate.

Rosa looked at Charlie. He was a poor specimen. No idea how to handle the occasion. God help him when the enemy confronted him. While he was making up his mind what to do he would be dead.

'Well,' she said.

Charlie grinned fatuously. 'Well,' he said.

Rosa spread herself on the sofa. Charlie stood over her, grinning uncertainly. He was like a man who had been waiting for a long time for a train to arrive, and now that it had steamed into the station wasn't sure whether he wanted to go anywhere.

'When are you going?' Rosa asked.

'Too soon,' he said.

'Well, you'd better hurry up,' said Rosa, 'before the siren goes or your sister pops back for a light.'

Charlie interpreted this remark as the green light. He sat down beside her and pressed his face against hers, breathing in her ear. 'Shall we go upstairs?' he murmured, in what he thought was a thrilling invitation.

'No,' she said. In that cow's bed? It would be a travesty. 'No. Just put the light out.' In the dark she couldn't see his silly face, which was beginning to dream in advance. Any minute he might go into a trance.

He put the light out, and it was pitch dark. He stumbled his way back to the sofa. He found her face. His lips connected with hers and went to work like the nozzle of a vacuum cleaner, as though making a supreme effort to suck all her teeth out. She pushed him away. She needed to breathe.

To speed things up she took his hands and placed them on her breasts. He gurgled with delight when he found her nipples, even through her jumper, vest and brassière. The night-club band on the wireless had started playing 'Amapola', and he jiggled her breasts on and off the beat.

'Switch it off,' she said. He climbed up again, got his legs trapped between the sofa and one of the armchairs but leant over and switched the music off. When he returned he seemed more determined, getting his hand up her skirt and grabbing the waistband of her knickers.

'All right,' she said, and tried to lift her bum up to make it easy for him, but now Charlie was at full steam. He pulled and there was a sharp whipping sound like a missile being released from a catapult.

'What was that?' he said.

'You snapped my elastic,' she said calmly.

'Sorry,' he said. 'It'll be all right, won't it?'

'Except that when I stand up my knickers will fall down.' He slackened off. 'It's all right,' she said, 'I've got another pair.'

'Eh?' Charlie said, puzzled.

'You'll have to get your trousers off,' she said pointedly. 'And get on with it. For God's sake.'

'Oh, er, right,' Charlie said and started on his flies.

Rosa, who hadn't been at all keen on the idea in the first place, was now thoroughly exasperated. This novice boy was practically committing an assault. She wanted to call it off, but the lad was aroused to fever pitch, breathing heavily. She couldn't see his face, but she guessed that it would be flushed and his eyes in a dreamy trance-like state. Eventually he got on top of her.

'Oh, oh,' he was saying, 'Rosa.'

'Wait a minute. Haven't you got a thing?'

'Eh? What?'

'A thing, you know. To put on.'

He went silent. It was obvious that he had shirked the vital task of purchasing the all-important French letter. 'It'll be all right,' he said weakly.

'It jolly well won't,' said Rosa. 'I'm sorry. No admittance without a ticket.'

'Oh Christ,' Charlie said. 'I can't stop now.'

They had just reached this impasse when the front door opened sharply and a blast of cold air entered the room.

'They're coming over,' Renee shouted wildly. She switched the light on and switched it off quickly. 'Don't mind me,' she shouted cheerfully. 'I didn't see anything.'

'The siren hasn't gone,' said Charlie, struggling with his buttons.

'It was on the wireless,' said Renee. 'They're coming over. You'd better get down the Anderson.'

Charlie scrambled to his feet, leaving Rosa exposed from the waist down. She sat up and discarded her knickers, rolling them up into a ball and stuffing them into her coat pocket.

'Come on,' said Charlie. 'We'd better go down.'

'I'll go home,' Rosa said.

'You can't,' Charlie said. 'Come down the shelter.'

The way Rosa was feeling, it was preferable to get blown up in the street than be secluded with Charlie and his horrible sister in a tin box and a foot of water. 'No. I'm going.'

Charlie hesitated. 'There won't be no buses running.'

'I'll go down the Tube.'

'I'll come with you.' He went to the back door and shouted, 'Reen!'

'What?' came from the depths of the Anderson shelter.

'I'm going out.'

'You're what?' Charlie didn't bother to reply. Rosa was already at the front door.

It was strange out. It seemed as though they had the whole street to themselves.

'I'm going for the Tube,' Rosa said. 'Be safer there, anyway.'

As they hurried along the air-raid siren started its mournful warning. Suddenly there was a humming sound, coming closer. There was an ARP warden on the corner, fidgeting with his arm band. 'Put that light out,' he shouted unnecessarily. There were no lights: no streetlights, no lights from houses, no car headlamps. It seemed that even the moon and stars had been blacked out. The humming sound came nearer, and suddenly there was a whooshing in the air, like a firework rocket setting off near by, and the pavement seemed to skid to the left and then right itself. Then there was a dull thump, which seemed to be quite near but was probably three miles away.

'Christ,' said Charlie.

Involuntarily, almost as if they had heard a starting pistol, they began to run. The nearest Underground station was at least half a mile away. At first they ran full pelt, out of panic and fear, and then, breathless, they loped and stumbled like drunks trying to negotiate their way out of a swaying pub, sucking in huge breaths of air and sounding punctured and constricted. They reached the station, but the gates were across.

'It's closed,' Charlie gasped and collapsed, exhausted, on the pavement.

It was not the regular time for closing. The authorities had realized that the whole Underground network was crammed and had decided that it would be dangerous for more people to be allowed in. In fact, a lot of people bought a cheap ticket and stayed there all day and night, taking it in turns to slip out for supplies. They brought sandwiches and thermos flasks, blankets and a change of socks. It had become their home. New communities had sprung up. Plots and places were claimed, saved and spoken for. These people became neighbours. They bought each other birthday cards and planned Christmas parties. They gossiped, laughed and sang, taking up an entirely new existence in the bowels of the earth.

Rosa and Charlie sat against the door of an ironmonger's shop. On the dusty window a finger had drawn Mr Chad, his long nose peering over a wall, with the message 'Wot No Sausages?' They could hear the drone of planes, and saw occasional flashes of ack-ack fire, and then those awful thumps that seemed a long way away but still caused trembles in the masonry of the buildings near by.

Charlie was frightened, and Rosa knew it. She knew she was on her own. If anyone was going to save the situation it wasn't going to be him. There was a slight buzz coming towards them, something in the road. There was no light to see, and if it were a vehicle of some sort it wouldn't be showing lights. Rosa got up and went to the edge of the pavement, stood on the kerb and peered into the gloom. There was something. It was a car. No, even better, it was a taxi. She shouted, screamed. Charlie came over and they both stood shouting like crazy people. Charlie stepped into the road. The car pulled up.

'You want to watch where you're going, mate,' said the driver.

'Can you take us?' Rosa said.

'I'm on my way home,' said the driver. 'If you're going my way I'll take you, but I'm not going back. A bit too hot for me up town.'

'Tooting,' said Rosa.

'If we can get there. I hear there's a bloody great hole in Balham High Road.'

They bundled into the taxi, which proceeded slowly and carefully past Clapham Common. Once the taxi mounted the pavement.

'I can't see,' said the driver through gritted teeth. On Balham Hill there was a row of policemen and ARP wardens. The driver stopped and a policeman came over.

'Can I get through to Morden?'

'Not this way you can't. You'll have to take the back doubles.'

The taxi turned off the main road, and, in a sudden flash from above, Rosa and Charlie could see a bus that seemed to have been shot in the leg, gone down on one knee, its left front wheel in a crater, the rest in a crazy drunken abstract of red steel. A cloud of dust and smoke got into their throats.

The back streets were deserted. There was no sign of human habitation. It was difficult to see where to turn. It was a matter of guesswork and instinct. Once they got to a parallel road the driver was a bit easier.

'I wish old Hitler was here now,' he said. 'I'd tell him a thing or two.' It was just the morale-building talk that was going on all over London. They stopped several times while the driver got out and tried to find the route. 'Emmanuel Road,' he read. 'Where the hell is that?'

Eventually they came out at the side of Balham Station and were able to join the main road. All the time Rosa and Charlie were absorbed in peering out of the windows. Charlie seemed to have gone to pieces, muttering unintelligibly to himself. Rosa felt protective towards him. Next week this stumbling awkward lad would be one of Britain's brave soldiers, and a few weeks later he would be lost in the thick of fighting in a foreign country far from home. She put her arm around him.

'Sorry,' he said. 'Sorry.'

After a long weary search the driver found the Tcherny home. Rosa found her key. Charlie settled with the driver.

'How much do I owe you?'

'Christ knows,' said the driver.

'Two pounds,' said Charlie. 'I've only got three and I've got to get back yet.'

Charlie followed Rosa into the house. In the sitting-room there was a big white shape under the table.

'What's that?'

'It's my mother. She's in the Morrison.' The Morrison was an alternative to the Anderson. It was an indoor shelter for people who did not have gardens. It was a steel cage that fitted under a table. The sight of Rosa's mother like a large white rabbit in a cage cracked Charlie into hysterics, but there was no humour in his insane cackle.

Rosa's father was standing at the back door. 'Is that you, Rosa?' It was an educated foreign voice, somehow calming in its steadiness.

'It's all right,' Rosa called.

'No, it isn't,' said the voice. 'It's crazy. You should have come home.'

'That's what I've been trying to do. It wasn't easy.' Rosa wasn't apologetic, Charlie noticed. She was an equal in this house.

Rosa relaxed. It was illogical. She was in as much danger here as anywhere else, but it was her home. If a bomb fell on the roof, so be it. It was much better than being stranded somewhere strange. She took Charlie's hand.

'Come on,' she said. 'We'll be all right here.'

It seemed strange, sitting at a table with a woman crouched down underneath.

'Do you want a cup of tea?'

'No!' came a shriek from under the table. 'Don't start the gas.'

'It's all right,' said Rosa. 'They've gone over.'

'No all-clear,' said the muffled voice.

'Well, I know what I'm going to do,' said Rosa. 'I'm going up to bed.' She took Charlie's hand and led him up the stairs into a bedroom at the back of the house. 'I'd just as soon die in bed than under a table,' she said lightly.

They sat on the bed, in the dark, holding hands. Charlie was completely unnerved by the turn of events. 'Won't your mum mind me being here?'

'No.'

'What about your dad?'

'He's all right.'

'But –'

'Shut up.'

'Wha –' A hand came over his mouth. A face was next to his. 'This is what you wanted, wasn't it?'

'Yes, but . . .'

'We can chance it, if you like.'

'I don't know.'

'Of course you do,' she said.

10

BERT Penrose did what he always did at the end of his day's work: he flung the sticky dishcloth against the wall, where it stuck for a few moments before it peeled away and fell. It was a moment of triumph and a moment of disgust.

He'd been looking around, making enquiries. There might be a porter's job going at the RAC Club in Pall Mall. Surely Claridge's would give him a reference after his dutiful service as a KP in their stinking basement? He'd been around to the Mall for an interview, and he was in luck. He was the same size as the bloke who was leaving, so they wouldn't have to order a new uniform. He would be well down the pecking order of hall porters, only just above the page boys, but it was a new start. It took years to work up to the plum job of head porter, the one who shot up the umbrella and pocketed five bob for his pains.

Bert put on his jacket and lit a fag. It was late tonight. There'd been a whole shipload of bosky admirals and their starchy wives. They made mountains of washing up. Must have had fourteen courses. Where did they get the stuff from? Of course, Claridge's wouldn't get anything from the black market, but they had their sources: gentlemen farmers on day trips to London, sporting fishermen with boats in quiet estuaries. It all came in through the back door. Even if they were questioned, which was unlikely, they had people in high places that would soon put a lid on it.

In Bert's mind the RAC Club had one drawback: it was strictly a men's club. Women were allowed in, just for a meal, but they couldn't be members and they couldn't stay the night. Despite this monastic prospect Bert had decided to make the move. It all depended on the reference.

He liked to just relax a minute with a fag before he left. There were still sounds of jollity from upstairs. They'd be doing the rugby scrum bit before midnight, falling about like schoolboys after their first taste of cider. He patted his pockets to locate his keys, and then he noticed a bunch of keys on a table. It was a big bunch of important-looking keys. Not to a safe, surely? He picked them up. Good pair of knuckle-dusters these would make. He tried one in the door. It didn't fit. Then he tried them in various cupboards, with no result. He then went into the passage outside and tried them on the cold-larder, and the lock turned, as sweet as a nut.

He peered in curiously. It was dark and cold. There was a fan-light over the window letting in a faint breeze. He ran his hand along the shelves. There were serving plates, all covered over with wire-mesh covers. He lifted one of the covers. Christ. A hand of ham, that was. He could smell it. The next was a chicken, and the third smelt like fish. They ate well, did the people who came to Claridge's. No rationing or restrictions for them. And, of course, none of them thought otherwise than that they were entitled to be fed better than the rest of their fellow countrymen.

Bert fingered the fish dish. It wasn't kippers, that was for sure. It could be salmon. He had never tasted salmon, except from a tin. He pulled a large piece out and ate it. It was delicious. Best food he'd ever tasted. It wasn't like cod or rock salmon or haddock. It was smooth and had a subtle flavour and melted in the mouth like ice cream. He pulled off another big slice. Hey, what was this? A knuckle of bacon? Bacon was something that Bert missed. The scrimpy little rashers that Edie got weren't even a taster. He wanted gammon. Good thick slices of it. This knuckle of bacon, it wasn't very big. Would anyone miss it? If they did, were they in a position to say anything?

It was under his arm, under his coat. Suddenly he shivered. It was cold in here. Best to be off home, after he'd had another slice of that salmon. He locked the door and put the keys back where he found them. And then upstairs and out the back to the trades-man's entrance and off down the road.

It was nearly ten o'clock. In a couple of hours Jerry would be over again. He was all right in the West End. Jerry wouldn't dis-turb the smart hotels and palaces. He'd be stone bonkers safe in the RAC. The fact was that most of the toffs agreed with Hitler, especially about the Jews, and Hitler would be handy to see off Stalin and them Bolsheviks. Britain and Germany ought to be on the same side sorting out the Russians. It was wishy-washy Chamberlain that had landed Britain in the soup, and, now he was gone, there was no hope with this Churchill who seemed to enjoy the whole business, dancing around in a siren-suit like a big romping baby. Hitler knew who his friends were, and he didn't want to upset people who lived in posh houses in Mayfair and Belgravia. There hadn't been a single bomb dropped in White-hall or Chelsea or Kensington. No. He'd concentrated his attack on the East End because he knew that that was where all the Jews lived. The docks were a convenient excuse to do what he wanted.

Bert made his way to Green Park station. The gates were across. He rattled them and shouted, and a porter appeared.

'Open up, mate. I've got to get home.'

'Sorry. It's orders.'

'Don't be bloody silly. I can't stand out here all night.' The porter hesitated. 'I've not been out on the razz. I've been working. At Claridge's.'

'There's not many trains,' said the porter. 'Where do you want to get to?'

'Clapham North.'

'No chance.'

Bert briefly considered finding a bench in Green Park, but he knew that the park was full of dossers who might strip you naked and only give you fleas in return, so he wandered along Piccadilly towards the Circus. Piccadilly Circus: it was a joke. A place where visitors came to gawp and wonder, where fathers used to bring their children to see the sparkling coloured lights, where hundreds looked up to see Moussec being poured into a cocktail glass and figures skiing in Biarritz. It was a magical place, epitomizing the centre of the whole mad merry-go-round, the hedonism and raffishness of London on the spree, but now dark and gloomy, with slow muffled traffic proceeding at a funereal pace, and Eros, the symbol of wild excesses of body and mind and spirit, boarded up for the duration.

Even though it was getting near Christmas, there was little sign of seasonal good cheer in the shops. It would be a half-hearted Christmas, almost as if it was something to be hushed up, like it was in some way unpatriotic.

There were still people about. Nightlife seemed to continue. It was a patriotic duty to get out and about. These toffs weren't going to let Hitler stop them whooping it up. In the dark it was much more fun. There were some people making a packet out of the war, and they were determined to spend it. The war had cured the unemployment that had preceded it. Even the working class had money. The joke was that there wasn't anything for them to spend it on. So many men had been called up that they had left thousands of jobs vacant. He wouldn't even need a reference.

A bag of rags staggered towards him, a tramp. He smelt vile. 'Could you?'

'No, I couldn't,' Bert said viciously.

'Thanks,' said the hoarse voice. 'God bless you, guv'nor.'

'Hello, love,' said a voice from a shop window. They were still there. They made Bert sick. The man who spent most of his days and nights visualizing sexual activity could not bear to have it degraded to a simple cash transaction. The woman came close. He stared into her face. Bloody hell. She looked about ninety. She looked like a man done up as a woman, a pantomime dame. He felt a wave of disgust.

'No. Go away.'

'Didn't mind me asking, dear, did you? No offence.'

He was walking in the direction of home. There used to be all-night trams from the Embankment. Maybe he could catch one. He knew the way, although he had to look out for familiar landmarks. But he didn't relish the thought of walking around six or seven miles.

Further on he saw two sailors holding on to one another as though each thought that the other was a lifebelt. One fell down and the other fell over trying to pick his companion up. They ought to be on the Halls. Then he heard the planes. They seemed to be coming from all directions. They were low and threatening. He started to run like they were following just him. He stopped and told himself that they were just passing over, on their way to their target in the East End. How long was this going on?

He was only vaguely aware of the bomb that fell only fifty yards in front of him. There was a sound like the devil whistling through his teeth and a lightning flash, and a crumbling sound like a granite statue grinding its teeth. Great clumps of masonry thudded into the road. One piece seemed to knock his legs from under him: LBW in a crazy cricket match played by giants. He went down, and a shower of dust covered him and got into his mouth. His legs hurt. His shoulder hurt. He couldn't breathe. He couldn't see. He'd lost his knuckle of ham, which had fallen down inside his coat and rolled away to safety.

He didn't know how long he lay there. He presumed he was dead. He didn't see any angels, and he didn't hear any tinkly music or choirs, it was just quiet and peaceful. God knows how he was going to get on upstairs. He'd done some things. He'd not been a good husband. He hadn't had the breaks. Nothing had gone right: no good luck, only bad. It wasn't his fault. But God was merciful. That's what they said. He would understand, wouldn't he? Of course, it could all be nonsense. Nobody had ever been back to tell. On the other hand, it didn't do any harm, in the circumstances, to offer up a little prayer?

Then he heard a shout. 'Anybody down there?'

Down where? Someone was scrambling about above him.

He shouted, 'Yes', but nothing came out. His mouth was full of sand. He tried to spit it out.

'Quiet! There's somebody here. Down there. Hold on, mate. We'll get you out.'

He didn't know whether to laugh or cry. He was alive, but then it hadn't been much of a life. He wouldn't have really minded if it had been all over.

'Can you hear me?'

The call from above needed an answer. He tried to clear his throat, and managed a dry 'Yes.'

'Good. Now listen. We can't get you out just yet. There's an unexploded bomb just up the road, so we'll have to wait until bomb disposal have dealt with it. It's a big 'un. Might be a land-mine. But chin up. It'll be all right.' He wanted to laugh. It was marvellous. Bloody marvellous. It was like Mona Lott in *It's That Man Again*, who, after relating string of disasters, would always finish up by saying in a doleful voice, 'It's being so cheerful that keeps me going.' It was a scream. You could die laughing.

Mrs Bennet had just made herself an Oxo. She'd had a tin of Oxo cubes for ages, since long before the war started. She supposed that you couldn't get them any more. She sipped the hot fluid. It was just like hot water. Maybe keeping them so long had made them lose their flavour. She sprinkled some salt into the cup, just to make it taste of something. The planes had been rumbling around all night, like summer thunder. How did they expect a person to sleep with all this going on? They didn't have all this fuss in the first war. It was all overseas. In France and Belgium. Her Tom came back and told her all about it. Wars and fighting was for men. They liked it. They liked the dressing up and firing things off. It wasn't right to drag women into it. She wondered whether them upstairs were asleep or those funny people underneath. He went out in the evenings, to work, he said, but she had her doubts. He was a funny little bloke with a moustache like Charlie Chaplin. If you were going to have a moustache you might as well have a proper one like her Tom had had – right across his face and curling into his ears, not that little toothbrush bristle just under your nose. She took up a broom and banged it on the floor. After a few moments there was a bang back. That'd be Edie. She went into the passage and to the top of the stairs that led to the basement.

'Is that you, Edie?'

'Yes,' came a muffled reply.

'Is hubby home?'

'Not yet.'

'Do you want to come up?'

'No thanks.' Please yourself, thought Mrs Bennet. Only trying to be friendly. No use banging on the ceiling. That Bunty couldn't hear anything, poor thing, although she kept herself cheerful did Bunty. More than her husband did, miserable little bugger.

Who would have thought that the war would start up again after all those years? Surely it was all done for. Old Kaiser Bill made a run for it, and then they signed up to say that they wouldn't do it again. But there it was, rumbling around in the background all the time. Those Germans never knew when they were done for.

She looked out of the window. What a red sky. It was way in the distance, but it was bright, like the sun going down after a summer scorcher. The red glow seemed to get larger and then to shoot out beams. It must be a fire, but there was no sound of fire engines. She felt vaguely disturbed. She pattered out to the passage again and banged the broom handle at the top of the stairs.

'You there, Edie?'

'Yes. Hello.'

'Can I come down? I don't like it.'

'What?'

'Everything.'

'Come down if you like.'

Mrs Bennet peered down the stairs. There was a banister, but she couldn't see the stairs very well. Edie appeared at the bottom, holding a candle. Mrs Bennet made her way slowly and carefully down the stairs. When she got down she was surprised to see all her neighbours down there. There was Bunty in her dressing-gown, and her Tim, who was talking earnestly to young Mrs May; Mrs May looked like she was embarrassed about something, while her husband smoked a fag as if the whole business of hiding in a basement was beneath his contempt.

'I didn't know we were having a party,' Mrs Bennet said.

'Well, it's been going on a bit,' Edie replied, 'and Bert's not home yet. I expect he's decided to stay where he is.' Edie's face, above the candle, was scared to death.

'He'll be all right, dear, you'll see,' said Mrs Bennet. She was pleased to be included in the company. Them Mays were a stand-offish pair. Bunty was all right, although Tim was a pig. Whatever he was saying to Mrs May, she was looking uneasy. Surely he wouldn't be trying something on, right there in front of her husband?

The planes had stopped humming above, but there was no all-clear. Edie found a card-table and a pack of cards, and they started a game.

''Ere, I'll tell your fortunes if you like,' Edie volunteered, but nobody took her up on the offer. Instead they played New-market, with pennies and ha'pennies, hardly speaking, just going through the ritual in a moody, listless fashion. Bunty scooped the pool, then dashed upstairs and came back with a bottle of port. Bunty was always keen to make a night of it. It was funny, Mrs

Bennet thought, these people hardly spoke to each other most of the time, but there they were, huddled together, around two candles, as cosy as could be. They gave her a glass of port. This was a bit of all right: a drink, and company.

She had been alone since Tom passed away. Her son Norman left soon after his father died. He'd got fed up with not getting a job, so he went to Australia. He must be getting on all right because he never wrote. Of course, she was all right. Tom's pension from the Army for having a busted foot and his bit from the town hall kept her going. She didn't want a lot. She didn't always use up her rations. She didn't really want anything you could buy. She wanted company. Someone to talk to. In this house full of people the only one who responded to her in a friendly way was Bunty, who couldn't talk at all. She was sure that Bunty was at it. Couldn't blame her in a way; she was a fine figure of a woman, and that Tim didn't seem to appreciate her.

They'd stopped playing cards and were just looking at each other in a kind of hopeless way.

'I expect Bert's stayed over,' said Edie. Nobody said anything and the remark hung in the air as if waiting for affirmation.

'Well, I don't know about you people,' said the young Mr May loftily, 'but I'm going to bed. I've got work in the morning.'

'What time is it?' asked Mrs Bennet, desperately trying to prolong her outing, but nobody answered her. One by one they all trooped off, leaving Mrs Bennet and Edie. Edie started putting things away. She seemed distracted, on edge.

'He'll be all right,' said Mrs Bennet.

'I've got a funny feeling,' said Edie, with a throb in her voice.

'He'll turn up in the morning. Right as rain. You'll see.'

'I hope so,' said Edie.

Tim Melrose ascended the stairs with a feeling of satisfaction. That Betty was an awkward bitch, but his persistence had worn her down. She didn't want to tell him. It was only after he said that he needed to know where Bunty was, and that, of course, Bunty couldn't tell him herself, that she came out with it. She didn't know where the place was but she knew what it was called – the Hostess Club – and that was enough. It would be in the telephone directory. As he lay in bed beside Bunty, he knew he had the lever that would give him control over the situation.

Betty May knew that she had done something wrong. That Mr Melrose had kept on and on. She didn't like the intensity of his questioning. The way he put his face close to hers, staring into her eyes like he was trying to make a connection with her brain, read her mind. Of course, it was dangerous for Bunty to be out on her own. If anything went wrong she couldn't even ask a policeman. On the other hand, she was uneasy that she'd sort of snitched on Bunty, given the game away. If Tim Melrose went to that dreadful dancing place he would soon see what went on there. Betty knew that Melrose was a violent man. There was that time when he tried to hit Bunty with that iron thing that he used to switch off the water. He had lost his temper completely. She wanted to talk to Stephen about it, but he had lost so much sleep already, and he had to get up in the morning.

The next day was all hustle and bustle for Tim. A water main had burst at Kennington. As he cycled to the site he was proud to see that the connected pipes were all along the route and continued beyond. Surprisingly, considering the bombardment last night, there was no damage to be seen. The burst main was down to some other, more normal cause. He found the hydrant and switched the water off. At this point he thought of nipping over the bridge and finding this place where Bunty went, but there was a message for him to attend another site in Camberwell. And so it went on, all day, and everywhere he went there was this snake of hosepipes stretching along in the gutters. Despite the busy day he felt much more at ease with life. He was on to her.

II

MAURICE was having a terrible time with Clare. The nub of the trouble was that Clare had immersed herself in civic duties, the WVS, beetle drives for soldiers' comforts, knitting socks that needed misshapen feet to wear them, collecting old newspapers for salvage and old books to send to the troops, giving cookery classes to show how you could make the miserable rations go further and innumerable coffee mornings and fêtes worse than death. Maurice wasn't doing any of these things. Clare always seemed to be at the head of a column of charging females, carrying things from one place to another, stuffing bulging sacks of things into cars, making piles of other things to be shifted to another pile somewhere else.

To Clare Maurice was a let-down. He wasn't a fire warden, in the ARP or the Home Guard. He just carried on as if nothing had changed. As far as possible Maurice ignored the war. He went to work and came home. Likely as not he would spend the whole evening reading a book. All hell might fall in overnight, the house might crumble, the Germans might invade, a bomb might fall down the chimney, and, if any of these catastrophes occurred, Maurice would still be sitting in a chair, reading. Clare had nothing against books. It was just that there were other things in the world. The times demanded action, not indolence. It was unpatriotic, bordering on treason, to ignore the war.

She couldn't imagine what she had ever seen in Maurice. Whatever it was it had entirely evaporated. He had been a dreamy young man but a lazy lover. She might have enjoyed children, but Maurice couldn't even get that business right. His mind always seemed to be somewhere else. Maurice was her first flush of romance, and she was convinced that she could knock him into shape, but after a while she realized that he was not going to change. You couldn't even get through to a man whose attention was focused on the world of literature, to whom fiction was more real than reality and reality was too mundane to contemplate.

To Maurice, Clare had become a comic figure. One of Wode-house's dreadnought aunts, perhaps, or a quirky spinster from Joan Butler. There was always the suggestion that Clare, in her Boadicea role, was actually leading this band of housewives, maiden aunts and gangling young girls into battle. He wouldn't have been surprised if she had shouted 'Charge!' as she led the assorted females into their next task.

In Cheam village he felt removed from the conflict. After all, it was a bus ride to Morden, through mock-Tudor land, and then a long trip on the Underground to get to the City. When he was at work he felt nearer to the front line, but at home he felt perfectly safe. All the more incongruous, then, was Clare's barging around as if the Germans were just behind the garden hedge.

He knew that Clare resented his calm approach to life, his refusal to be panicked into defensive action. His task, as he saw it, was to keep the business going, to preserve the normality of the book trade. For this he had to read the reviews, had to know what was likely to be in demand, so he could stock up. He'd been caught out before. He never thought that *Mathematics for the Millions* would be a bestseller, despite its favourable reviews.

He was just trying to get the drift of *An American Tragedy* when Clare barged in, wearing her ridiculous uniform. She had a large sheet of paper, which she spread out on the dining-room table and proceeded, with a ruler, to mark it out in neat little boxes. Everything that Clare did needed a rota mapped out, headed by the days of the week and divided, down the side, by two-hour intervals. The chart detailed who was doing what on which day and at what time. Clare spent hours on these charts, which were displayed in the church hall. The hall had become the centre for WVS activities, and she was always nipping in to cross out one name and substitute it with another, until the chart assumed the proportions of a giant crossword.

'Shall I get some tea?' Maurice said.

'You'll have to get it,' said Clare. 'I've got to get this going.'

'Of course,' he said, tolerantly.

How would Clare feel if she knew that he was meeting a young woman, secretly and regularly? Would it even register? And would she believe that this was a truly innocent friendship?

Would she even care? Would she even pause in her quest to collect milk-bottle tops to build battleships? Had the war been invented to salvage women like Clare from meaningless activity and give them a role in life?

It was getting dark now, and back in his real world they would be scuffing down for the night. As soon as it was dark the bombers came over. At home, on the borders of Surrey, they scarcely noticed them. There was a droning in the distance, but Cheam was not on their route.

He made some tea and cut some bread, which he buttered and then spread with blackcurrant jam. The preserve had been bought at a fête in aid of God knows what. It was a bit tart, but then sugar was a scarce commodity these days. He had given up taking sugar in his tea to save some for making cakes.

He wasn't sure whether he was looking forward to tomorrow. He had put off considering the problem all through Saturday, but now it was Sunday evening. He had promised to meet Betty on Monday and take her to the warehouse, to show her the rows of books, the yards and yards of shelving, to explain the cataloguing system. He hadn't been able to put it off any longer. She had been getting petulant lately. On the surface he liked nothing more than to boast in his domain. The whole place was a wonder of organization. He could turn up a request in minutes, and it gave him great pleasure to display his efficiency. But, having seen the place, the girl would naturally think that the time had come to offer her a job, and he didn't really want her about the place. She would soon become one of the staff, and the delightful conversations with him lording it over her ignorance would come to an end.

After eating, Clare announced that she was going to bed early; she had a big day tomorrow. She made it sound as though she had been given the job of liberating France single-handedly.

He sighed but said nothing. He could settle down in a chair next to the Christmas tree with the *Sunday Times* book reviews for an hour.

As he read, fifteen miles away German bombs were taking a hand in Maurice's order of events. Betty would never now see the warehouse in all its ordered glory, never smell that special smell that comes from freshly printed books, never get to know how a dusty ancient copy could be rubbed up to look like new. Never sample the temple-like atmosphere of Green's warehouse.

The day before, Saturday, had been Jimmy's big day. Helen had agreed to meet him for an afternoon at the pictures. He had tempted her with a Norma Shearer film called *The Women*. He didn't know what it was about and didn't care much. If he had his choice it would have been an unremitting run of Laurel and Hardy, Abbot and Costello, Popeye and Our Gang. Norma Shearer spelt dreary, and so it proved. The film seemed to have got together half the female stars in Hollywood. Besides the tearful Norma, there was big-eyed Joan Crawford, Rosalind Russell, Joan Fontaine, Paulette Goddard and heaps more. Jimmy didn't follow the plot but, nevertheless, sat through it in a haze of contentment.

In the morning he had got on to his mum about some new clothes. She said she hadn't got any coupons, but he knew that his dad could get stacks of coupons up Fleet Street. In the end she took him to the walk-round shop, where there were hundreds of pretty standard jackets and trousers all renowned as being 'hard-wearing'. She was astonished when he went mad for a pair of grey flannel trousers and a blue blazer. 'Going to Oxford, are we?' she said. He couldn't tell her that he was getting as near as he could to Greyfriars. She wouldn't understand. If he could have got a striped blazer as seen illustrated in the *Magnet* he would have been better suited. He went home, had a bath and put some brilliantine on his hair. In the end he looked like one of Hollywood's young stars scrubbed up for the finale of an end-of-term – and end-of-film – musical at Carvel High or some other fictional co-ed college.

He had met Helen outside the cinema. It was a big place, the poshest in the district. It boasted 'perfected air', although, even if you sniffed hard, you couldn't notice any difference. Inside there was a dark-blue sky with stars twinkling and high up in the ceiling a display of classical statuary of Greek gods jumping and crouching, bending and stretching in various poses of athletic endeavour. It was worth a tanner just to get into the place.

When they met she seemed a little cold. It was clear from her manner that she didn't want Jimmy to think that she was in any way keen to be in his company. She'd only come just to please him. She was quite capable of going to the pictures on her own or with any of her wide circle of friends. He had to be put in his place, and if he settled for it she might melt a little. There was a slight crisis when they bought their tickets. Jimmy thought it was up to him, but Helen wouldn't hear of it. He insisted on paying for them both, but when he got the tickets she wouldn't go in. She pressed her sixpence into his hand and when he wouldn't take it slipped it into his pocket. Then, independence established, she allowed him to buy a box of chocolates from the girl selling them from a tray around her neck.

When they sat down the organist was still playing. He swung around and smiled smugly, and then he and the organ gradually disappeared below the stage. The place went dark and the Three Stooges started bashing each other about. They weren't as good as Laurel and Hardy. They were crude and brutal and spoke in jerky shouts. Helen plainly thought that they were beneath her consideration, and Jimmy didn't dare laugh in case she thought he approved of their animal antics. Then it was the news. The same pictures of soldiers looking cheerful while up to their eyes in mud, Churchill giving the V-sign and the King and Queen being cheered by people who had just been bombed out of their homes.

It was time for the stage show, but the house lights remained low and a notice came up on the screen: 'An air-raid warning has been sounded. If anyone wants to leave, will they do so quietly.'

Jimmy looked at Helen. 'What d'you want to do?'

'I've paid to see the film,' she said. 'You can go if you want.'

'No fear,' he replied, feeling a bit stung by the inference that he was keen to make a cowardly exit to the nearest shelter. However, the slight *frisson* gave him the excuse to slip his arm around her shoulders, and she appeared not to have noticed.

The stage show wasn't much: acrobats, all white powder, who did everything in slow motion. They were followed by a conjuror, who talked all the time, nervously, as though he expected someone to rush the stage and shoot him. He made jokes about Hitler and rationing and finished his act by extracting a huge

Union Jack from a small cylinder, which got him a round of applause. He went off sweating but relieved.

Throughout the second feature he enjoyed the closeness of her, the smell of her, the little tickle of her hair when it brushed his face, the sight, in the dim light, of her slightly pouting lips. This was it. She was real. He thought of his mum and dad and shuddered. Had they experienced this delight when they first met? This feeling of oneness, of being in a perfect harmony with another person? He drew her head closer and felt her tighten. Steady. Too quick. But then her hand found its way into his. She still stared at the screen, seemingly oblivious of the way her errant hand was behaving. He shifted nearer to her so that their faces were touching and sat there in bliss.

When it was all over they debated whether to stay on and see the programme all over again, but, thinking of a second dose of the Three Stooges, Helen said she wanted to leave. It was, after all, six o'clock, and she had to get the tram to Battersea, and, although the all-clear had been announced on the screen, there was always the chance of another air raid as soon as it got dark.

He went with her to the tram and got on with her, upstairs.

'Where are you going?' she said.

'I'm going with you,' he said. 'To see you home.'

'It's all right,' she said. 'I can get there.' But he could see that she was pleased.

The tram clattered up to Clapham Common and then down Cedars Road. She lived somewhere off Latchmere Road. He walked along with her, determined to extend his outing with her as long as possible.

'Good, wasn't it,' he said.

'Norma Shearer was good,' she said critically, 'but I didn't like Joan Crawford being in it.'

'Nor did I,' he said loyally.

They stopped at the corner of her street.

'Well,' he said awkwardly. It was dark but he knew she had started blushing again. He pulled her to him and kissed her cheek. It was soft and cool. She drew him into a dark shadow. 'We can go again,' he said. 'I'll see you at Hodder's. We'll fix it up.'

Suddenly her arms were at the back of his neck and her open lips were seeking his. He responded. It was like strawberries and cream, sausages and mash and cream soda. It was an extreme sensation of pleasure, like a mild electric shock, which gave some zing but didn't hurt. It was something that he tried to fix in his mind so that he could recall the feeling later. He would dream about it, conjure it up in daydreams, live it all over again.

He took her to her front door.

'Helen,' he said, with some depth of feeling.

'What?' she said.

'Nothing. You've been great.'

She looked down. 'Not so bad yourself,' she mumbled.

All day on the Sunday he relived the moments, tried to recapture the cool, velvet feel of her skin, the feel of her lips on his, to imagine her voice, her looks, her smell, her presence.

Betty gave herself an all-over wash in the small sink in the kitchen. It was easier than trying to negotiate a bath. It was always difficult if anyone wanted to come in to use the lavatory, and she was frightened to death of that brown geyser thing that spat small blue flames and sparks and rumbled as though it had eaten something poisonous. But she was determined to be at her freshest and smartest tomorrow. She wouldn't just be seeing Maurice but all the staff at the warehouse. She wanted the make a good impression. She had ironed her blue skirt and jacket and a cream blouse that Bunty had given her some time ago and smoothed out a pair of silk stockings that had come from the same source.

Stephen was lying on the bed reading a newspaper. She put on her dressing-gown. It was cream with a blue edging. She had it as a Christmas present when she was sixteen. There was just room in the small kitchen to make tea and toast. They had it every night and looked forward to it. There was no fire, but there was a fireplace. She sat down in front of it like it was a source of glowing warmth. Stephen looked up.

'You going out tomorrow, Bet?'

'You know I am. I'm going to Green's. My first day.'

'Ah yes. I'd forgotten. Well, good luck.'

The truth was that Stephen was preoccupied with another matter. He had been for his Army medical, and they had found that he had a weak chest. He hadn't known whether to jump for joy or start praying. The last thing he wanted to do was go into the Army, but, on the other hand, he didn't want to go into a TB hospital either. He didn't feel anything yet, but it seemed that it was inevitable that he would start spitting up blood one day and that would be that. His father had died of consumption, and Stephen remembered the skeletal figure racked with coughs. The worst thing about it was that there didn't seem to be any cure. The Army had rejected him, and he knew that they didn't do that lightly. He didn't want to say anything to Betty: time enough for her to worry when the symptoms became obvious. And yet the discovery that he would still be available would open up new vistas in his career. People in the shop were being called up all the time. They put a brave face on it, with leaving parties and kissing all the girls, but you could see that they were scared to death.

He put his arm around his young wife. He enjoyed being with her. She was a smashing looker, but it was clear that she wouldn't get far in an intelligence test. There was no doubt about it, Betty was a bit dim. Look at the way that Bunty bitch had led her on – anyone with half an eye could see that Bunty, dressed to kill a whole regiment, didn't spend her afternoons at a vicarage tea party – and now this man, Maurice, what was going on there? Surely Betty's potential as an assistant in a firm that dealt with books was nil, and yet this man was paying her fifty bob a week, just for meeting him up to now. It had made a deal of difference to them, but where was it leading? Betty was an innocent abroad. London was full of spivs, crooks, soldiers on the run, prostitutes and their ponces. She didn't know what went on. She floated on a cloud above the sordid reality of wartime life. She was all right with him – he could have sex with her any time he wanted – but there was something missing. It was as though she was submitting to him because he was her husband, and so he was entitled. There was no feeling that she was joining in. God knows what would have happened to her if he had been called up.

'Do you love me?' he said.

'Of course,' said his wife primly, as though her loyalty or honesty was being questioned.

'I may be made a buyer soon,' he said. She smiled, but he could see that it meant nothing to her.

'What was that Tim chap saying to you?'

'When?' Her eyes registered surprise.

'When we went down, to the basement.'

She frowned and looked worried. 'I didn't want to tell him, but he kept on so.'

'Tell him what?'

'Where Bunty goes. In the afternoons. You know . . .'

'You mean he didn't know?' Stephen shrugged. It wasn't his business. He started undoing the buttons on his wife's dressing-gown.

'Would you like children?' he said.

She looked at him with a serious face, like a child, solemnly trying to learn to read or cope with some problem outside its limited experience. 'Is that what you want?'

'Well,' he said. 'It's best while you're young.'

'But why? Why have you brought it up today? Just when I'm about to start a new job.'

He laughed. 'Betty, my love. This man isn't going to give you a job. I don't know what his motive is, but it's not to offer you regular employment. You're not qualified.'

She refastened the buttons that he had undone. 'You don't know anything of the sort. Maurice is a gentleman. He wouldn't lead me on like that.'

In Stephen's experience, so-called 'gentlemen' were the most likely to be leading girls on. He had barged into the manager's office one day and found one of the young shop girls lying on the desk looking guilty. And this was a public-school man.

'Well, you just watch it,' he said. 'That's all.'

Stephen need not have worried. Circumstances were conspiring to protect Betty from her gentlemanly predator at least for the next day – but these same circumstances were also to release forces in Maurice that had been kept comfortably below the surface for at least a couple of decades.

The next morning Maurice set out at the usual time. There had been some heavy bombing overnight, and Fleet Street and Ludgate Circus were jammed with traffic, while newspaper vans skirted in and out and up on to the pavement in an effort to make their deliveries.

He turned into the street and saw Miss Tcherny on the corner looking shocked.

'Good morning,' he said briskly.

She just looked at him and did not reply.

'Good morning,' he said again, thinking she may not have heard him. There was a lot of bustle going on. There was a fire engine at the corner of the street and a few ARP wardens stamping about.

His second greeting brought forth a sort of horrified glance, and she turned away. Perhaps something had happened during the night? Maybe she'd heard some bad news, about a relative or something? He turned the corner. The street seemed full of activity. There was a fire engine half-way down with its ladder extended. A fireman was at the top holding a hose that was spurting water. My God, there must have been some damage in the street. Why? It was a street full of warehouses, clothing firms and a wine importer, some offices, but nothing of any importance to the war effort or threat to an enemy. There were great clumps of masonry in the middle of the road and bricks and stray files flapping about. There was water running swiftly in the gutters and smoke and dust, great clouds of it, swirling about, so thick that he could only see half-way along the street. He picked his way carefully, sometimes stumbling when he found a hole in the pavement that he could not see. He began to tick off the premises. There was Zack's, the theatrical-costume business, and there was the coffee importers and the curious tiny place that dealt in antique jewellery. There was a fire still burning somewhere. He could feel the heat of it. These incendiary bombs caused as much damage as the high explosives.

Then he was suddenly filled with a deep feeling of dread. Involuntarily he quickened his step, slipping sometimes on the wet pavement, kicking the occasional brick, until he was running headlong, hardly seeing where he was going. Before he got there he knew what he was going to see. The old Victorian façade of Green's was no longer there. Where on Friday there had been three storeys of books, painstakingly gathered, all catalogued and preserved against dust and damage, there was now just a big hole. His empire had vanished. He staggered and fell to his knees with the shock of it. He stretched out and found a book, wet and mushy and covered in dust. He wiped the mess off with his hand so that he could see the jacket: *The Health, Wealth and Happiness of Mankind*. Why had it come to this? A whole civilization, a history, a record of man's existence and achievements, the process of thought, of logic, of reason, of manners, of life itself, all now a charred bonfire. Could it ever be reassembled? Where? He could hear someone sobbing. Deep sobs, full of anguish and emotion. It was him.

'Come on, sir,' someone was saying. It was a policeman. 'I shouldn't go down there. It isn't safe. Come back up here, will you?'

He turned, uncomprehending. 'This is my place,' he cried. 'I work here.'

'Not today I shouldn't think,' said the policeman. 'There's a van over there. You can get a nice cup of tea.'

Tea? For God's sake, who wanted tea?

The policeman was beginning to get official. 'I shall have to ask you to clear this site. There's stuff still coming down from them roofs. Come on, sir. We don't want another casualty, do we?'

'You don't understand. This is my business.'

'I know. I know. Must be a shock and all that. But don't forget you're still alive. There's a lot in London who weren't so lucky last night.'

He wished it had been him. What was there to live for now? No business, thousands of books destroyed: his life's work wiped out in one night of pointless carnage.

12

J IMMY arrived on his bike with a smile on his face. He had ridden
practically all the way without holding on to the handlebars. It
was a sort of dare and a celebration. It had been tricky around the
hosepipes, and the tramlines were always a hazard. When he got
over Blackfriars Bridge the whole place seemed to be alive with
people. People walking, stepping carefully over all the obstructions,
staring in surprise and amazement, walking quickly, looking
worried. Maybe the Tubes were closed. His dad had said that
there had been a bad night with the bombing. His mum and dad,
after he got in on Saturday, had stayed downstairs all night, with
him sleeping on the sofa with a soppy grin on his face. He couldn't
stop smiling. It was how he felt.

'What's the matter with you?' his mum enquired, more than
once. He knew what was the matter. He'd got a girl, a nice one at
that, a looker who kissed him as though she meant it. It had
transformed his whole existence. He wasn't just a scruffy book
collector, carrying his job on his back; he was someone who lived
it up, had a romance going, meant something to somebody else.

His mother had looked at him suspiciously that night when
he came back from the pictures. 'Had a good time?' she said, as if
she suspected something.

'Not bad,' he said. Nobody in Jimmy's family ever said that
something was good. They always tempered every opinion by
negative downgrading. 'Not bad' really meant good. If they
weren't sure they would say 'not too bad'; 'not half bad' meant
that whatever it was, it was superb. But he didn't want to give
everything away, so he stuck to 'not bad'.

But the fact was that the day out with Helen had been great and
he was looking forward to many more. More pictures – not Norma
Shearer though – more kisses, walks in the park, days out somewhere; pity that Brighton and all the seaside towns were fenced off.
He could always see her at Hodder's as he went in there most days
for bibles and prayer books, stuff from EUP, as well as bits of fiction.

On the Sunday Jimmy's dad had been to Club Row, where you could buy dogs in the street. You could also buy cage birds, and Jimmy's dad, already missing his hobby, had gone there to buy a pair of breeding canaries. He wasn't intending to start the aviary up again, just to have a pair in a cage in the house. He came back and solemnly displayed the cage in which there were two bewildered-looking birds that had some yellow colouring but were mostly brown. They turned out to be sparrows that had been doused in a yellow dye. Jimmy's mum said they had put mustard powder in to make it stick. His dad let them out and they flew away, sprinkling yellow dust as they went.

On Monday, when Jimmy got to the street he found it was cordoned off. There were barriers, so he went around the back of St Paul's to get in through to Paternoster Row. There were great piles of bricks and dust everywhere and the sullen, smoking remnants of fires. The whole area smelt charred and foul. He got under the barrier, as there was no one there to stop him, and walked down Paternoster Row. Where was Longman's? Where was Nelson's? Where was SPCK? Harrap's? He wheeled his bicycle nearer into Warwick Square. Surely that battered building wasn't OUP? Warwick Square looked like a pond with bits of stationery floating in it, like paper boats that had come apart. You could paddle in it. Where was Stanley's and, more importantly, where was Hodder's? He sighed with relief when he saw that Hodder's was still standing. It looked badly knocked about, with broken windows and scars on the brickwork, but, substantially, the building itself was still standing. But it was deserted. He peered in one of the windows. The whole placed seemed to be under water. The door of the trade counter was hanging wonkily, as though someone had tried to wrench it off its hinges.

He looked around him. This place was done for. No business would take place here today or for a long time after. He was bewildered. This was his world. The landmarks with which he had got so familiar. What would happen to all those books? What would happen to all the people that worked in these places? What would happen to Helen? Just as he's got something good going, along comes bloody Hitler and buggers it all up.

Then he caught site of the yawning gap that was Green's. The other buildings had been knocked about – not that there wasn't plenty of damage, the whole area was shattered – but you could recognize the buildings. But Green's simply was not there. It was just a big hole, piled with shattered bricks and masonry, broken slates, glass and sodden books and paper. He propped his bike against a wall and stood there, mouth open, trying to take it in. What was he supposed to do? Would he get his money on Friday? Where was old Maurice? He was supposed to be in charge, wasn't he? Was he still working there? Would they start up somewhere else? But all those books. Hundreds, no, thousands, maybe a million. How could old Maurice get them all together again? Must have taken years to get in all that lot. Some of them must be out of print by now. Where would the letters go? There was no letter-box, no door, no building, no Green's.

It was the overwhelming magnitude of what had happened that was a shock. And why did anyone think it was going to help the Germans to win the war? It was like some giant wind had come along and simply blown Green's away. Where was the rest of it? Three floors of books simply gone. Just a pile of old bricks, chimney stacks and shattered concrete, with red steel girders pointing at the sky, as if they were set to shoot up and do battle with the enemy in the doom-laden clouds. There was nobody about, no firemen, no ARP, no policemen. They must have given up on Green's and turned their attention elsewhere.

What was he supposed to do? Hang about and see if old Maurice turned up? And where were Miss Tcherny and Harry the packer? Had they turned up, taken one look and gone back home? How was he to contact anyone? And what about Helen? Was she around somewhere? How would he get in touch with her again? He knew where she lived. That was it. He would have to go to her home. Having sorted that out he felt a bit better.

He retraced his steps, picking his way through the rubble. He was surprised to find that the ABC was open. People were sitting, drinking tea and eating toast, in a dazed, abstracted way. Nobody was speaking. The shock seemed to have stunned everyone into silence.

Who was going to clear all this mess up? The roads needed to be cleared. There were some places untouched, still standing, although their next-door neighbours were missing. Should he go to the Labour Exchange and see about another job? Would they give him one if he were still supposed to be working for Green's? Of course, if Green's carried on paying him he wouldn't mind hanging on while they got things straight. Green's knew where he lived – but wait a minute, all the records, including his address, could have been destroyed. It was a right old pickle and no mistake.

Suddenly he saw Miss Tcherny. God, she was looking fed up. She saw him but gave no sign of recognition. It seemed that everybody was immersed in his or her own private world. He sat down opposite her.

'What's going to happen, miss?'

She just looked at him. He had always liked Miss Tcherny, with her tight jumpers and dark eyes that sometimes seemed to be saying something without her speaking. Now those eyes were dull.

'What's going to –'

'I don't know,' she interrupted crossly. 'What makes you think I know anything? I saw Mr Maurice and then he disappeared.'

'It's all gone,' he said, wonderingly.

'I know,' she said. 'I've seen it.'

For some reason he couldn't understand, tears started in his eyes.

'Oh for God's sake,' said Miss Tcherny. 'Don't start that.' But even as she said it there was a catch in her voice and she, too, found tears welling up.

'I don't understand it,' said Jimmy. 'Green's wasn't doing no harm.'

Suddenly both of them felt a shiver of fear, a sense of desolation. Churchill's voice was on the shop radio. Somebody turned it up. So he was all right, then. Probably in an underground bunker two miles under the earth. 'We can take it,' he was saying. He had no bloody idea.

They came out of the teashop and stood on the pavement, lost, not knowing what to do, where to go.

'What are you going to do, miss?' Jimmy asked.

Miss Tcherny replied, in a small, frightened voice, 'I think I'll go home.'

And then they saw Maurice, across the road. He looked terrible. He had mud on his suit and his face. He looked like a man who had just discovered that his worst nightmare was real.

They didn't know whether he had seen them. He was looking at them, and yet he made no sign of recognition. Miss Tcherny went towards him, but he turned his back to her. From across the road Jimmy saw that Miss Tcherny had spoken to him and he had reeled around as though he had just heard a voice from his past. Miss Tcherny took his arm and brought him over the road.

They went back into the teashop. There were no waitresses. Jimmy went to the counter. Old Maurice was staring around as though he suspected that there was a plot to assassinate him. Jimmy got a pot of tea and brought it over. He didn't have the heart to ask for the tuppence. Miss Tcherny was holding old Maurice's hand while he blinked and kept twisting his head around. It must be his nerves, Jimmy thought. Must have been a shock for the poor old bugger. Maurice's face was white and his eyes were creepy. He looked like some crook at the end of an American gangster film who knows he is going to be found out and sent to the electric chair.

In fact, Maurice was only one of a tribe of walking zombies who roamed around like ships without rudders, people whose lives had taken a sudden turn, for whom life would never be the same again. This was a day they would look back on. When they were forced to find a new path to success, to survival.

Jimmy, waiting for Maurice to say something about what was going to happen, realized that Maurice was as lost as he was.

'Come on,' said Miss Tcherny, 'I'll see you to the station.' And old Maurice got up, like he was sleep-walking, and went out with Miss Tcherny. Jimmy followed, not knowing what else to do.

When they got to the station Miss Tcherny had the bright idea of writing their names and addresses down and putting them in old Maurice's pocket. Old Maurice still seemed dazed, but he thanked Miss Tcherny and patted Jimmy's head before he went down the Tube.

'Well, goodbye, miss,' said Jimmy, feeling somehow that something formal should be said.

'Goodbye, Jimmy,' Miss Tcherny said, and added, very seriously, 'Good luck.'

Betty was getting impatient. She was standing outside the Gaiety Theatre, with its old and faded posters of a show starring Leslie Henson, Richard Hearne and Fred Emney. The trio was popular and had been on before at this theatre. Henson and co. might have been amusing, but Betty had already had enough of their drollery for one day. She had read every word about the show, how it was a 'Smash Hit' and a 'Tonic'. She must have walked around the whole block of Bush House half a dozen times. How long was she expected to wait? Maurice had sometimes been late but never more than five minutes. Something might have happened, of course. He could have been taken ill, knocked down by a car. She had only a vague idea of the location of the business from the address on the business card he had given her. But he had said that he would meet her here.

She noticed that a man was watching her. He was smart – well, more flash than smart. He had a dark-blue suit. The jacket seemed to be too large for him. It flapped about and hung from the shoulders in a straight line. He had a light-grey trilby that seemed to be sited at a cocky angle. He was clearly someone who thought a lot of himself. He sauntered towards her, and she turned away quickly and started walking back the way she had come.

'You all right, love?' The hoarse voice was right behind her.

'Yes, thank you,' she said.

'Only I've been watching you. I thought you might be waiting for someone.'

'I'm perfectly all right, thank you.'

'Will I do? You sure?' the voice persisted.

She panicked. 'If you don't go away I'll call a policeman.'

'I think they're all busy, love.' But he went away.

There was a lot of activity at this end of the Strand. Fire engines passed, with bedraggled firemen looking exhausted, and dust carts from Westminster City Council, leaking wet red and yellow earth and clay, like droppings from giant snails, all the way down the street.

Maurice was an hour late. This was significant. Stephen had said that she was never going to be offered a job, and this was the day when it should have happened. Would she ever see Maurice again? Had she been wrong to press him? She resolved to walk around the block once more, and then twice, and even when she left to catch the 88 bus, she kept looking back in case he had turned up after all.

Maurice sat on the Underground train feeling as if he had been drained of all life. He had died in his head, but his body continued to walk about, getting in everybody's way. What should he do? Should he report something to somebody? Surely some record ought to be kept. The train eased into stations and out again, rocking and roaring along to the next, Maurice not registering the names. In any case, he didn't get out until the end of the line. And yet somehow he felt uneasy. Was there something he had neglected to do?

Suddenly, in a pitiful close-up, he saw the face of Betty, looking cold and lost and anxious, at the end of the Strand. He had arranged to meet her. Was that today, Monday? What day was it anyway? He looked up as the train stopped again. Balham. Not far to go. But what about Betty? Would she still be there? He knew that she had a faithful, dogged quality. He had the feeling that if you told Betty to wait somewhere she might be there to the end of time. The trouble was that he hadn't got an address for her. He had preferred it that way, just two souls meeting without encumbrances and backgrounds. It was a romantic notion that he liked.

He got off the train and sat on a platform seat. Whatever happened now, he was over an hour and a half late. Should he go back? Would there be any point? If not, how could he get in touch with her? She was someone he could talk to, who just listened. He was in need of someone to talk to, someone who wouldn't interrupt. Who would let him pour out his feelings about his great loss? He was going to miss Betty. She was perfect for the job.

Bert Penrose woke up. He tried to look around him, but his head wouldn't move. Everything he could see was white. White ceiling, white walls, white sheets, women dressed all in white, who came and peered at him once in a while. He felt stiff, but at the same time he felt as though every bone in his body was broken. His skin felt clammy, his mouth dry. He found that he couldn't focus. When he set his eyes on something it began to duplicate itself and then float about. He could hear whispering. What was going on? Where was he? What time was it?

Suddenly, right in front of his eyes was a pink blob with bulging eyes that were looking at him as if he was something that ought to be put out of its misery.

'How are you feeling, old chap?' If he could have laughed he would have burst his sides. The pink blob seemed have acquired a moustache and glasses. 'We're sending you off to Epsom.'

Epsom? What for? The Derby? His leg was hurting. It was really giving him gyp. He tried to bend it, but it wouldn't shift. He caught a glimpse of a white bed opposite, and, as he widened his vision, he took in other beds, in a long, neat row. God Almighty. How many people were in here? It was all too much for him. He decided to sleep it off. Whatever was going on here was clearly bad news.

The next time he opened his eyes he saw Edie looking down on him as though she had had a nasty fright.

'Bert,' she said, 'you're all right', but he could tell that she didn't believe it. He tried to lever himself up on one arm. 'No,' Edie said. 'You mustn't move. You've got to lay still. The doctor said . . .' She looked worried to death. There was fear in her eyes and her hands kept stroking him as if she was trying to calm him down.

'What's up, old girl?' he said.

'You've been hurt,' she said. 'In Piccadilly.' For some reason this piece of news struck him as being wildly funny. He was hurt all over. Not in Piccadilly.

'It was a bomb,' Edie said. 'It hit a night club.' He hadn't been in a night club, had he? He certainly didn't remember it. By God, Edie looked worried.

'You all right?' he said.

'They're taking you to a hospital in Epsom,' she said. 'It's a bit quieter there.'

'They told me. Where are we now?'

'St Thomas's.'

'I've got a new job,' he said. 'At the RAC. But I've got to get a reference.' Edie looked down the bed. 'What's up?' he said.

Edie looked at the ceiling. 'Haven't they told you?' She looked frightened.

Something was up here. 'What is it?' he said.

Edie gulped. Something was sticking in her throat. 'Bert,' she said tremulously. 'You've lost one of your legs.'

This also struck him as being hilarious. Lost one of his legs? Bloody careless that was. Should have looked after it.

'Edie,' he said. 'There's some fags in my pocket. Get one out, will you?'

And so the ordinary people of London would check to see whether their part in the life of the capital was still there. Some shrugged and went home. What could they do? It was all bloody silly anyway. Knocking the place about. Didn't they know that people had work to do, their living to earn? But many hung about in shiftless groups. Now and again there was a show of mass hysteria. The appearance of a dustcart got an ironic cheer. Somebody standing outside a ruined building started to sing 'There'll Always Be an England' in a loud defiant voice, but nobody joined in. There was an air of grumbling resentment in the air. This crowd could easily become a mob. What had they done to deserve this? War was one thing, but bombing cities like this just wasn't on. Somebody would have to pay for it – probably them. The bloody government took half their money in taxes already, and it was certain that the insurance companies wouldn't pay up. It wasn't only the damage, it was the loss of earnings: days off, probably months off, it wasn't good enough.

That morning Charlie was sitting in the front of a ramshackle lorry heading down the A1 to London. He had hitched a lift because he didn't dare go on the railway because of the redcaps. He had found this bloke who had been up to the Potteries in search of seconds in the way of ironmongery and china.

'You can't get nothing', he said, 'unless you fetch it.'

So the lorry rattled and clinked with tin and china as it hobbled its way to the capital. The driver stopped at a roadside café that looked like a benighted shack in a western film. He ordered the full works: a whole plate of sausages, tomatoes, fried bread and an egg. It seemed like three breakfasts rolled into one. The driver scoffed his down, but Charlie found it too much in the end. When he offered to pay, the driver wouldn't hear of it.

'Nothing too good for our boys,' he said. 'You on leave?' he enquired.

'Yes,' Charlie said. 'Wife's having a baby,' he added, to lend credibility.

'Gawd bless you, son,' said the driver.

Charlie had only been in the Army for three days, but it had been enough. The clothes were rough and didn't fit, the boots were impossible, the food was all right, but it wasn't what he was used to. He could have put up with all that, but it was the way people behaved that was so awful. Did they need to shout all the time? Standing so close and bellowing in his ear. And did they need to be so vulgar? Some of the chaps at work could let it rip at times, but nothing like this. It was like he had been sent to a tribe of savages. And the threats . . .

'You may have broken your mother's heart but you won't break mine.' This was all said without a hint of humour. 'If you know what's good for you you'll shape up, you shit-faced bastard.' Was there any need to be so threatening, so loud, so crude?

He was in another part of the world. He'd been given a train pass to get to Crewe, which looked like a railway station on the edge of the world, and was bundled on to an Army lorry when he got there. Then through some bleak and cheerless countryside that seemed an altogether darker and bleaker world than London: tiny little towns, no shops of any size, rabbit-hutch cinemas, it was like going back fifty years. And then this vast estate of wooden and tin huts, with hundreds of strangers, all living a sub-human existence, ruled by shouting madmen.

After two days he was shattered in mind and spirit. Most of the other intake seemed to be taking this outright bullying as though it was a normal way of carrying on. Then came the cross-country run, wearing the boots, with somebody shouting at him all the way. And it wasn't in the country at all. It was on the road, with women and schoolgirls giggling as he strove to keep up. Was all this humiliation necessary? The people who inflicted all this, the teak-faced sergeants and their arsehole-licking corporals, seemed to be enjoying it. Who had given them permission to inflict this kind of torture on unwilling recruits? After all, he wasn't a volunteer. No bloody fear.

The accommodation was bad enough: bunk beds, up and down, bolted together in series so that when somebody moved the whole lot of them moved, and no privacy. Everything was done in public. He was amazed at the way such ordinary matters as folding a blanket had been elevated into a precise art form and the way what they called his kit had to be laid out as though it was an exhibit in an art gallery.

The only thing he had to relish was that last night with Rosa. It had been so sweet. She had taken all her clothes off, and the revelation had filled him with a kind of tenderness. He had stroked the contours of her body lightly, with reverence almost, feeling her skin tighten in response. It was what he wanted, but he wanted more. He wanted to claim her. To have some promise for their future life. He was going away, but that needn't be the end of it. He would get leave.

But when he got to the town of Nissen huts he was told that he wasn't allowed out for eight weeks. They started on him the first day. Marching up and down like cartoon characters, shouting in unison. It was mad. The people who ran the place were completely crazy. They walked funny and talked funny. The sergeants and corporals had strange accents. Half the time he couldn't fathom out what they were saying, and his inability to understand the instructions made them madder than ever. How could anybody think that this was reasonable behaviour?

After two days he knew that all he could do was run away. If he stayed in this place he would break down and be no use to anybody. He thought about going to the doctor, but he had seen the doctor on the first day and he knew that the evil-looking medical man was in on the conspiracy.

The next day there was an incident that forced his hand. There was another run in the morning, and he had a stroke of luck as he was named as room orderly. That meant that he didn't have to go but instead had to stay in the hut and clean it up. Twenty-nine men trooped out in their white singlets, blue shorts and boots and clattered down the drive. It was a brisk, cold morning, and they would need to run to keep warm. When they had gone he luxuriated in the thought that he was alone. The first moment of peace he had had since he arrived at the blasted place. He didn't know what his duties were. The place seemed clean and tidy enough. He moved a black screen black-out frame to sweep behind it and saw a pair of fat hairy thighs crouching there. It was one of the corporals, the fattest, dressed for the run, who straightened up and said seriously, 'You haven't seen me. Right?' What was this? The Marx Brothers? It must be a lunatic asylum, thought Charlie. The corporal went outside the hut and rubbed grass and mud on his legs and shorts. He came back in.

'You the room orderly?' Charlie nodded. 'You have to light the fire. Come here.' He pointed through the window. 'See that pile of coke? Get some in that bucket.' So Charlie fetched some coke. 'Now then. You want some paper.' Charlie scuffed around and found two newspapers.

'Why aren't you on the run?' he asked.

'Because I didn't feel like it,' said the corporal. 'So keep your mouth shut or I'll . . .' He didn't specify what might happen if Charlie snitched on him, but Charlie knew it would be some embellishment on the 'guts for garters' theme. He lit the paper but it all burnt away without igniting the coke.

'You need some wood,' said the corporal, and reached out and wrenched a strut off one of the bunks and gave it to him.

'It's too thick,' Charlie said.

'So?' said the corporal impatiently. 'You got a bayonet, haven't you?' So Charlie was calmly engaged in chopping up Army property with his bayonet, that should never be out of its sheath except for dire circumstances, when the colonel of the camp marched in followed by a string of attendants: the adjutant, the RSM, the company commander and a string of assorted non-commissioned officers, all sparklingly dressed, looking as though they were in a musical comedy about military life in India or somewhere.

'What are you doing?' said the colonel mildly.

Charlie looked around for the corporal, who seemed to have

vanished. Behind the black-out, of course. And Charlie hadn't seen him if he didn't want his guts as garters. 'Chopping wood for the fire, sir.'

'Stand up, lad,' somebody shouted somewhere down the line.

'With your bayonet?' said the colonel. He turned to the adjutant, a fleshy handsome man, who looked like Nelson Eddy in *New Moon* but lost without Jeanette Macdonald. 'Is this man all right?' The colonel nodded as he walked out, with the others following at a respectful distance, except the RSM.

'Report to the MO in the morning. What's your number?'

Charlie couldn't remember the number they had given him.

'I figured not,' said the RSM thoughtfully.

Why the doctor? Did they think he was mad? Would they lock him up somewhere? Maybe they would chuck him out of the Army for being too daft. Anyway, he wasn't going to wait and see.

The corporal came out from behind the black-out screen. 'Christ,' he said. 'That was a close shave.'

'They thought I was mad,' Charlie said.

'Yeah. You did that well. Keep that up and you'll get your ticket.'

Getting away was easier than he had thought. He slipped out of the hut early morning and just sailed up to the main gates and walked through. The sentries, raw and inexperienced like him, naturally thought that he had a pass or some sort of permission to go down to the town, which was about four miles away.

He thought it best not to go right into the town. He reached the outskirts and was lucky enough to get a lift on a bread lorry that dropped him near the main road where he ran into a group of women coming off a factory night-shift. One of them calmly took his arm and walked with him as though he was a trophy, while the others made coarse remarks. She lived in a terrace of cottages near by. He went in with her and she made tea in a big mug and gave him some. There was a picture of a smiling sailor on the mantelpiece. In the harsh morning light the woman looked exhausted.

'I'll have to have a little rest, soldier, and then I'll see to you,' and she winked, her face lighting up briefly into a saucy grin.

He sat on a busted armchair. It was a tiny room, with a low ceiling and poky window. The woman had fallen asleep as soon as she sat down. There was a dead fire in the grate. When the woman was sound asleep he went to the door. He could see traffic going by not so far away. That must be the trunk road. He went out quietly.

He had to skip over the hedge a few times as military vehicles came along, but eventually the traveller in pots and pans picked him up. He felt at peace with himself. All he had to do was to get home and get his ordinary clothes on. He couldn't stay there, of course, because they would have his home address and come looking for him. He would stay with Rosa until things had blown over. He was back in London. His home town. London would protect him.

Mrs Bennet packed a bag. She had enjoyed herself last night, and she hoped that there would be another raid tonight. She put the kettle on to make a thermos. This was a different twist on life. All the people in the place had been together. Of course, she'd always kept herself to herself, didn't poke her nose in where it was not wanted, but this was different. They were all in the same boat. The war – well, the bombing, really – had rescued her from her enforced isolation. They weren't all nice people, but they were people, and they had been forced to notice her.

The best thing about it was that she had come to no harm. The bombs had fallen miles away. She had heard someone talking about a landmine in Peckham, caught up in telephone wires and swinging back and forth in the wind while everybody held their breath. Even if there had been an element of danger, it was probably better than being on her own all day and night. She liked people. Tom knew that. He used to fall asleep when she was speaking to him. 'You're a right old chatterbox,' he used to say.

Of course, when it was all over all the people would go back to leading their own separate lives, and it would be back to 'good morning' and 'good afternoon'. What she really wanted was someone to say 'good night' to.

13

BERNARD viewed the destruction of Green's with an equanimity bordering on grim satisfaction. Nobody had told him. He went there that afternoon to collect some supplies, and found himself viewing the ruins. He was surprised at the complete destruction: like Green's had never been there. There were buildings on either side, badly damaged but still standing. He immediately thought of compensation. There was a fund for war damage, wasn't there? But they weren't likely to get it until the war was over – that is, as long as Britain was on the winning side. In the meantime, could the business function? Well, his side of the operation certainly could. He didn't need vast storage space. His area of the business was quite compact. Not more than a hundred titles in all.

Bernard had never felt a part of the Green's enterprise. It was Maurice's domain, Maurice's castle, which he had run as though it was some kind of noble calling. Bernard had only been a hanger-on. He had never been given any standing. His contribution had been largely ignored and disapproved of, even though it brought in a healthy return. Now he could run that side on his own. It was obvious that Maurice's part of the business could not continue, but the stuff that Bernard dealt in was in and out. He could run it from his big garage at his house in Ealing. He could load books into his car and carry on with the distribution of the select titles. It seemed like providence had intervened, as the whole area to one side of St Paul's had been destroyed, but the other side, which housed the publishers that Bernard dealt with, was still intact. All the purveyors of religious works, bibles and prayer books had been wiped out, but the publishers who dealt in the racy stuff were still there. Whose side was God on?

Once Bernard realized that he was in control of his own destiny he felt a sense of release. He had never had much regard for Green's standing in the trade. He had always thought that

Maurice made too much of their reputation for reliability and service. After all, they were in business to make some real money, not just the few coppers scraped from reluctant publishers' profits that they got servicing lazy booksellers. To make anything out of such an arrangement you had to sell in large quantities, as he was doing on his Leicester Square run. It was quick profits and quick returns.

Bernard had no intention of consulting Maurice about his plan. It wouldn't be a part of the Green's enterprise. He was going to strike out on his own. A new business using all his old contacts. He would call it something else, Star Books or something, and register it in his own name. The bombing of the claustrophobic old firm could be a new start, away from his stuffy brother.

Having decided on a course of action Bernard thought that he ought to celebrate. He thought about the Hostess Club but dismissed it. There were no surprises there, and, besides, he fancied something with a bit more class.

He got on a bus. By God, the passengers all looked fagged out: white-faced and hollow-eyed, all in a sort of cloud of collective misery. Where was the cheery cockney, full of optimistic wit – down maybe but never out? Where were the joyful pearly kings and queens, doing the Lambeth Walk? Where were the spivs, dazzling money into their pockets by sheer force of personality? Where were the buskers, working themselves into a lather while their bottler collected the dibs? This lot looked tired, frightened and defeated. They looked as if they had been up all night praying but did not have the faith to expect a result.

It was a depressing time, but Bernard did not feel depressed. He was at the start of something good. Soldiers and sailors, away from home, read a lot. Tucked up in their little barrack beds or bunks they liked to read about life in an Istanbul harem, about lowlife in Paris, agonies in Egypt and downright degradation in South America. The life of an American gangster was a damned sight more interesting than the memoirs of some crusty old general. Who wanted to know what Marx said or Freud and Byron, Shakespeare, Darwin and all that crowd that Maurice was so keen on? You couldn't read the stuff, even if you wanted to.

People wanted something in their own vernacular, something they could relate to, something that would add to their nightly fantasies. He got off the bus in Coventry Street and strolled, feeling relaxed and triumphant, until he got to Piccadilly Circus.

It had been no use boarding up Eros. Was it a symbolic gesture, to put away the nation's pleasures until the war was over, to concentrate minds on the job in hand? Was it to hint that you should put away anything that detracted from the war effort? Well, it hadn't stopped anyone's feelings, yearnings. And there was more activity in the sex business than ever before. The troops thought of London as a Mecca. London, after all, was a garrison town.

He turned into Piccadilly and saw barriers across the road. There was no traffic moving, but there were fire engines, ambulances and police cars, parked at odd angles all over the road. There was only a narrow passage to walk along on the Green Park side. There was dust and black soot everywhere. He walked along until he saw a big crater in the road. People were scrambling in it, calling hello. ARP men swarmed over the big hole like ants, frantically lifting concrete slabs with their hands, throwing bricks over their shoulders like a dog digging for a lost bone. Sometimes they would all stop, and someone would call out 'Quiet!' and it seemed as though everybody in the area, the birds in the Green Park trees, even the buildings, were holding their breath, for any sound of life from below the rubble.

Something big had happened here. There were gaps where buildings should have been and a putrid smell invaded the whole area. It was as though a child had tipped up a whole box of bricks, flung them in the air for fun, and they had landed forming odd shapes, leaving caverns and caves in between. The ARP men continued with their frantic efforts. They had constructed a tunnel, with stout wooden props like they did in a coal mine. Men crawled down into the tunnel, doubled up, and emerged, black-faced, with just their white eyes showing, like minstrels in a ragtime revue. If some poor beggar were under that lot they wouldn't have much chance.

Bernard continued, shaken, and up a side street he spotted Claridge's. It was a bit up the scale from what he was used to, but suddenly he felt that he might have gone up the scale a bit himself. He was the managing director of a newly formed business. A one-man band run by a real live wire who didn't have anybody to answer to. In any case, what did that sort of thing matter any more? They were all in it. Class barriers had been swept away by the common sense of danger. It didn't really matter if a fire-bombed corpse was a duke or a ragged-arsed tramp.

He walked through the imposing doorway into the hotel vestibule. The hall porter spotted him right away. 'Good afternoon, sir.'

'A drink,' said Bernard. 'I've just dropped in for a drink.'

The hall porter looked at his watch in an elaborate gesture. 'We seem to be out of hours, sir, don't we?' and he winked heavily. 'Of course there are soft drinks, or tea if you would prefer, but I suspect that you're a soft-drink man, aren't you, sir?' And he winked again, as though the wink was a code that Bernard would know.

'All right,' said Bernard, somewhat confused, and he was led into in inner bar area, with large leather sofas, elegant mirrors on the walls and portrait paintings of some bosky eighteenth-century notables, who all seemed to have puffed cheeks and red noses. The bar was inhabited by some very smart men and women, all of whom looked as though they might have fallen out of the pages of the *Sketch* or *Bystander*.

Bernard saw nothing for it but to order a lemonade, which was brought to him on a silver tray. He wished he hadn't come into the place. A lemonade. He picked up the glass and sipped and immediately discovered the reason for the pantomime wink. The drink was heavily laced with gin. So, there was life in the old town if you knew where to find it. When he finished the laced lemonade he immediately ordered another.

'Hot day,' he murmured to the waiter. Then he started to make calculations. He had been on a salary at Green's with only 5 per cent overriding commission, but buying and selling direct, with no rent or upkeep and no staff, he would be taking a third and a bit more if he could retain Green's terms. Maybe he could afford a small premises and perhaps someone to help him. He thought of the staff at Green's. That Miss Tcherny was a sensible girl and she knew the business, especially the accounts. She would be looking for a job, but how was he to find her? Would they be on the telephone, the Tchernys? More people were nowadays. If she was signing on, perhaps the Labour Exchange people could find her?

He suddenly became aware that a woman was looking at him. She was, he was certain, trying to catch his eye. She was at the other side of the room, sitting alone. She had an aristocratic face, high cheekbones and full lips, with a dark, lacy dress and a fur stole. She looked away, her mission accomplished. He got up and moved over to the table where she was sitting.

When he got close to her he could see that she was very smartly turned out but older than he had thought, more like thirty-five than twenty-five. Her face was skilfully produced, with arched eyebrows and the high cheekbones shaded in, the full lips painted on, entirely different from any of the women he might have met at the Hostess Club.

'Haven't we met before?' he said.

'No,' she said, seemingly amused at the crude approach, 'but it doesn't matter. You may sit down.'

He sat down. 'Are you having the lemonade?'

She laughed. It was a musical laugh, not spontaneous, but controlled, produced. There was something entirely artificial about this woman, and he found this exciting.

'Bernard,' he said.

'Well how are you, Bernard?' she said, with a hint of irony in her voice.

'Not bad', he said, 'for a chap who's just seen his business blown up.'

She frowned. 'That's terrible. What will you do?'

'Oh, I'll manage somehow. Start up again. Out of town, I think. And what about you?'

She smiled and showed a row of perfect teeth. 'Me? I'm out of work.'

He signalled to the waiter and two drinks were brought to them.

'Out of work? What kind of work is that?'

'I'm an actress.'

'Ah,' he said. It all slotted into place.

'Theatres closed: no work.'

'I see. Bad luck.'

'So that's why I'm sitting here, trying to get some kind man to buy me a drink.'

'It's a terrible business,' he said. 'It's hit all of us. What's your name?'

'Gloria – well, that's what I'm known as. It's not my name.'

He smiled. A West End actress, down on her uppers. 'Well, Gloria,' he said. 'Do you know any place where we could get a decent dinner?'

Maurice had got down as far as Bush House. He didn't expect Betty still to be there, three hours after their appointment, but he didn't seem to have anything more sensible to do. He crossed the road to Waterloo Bridge and stared into the muddy river. It was a bright day, an autumn day, a day for walking briskly, producing enough heat to keep warm. Well, they couldn't bomb the Thames, could they? The river would at least be there when all this non-sense was over. He supposed that he ought to call a meeting. Bernard and Bella would have to be consulted. Was there any point in starting up again? He needed to talk to somebody. Betty would have been perfect. It was unlikely that she would have made any sensible suggestions, but out of his ramblings there might have emerged a picture, a plan.

It was certain that Clare wouldn't listen. She was too wrapped up in her own affairs; and Bernard, well, Bernard might be concerned. Bernard would need to find some other way of earning his living. Maurice had wanted to talk to his solicitors about insurance and government cover, but the telephone lines were down and he couldn't get through.

Suddenly he thought of that dreadful club where Bernard had taken him. That was where he first met Betty. He didn't think she went there any more, but they might know where she was, her address or a contact telephone number. Could he find the place again? It was behind Cambridge Circus, wasn't it? If he went there he might be able to retrace his steps.

So he wandered slowly along the Strand. The Savoy Guild was still displaying smart clothes. There were servicemen everywhere, the officers looking as though they were in the chorus of a musical comedy, but the other ranks looking like bagwash tied around with string. The armed forces did not inspire confidence at all. They weren't soldiers, just ordinary chaps pressed into service in an emergency. They looked lost and bewildered. He reached Trafalgar Square. There was a crowd outside St Martin-in-the-Fields. That woman Myra – what was her name? – Hess was playing there during the day. It was a defiant gesture, and even people who didn't like classical music went in to see this woman serenely playing, and they seemed to get some comfort from the music and the gesture.

In Charing Cross Road the dusty old bookshops where he had spent many hours of sheer joy seemed somehow irrelevant. There was no time for that sort of thing now. All the civilized pleasures of life had been obliterated. Even books were on emergency rations. He went straight on until he reached the Palace and then plunged into Soho.

As soon as he got into Greek Street he felt vaguely apprehensive. It was the very foreignness of the place. So many nationalities, some looking cheerful but just as many looking evil: dark-skinned men with curly hair who could have easily been Italian. Weren't they all interned?

Was it near a market? He seemed to remember a row of stalls selling fruit and vegetables, and racks of clothes in distinctly un-English styles. He wandered up narrow streets, full of mysterious offices and warehouses. It was said that the police only ventured into this area in pairs. There was an air of menace, as though anything violent could happen as a matter of course.

He stood on a corner watching a hefty prostitute smiling at prospective clients in a manner that suggested she would strangle the first one who refused to take her on, and suddenly he saw the place. It wasn't drawing attention to itself, but those who wanted to find it would know where to go. There was no sign outside. Just a brick building, trying to be anonymous.

He stood outside, wondering whether to go in. A big grey Humber pulled up outside. The door opened, and the blonde, hard-faced bitch that had been there with Betty got out. She was more awful in the daylight than she had been in the shaded light of the club. My God, she was brassy all right, all bosom and tight skirt.

'Excuse me,' he said, but she ignored him. He touched her arm, and she turned to him and switched on a ghastly flirtatious smile. 'That woman who was with you, Betty, do you know where I could find her?' The woman looked puzzled but then assumed an expression that indicated that he had said something quite outrageous. She took his arm and pulled him towards the entrance to the club.

'No,' he said. 'Betty. Do you know where I could find her?' The woman smiled uncertainly. Was she loopy or something, or foreign? She couldn't understand plain English. She pushed open the door and stood there, as if daring him to follow her. When he made no move she just glared at him, and then, as if giving him his last chance, smiled invitingly.

Across the road Tim Melrose observed the little cameo with mounting fury. So this was the man who had been knocking Bunty about, sending her home bruised and scratched. Well, he wasn't going to get away with it. It was Tim's duty as a husband to see that he didn't. His eyes went dull and slightly crazed. He was like a bull, aroused to a fury by repeated taunting. With a roar of uncontrollable rage Tim sprang across the road in a tight ball of fury. He grabbed Maurice around the throat, pressing his thumbs into Maurice's windpipe. Tim was smaller than Maurice but he was stocky and fit, and he had the added element of surprise. Maurice saw the woman's eyes registering alarm, as he felt the juddering thud of Tim's knee in his stomach. He bent double with the pain. What was happening here? Where were the police? Did they take fights as par for the course in these dangerous streets? He had been set upon by a madman. What for? For his wallet? The crazy man had got his arm up between Maurice's shoulder blades and was forcing him into the back of a small van with 'Water Board' painted on the side. The woman was trying to stop the madman, but he brushed her off. Maurice was in the cramped space of the van, with various iron tools, damp sacks and hosepipes. Now the madman was forcing the woman into the front seat as she struggled and hit him about the face and shoulders. The man's face was set. It was clear that there was no reasoning with him. The only thing that would stop him was a strait-jacket. The man got into the driver's seat and started the van. The wheels jerked and skidded over the cobbled road. The man at the wheel drove steadily. There were many obstacles, some roads closed, but he carried on, determinedly, like a man on a mission.

Maurice soon recognized Cheapside and Aldgate and then Commercial Road. The further they went into the heart of London, the less there seemed of it, and when they got into East India Dock Road there was devastation on every side. Whole areas were flattened. An area as big as a couple of football pitches with hardly any buildings standing, just the odd chimney stack with a drunken pot lurching precariously on top. There were odd snapshots: a china cup, unharmed, looked surprised that it had landed on a mossy patch on the top of the single wall left intact; a washing-line with scorched and burnt clothing still flapping in the breeze; a brave geranium still flourishing in a broken window-box; and rhubarb growing on the top of an Anderson shelter. There were groups of people, all looking dazed and helpless. Some were walking, carrying suitcases and bags, with gas-mask boxes around their necks. Some were loading barrows with furniture and clothes. There were lorries and carts with crazy heaps of belongings snatched up quickly and piled on to any form of transport. This was an evacuation. These people were refugees, a sight often seen on newsreels in some foreign country but never before seen in England.

Despite his discomfort, Maurice's brain registered that this was an extraordinary sight. It put his loss into some perspective. He had lost his business, but these people had lost their homes and everything they possessed.

But where were they going? The woman in the front had settled into a profound sulk. The short gritty man at the wheel was clearly being driven by some inner force. He was clearly unbalanced, suffering from some delusion. He seemed to have control over the woman. The drive was taking them into the East End of London, to the Docks, where the worst of the bombing had taken place. In Mile End Road most of the shops were closed, although a street-market of a sort seemed to be doing a sluggish trade. There were groups of Jews, with long beards and tall hats, carrying cloth bags. They seemed more resigned than frightened, as though they always knew that their life in London was too good to be true, that they always knew the roof would fall in some day.

Then they ran out of people. There were just piles of bricks everywhere, warehouses gutted by fire, the road strewn with broken glass glistening in puddles, the sound of running water and the smell of gas.

Close to the river the van stopped and the stocky little man got out and opened the back door, indicating that Maurice should get out, too. Maurice got out. There was a foul smell from the river. He looked around at the scene of destruction. He had never realized it was as bad as this. This was like no man's land between opposing trenches. Just mud and bricks, a few hardy weeds and seagulls diligently scavenging.

The driver faced him, glaring at him. The angry man assumed a boxer's stance, managing to look heroic and ridiculous at the same time.

'Come on,' he snarled. 'If you want a fight . . .'

'Fight?' Maurice said bewildered. 'I don't know you. Why should we fight?'

The man looked impatient to be getting on with it. 'But you know my wife.'

'Hardly. I met her once. I went to find Betty. They were there together the one time I went.' The man hesitated. A flicker of uncertainty showed in his eyes. The woman had got out of the van and was looking at the man with contempt. There was a clatter as a rusty sheet of corrugated iron was lifted by a breeze, flew briefly and then crashed to the ground.

'Someone has been knocking her about,' the man said doggedly.

Maurice felt emboldened by the man's hesitation. 'I went there with my brother. I met Betty. She was there with your wife.'

'Betty?' the man said. 'Betty May?' It then dawned on Tim that it was he who had suggested that Betty went with Bunty, and that snotty young Stephen had cut up rough about it and Betty had never been out with Bunty since. He dropped his hands and looked vacant. He had made a stand, but it was the wrong time and the wrong place and the wrong man. It had all gone wrong. He looked defeated and lost. Bunty came over and put her arms around him. He let out a heart-wrenching sigh and began to sob.

Maurice felt relieved but angry. It was obviously a case of mistaken identity, but he had a pretty good idea of the real culprit. Bernard went with the brassy woman, and he knew that Bernard had a vicious streak. It occurred to him that he could put the madman on the track of Bernard, but there was no telling what might happen. This little bull of a man could find himself up for murder. No, he was lucky to get away without serious damage.

'I just wanted to ask your wife –'

'She can't hear you. She can't hear, can't speak.' It was torn out of him like a confession.

Maurice tried another tack. 'Why did you bring me down here?'

The man mumbled. 'Nobody down here any more. They've all gone.'

Maurice started to tremble. This demented, half-crazy little runt had brought him to a place where he knew he wouldn't be seen. Had it been his intention to murder Maurice and leave him here to be found, another victim of the bombing?

Suddenly the man regained control of himself. He shook off his wife and went back to the van. He got in, and the brassy wife got in beside him. Maurice went forward, but the man started the engine and drove off. Maurice watched the van as it crackled over the uneven surface. He was still trembling but relieved.

Rosa Tcherny opened the door. Charlie was standing there, looking foolish in his Army uniform. He smiled uncertainly. He looked unkempt, unshaven, as though he had left somewhere in a hurry.

'Can I come in?' he said.

'What are you doing here?' Rosa asked. He had only been away a few days. Had they found him too inept for service? Discovered some fatal medical flaw?

He came in nervously. 'I couldn't go home,' he said. 'They'll go there first. I was wondering', he said hesitantly, 'if there were any clothes?'

'Clothes?' she said. 'What sort of clothes?'

'Oh, any old clothes,' he said. 'Doesn't matter much.'

'But what for?' she said.

'I can't go anywhere like this.' He pulled at his tunic top.

Rosa was getting impatient. 'But what have you come for? Why are you here?'

He shuffled his feet and looked down at them. 'I couldn't stand it,' he said, in a low voice. 'You've no idea. Shouting. All the time. Ordering you about. Horrible people. All mad.' Tears started in his eyes and ran down his face, making white streaks.

'For God's sake,' said Rosa. 'I've just lost my job.'

'I'm sorry,' he said. 'I'll go. If you've just got some clothes. Anything of your father's that he don't wear any more.'

She looked at him and sensed his distress. He wasn't very bright, and he'd been thrown into something he didn't understand.

'But what are you going to do? You can't go running around in old clothes, can you? Where are you going to go?' Charlie sat down on a chair in the hall. He looked hopeless and helpless. 'You'll have to go back,' Rosa said.

'I can't,' he said. 'You don't know what it's like.'

'But you're a deserter.'

'I can't help it.' He wrung his hands in desperation. 'I don't fit in with it.'

'The place where I work has been burnt down,' she said.

'I'm sorry,' he said. 'What a mess. What a mess. Why don't they leave people alone?'

Rosa made a sudden decision. 'Stay there. I'll see what I can find.'

The telephone rang. She ran to silence it, feeling, irrationally, that someone was listening in to the fraught scene.

'Hello?'

'Is that Miss, er, Tcherny?'

'Who is it?' she answered cautiously.

'It's Mr Green. Bernard Green.' Maurice's brother. The dark horse.

'Oh?'

'I suppose you know that we're out of business,' he said.

'Yes,' she said. 'I went there today. I'm really sorry. It was a good firm, and I liked working there.'

'I know. Can't be helped. Bloody Germans. Look, I'm thinking of starting up on my own. I was wondering if you'd be interested in working for me?'

Charlie had stood up. He was clearly apprehensive about this call. She nodded to him and smiled and shook her head. He sat down again.

'Can we meet?' Bernard was saying. 'I'll give you an address. It's in Ealing. You know Ealing Broadway?'

'I've heard of it. It's a long way.'

'I know. I'll pay your fares. Can we at least talk about it?'

'I'm rather busy just now.'

'I'll give you my number. Ring me back when you can.'

She wrote the number down. 'All right. I'll ring you back.'

Rosa went upstairs. Her father had a wardrobe of clothes, some that he never wore. She took an armful downstairs.

'Thank you,' Charlie said earnestly. 'I'll never forget this.' He tore off his tunic. He had on a rough woollen vest, cream with blue streaks in it, like Gorgonzola cheese. He put on one of her father's shirts. The sleeves were too long. He rolled them up. The trousers were all right, but the jacket was too long as well and he was forced to turn up the sleeves inside. Shoes were a problem. They were all too big. When he was finally assembled Rosa thought he looked like a Guy Fawkes.

'Have you got any money?'

'A bit,' he said. 'Not much.' She gave him a ten-shilling note. 'I'll pay you back,' he said.

Rosa did not have any special feelings about Charlie, just an ordinary human regard for someone in distress.

'Where are you going now?'

'I'm going home. When it's dark. Get my own clothes.'

And then what? Rosa thought. Hide out until the war ends? Would his parents look after him, give him scraps from their rations, or persuade him to give himself up? Anyway, it wasn't her business. She had to find another job. He hadn't any claim on her, despite their frantic union of a few nights ago.

Bert Penrose felt for his cock with a sense of relief. That was all right, then. It had tweaked now and again as he watched the nurses bending over, making the bed of the chap opposite. Blimey. He'd lost a leg. He thought it might have been something serious. It wasn't too bad in this place. No stinking dish-washing. When he got stronger he would be mistaken for a wounded soldier. Get bought pints in pubs. Might get a sitting-down job. And in the meantime he was in this place surrounded by all these young bits of crackling. They had these funny uniforms, white and blue. Some were a bit severe, but some were softer, only pretending to be severe. They bent over him, took his temperature, held his wrist and washed him all over while he lay there, enjoying it. He knew he wasn't quite right in the head yet. He was quite muddled. He could swear that he was just walking home from somewhere when he was suddenly in the front line and a big tank was coming towards him. There were flashes and some heavy drumming and horses, and Edie shouted, 'Don't you dare', and that Bunty bit upstairs had undone his braces, and he was squealing with delight. It was a big party, and Mrs Bennet came up to complain about the noise, and it was dark and sweaty down here, and what was that knocking, and somebody lost shouting 'Hello', and what would he do with only one leg to stand on? He might as well have been in the Army. At least he would have got a medal.

14

BETTY May couldn't help it. She was down in the dumps. The business with Maurice rankled. Surely he ought to have been more straight with her. If he didn't want to give her a job he should have said so. Stephen had been quite sweet about it. 'A man like that isn't worth bothering about. He was just playing you along.'

But why? What did Maurice get out of it? After all, they only talked. If he had wanted something more he would have said so, wouldn't he? In any case, he knew she was a married woman and would have been off at the sign of any indelicate suggestion. And yet that sort of thing had never arisen. Stephen thought that Maurice just hadn't got the nerve, but had their meetings continued he would have got around to it in the end.

Now there were no meetings to look forward to she was so bored she could scream. The little trysts with Maurice, the harmless half-hours in which she learnt something new every time, had given her life some purpose. She was still puzzled. Above all, Maurice was a gentleman. Leaving her waiting just wasn't like him. Of course, something could have gone wrong. He could have collapsed in the street. He could have been blown up in one of the bombing raids – although he said he lived out of town. She had rung Green's several times, but the line was dead. Had the firm gone bankrupt? Was Maurice mixed up in some swindle and had to go into hiding? No. That was too fanciful.

And then, suddenly, her scarcely used brain lurched into action. She could go there, find the address in the telephone book and just present herself. See what he had to say for himself. In a fit of excitement she rushed down the stairs to get to the nearest telephone box. In the street she saw Edie coming up from the basement. Edie looked awful. Her face was set, but her eyes showed signs of strain.

'Hello,' Betty said brightly.

Edie stared at her. It was a somewhat hostile stare, maybe not for Betty but for the world at large. 'Bert's had it,' she said, and before Betty could ask for some elaboration she went on in a dry monotonous fashion, in a voice drained of emotion, 'The other night, as he was coming home from work.'

Betty was shocked. She knew that people were getting hurt in the raids, but she didn't think it would be anyone she knew. 'Is he all right?' she said, and then seeing this might be a tactless question, she added wildly, 'Where is he?'

'Epsom,' said Edie. 'They took him to hospital there.'

Ah. At least he wasn't dead. 'Will he be all right?'

'I don't know,' said Edie dully. 'He hasn't properly come round yet. One of this legs has gone.'

'Oh dear,' said Betty. She didn't have any feelings about Bert Penrose. He had a way of looking at you that made you feel that you had promised him something and had somehow let him down. You couldn't put your finger on it, but Bert had the capacity to embarrass her without saying a word. Even so, she didn't wish him harm, and it was clear that poor Edie was in a state of shock.

They walked along together. Edie took short, determined steps.

'I'm going out to see him. He needs some clean socks,' she said helplessly, realizing immediately that this was a useless remark in the circumstances.

Betty felt inadequate to the situation. What did you say in such circumstances – 'Wish him good luck. Tell him to get well soon'? When confronted by a real-life tragedy all commonplace phrases sounded trite. Finally, she settled on: 'Tell him to have a good rest and that Stephen and me are thinking of him.' She reached the telephone box. 'I've got to make a call,' she said. Edie grunted and marched on.

Betty May turned up Green's in the directory. Old Causeway? Where was that?

Maybe if she got into the area someone would know. She boarded the Number 88 feeling that at least she was doing something positive. She knew that a bus from Trafalgar Square would take her to Fleet Street. The bus journey was a dreary affair. Nobody spoke any more; the passengers sat in grim rows, all immersed in their own private thoughts. There were no children to break the silence with inane questions or grizzling. There seemed to be few children in London now; most had been packed off to safer places, lost in meadows, seeing new sights, smelling new smells, but miserable just the same.

One of the Fleet Street shops had a row of tin helmets used as hanging baskets for flowers. That was a brave gesture that almost made Betty smile. Of course, London would come through all this, be bright and gay and exciting again. She remembered the first time she came with Stephen, how vibrant the place was, how enormous it seemed. They had taken a long tram ride, must have been forty-five minutes, and she had asked, 'Where is the country?' because in any ordinary northern town there was a time when you ran out of houses and found fields, hills and rivers. But this London was vast. It never seemed to end. That was why it would always survive any attack. Not even the Germans could bomb all of it.

Eventually, after asking a policeman, she found Old Causeway. There were three- and four-storey buildings on both sides of the road, all in brown stone, going grey. She stared in at Salmon and Gluckstein, tobacconists, with its moving model of an old sea salt banging out his pipe on his wooden leg; the windows of Carnival Novelties were missing, and all the aids to wild gaiety were covered in a milky dust; the windows of the furrier's had gone, too, and all the fur was grey but safe behind a steel mesh. There had been some damage here. But where was Green's? Maurice had said it was near to St Paul's, and she could still see the dome, looking down as though keeping fire-watch over the whole area. This is my city, it seemed to be saying, damage it and the wrath of God will be upon you.

Towards the end of the street there were some buildings that had been hit. There were scars in the road like some giant beast had scratched the tarmac with long brutal nails. Demolition men were shovelling rubble into lorries, and she noticed some books mixed up with the stones and grime. Betty shivered. A shovel turned over another pile of books. Was that a title that Maurice had mentioned: *Rabble Without Arms*? And another: *What Katy Did*, a book she remembered from her schooldays. Poor Maurice.

She turned to one of the workmen. 'I'm looking for Green's.'

The workman took his cap off and wiped his sweaty face. 'That's it, love. What's left of it.'

She stood watching as the workmen lifted shovel after shovel of rubble and books on to the back of a lorry. It was all rubbish now. Thousands of books, millions of words, hours of work, of drudgery and inspiration, high thoughts and low thoughts, books wrought through pain and anger, good humour and bad humour, dashed off or painstakingly written with care and love, written for money or from some strong conviction, all mashed up with sand, burnt wood, brick dust and water. Before she had met Maurice she wouldn't have experienced the full horror of it all. It was Maurice who had taught her the power of books. Maurice. Where was he? He must be heart-broken. But there was no one to ask.

She hung about for a while. Maurice might be around here somewhere. She stared at people walking by, heads down. Scenes of devastation no longer made people curious; they were now an everyday part of London life. Then she retraced her steps. She knew that what she had seen represented a tragedy of the first order, and she now knew that Maurice had not casually let her down. God knows what he must be feeling. He was so proud of his old books. But it was the end of the Maurice saga. There would be no job, no future in the book trade. The gap in the row of buildings represented a gap in her life.

Jimmy felt light-hearted as the Number 34 tram rumbled down Cedars Road into Battersea. He wouldn't be seeing Helen at Hodders any more, but he knew where he could find her. He got off the tram and stepped out along Latchmere Road, turning off into the maze of small dwellings that fell in the concrete valley below. He found the street where he had taken Helen the night they went to the pictures, found the corner where they had kissed, and the thought of that pleasure made him smirk. He knocked at the door. She would be surprised to see him – delighted, he hoped. Nobody answered the door. He knocked again, more vigorously, but no reply. He stood back and looked up at the bedroom windows, criss-crossed with sticky tape. She wouldn't be at work, that was for sure. But there was nobody in. What about her dad and mum? After another brisk knock brought no reply, he sat down on the coping-stone of the small front garden. He could wait five minutes. He could wait ten minutes. He could wait the whole afternoon if needs be.

Some young boys were playing Spitfires in the street, zooming down the centre of the road with their arms out, making throttling noises, bashing into each other and shouting, 'You're dead.' It wasn't so long ago that he was indulging in similar antics, but the kids of his time were aping the last war, with trenches in hollows, going over the top to the opposing trenches on a piece of waste land. It was good fun at the time, until that soppy Stanley kid got a brick on his head and ran home crying with blood streaming down the side of his face.

A bread van was delivering, but he didn't bring anything to Helen's house. Jimmy banged the knocker again, hard. The next-door neighbour opened her door.

'Christ Almighty,' she said. 'When are you going to stop banging?' She had a rough-wool dressing-gown on, and her hair was mussed up as though she'd been sleeping.

'There's nobody in,' Jimmy said.

'All the more reason to stop banging the bloody knocker then. I'm on night-shift tonight.'

'I'm sorry,' Jimmy said. 'I'm looking for Helen.'

'They've gone away,' said the disgruntled woman. 'She's lost her job. Bombed out.'

'So am I,' said Jimmy. 'I worked near where she was. Do you know when they'll be back?'

'They've gone to Reigate,' said the woman. 'To her sister's to get a bit of peace and quiet.'

This was bad news. 'But how long for? When will they be back?'

'I don't know,' the woman replied, scratching her back with a long shoe horn she was carrying in her hand. 'It's nothing to do with me. They don't tell me everything.' And she went in and closed the door.

He found a tin can in the gutter and kicked it along the street. He kicked it all the way up to the high street. Another fairy-tale gone west. Would he see her again? Where the hell was Reigate? Was it a big place? What chance would he have of bumping into her? The bloody war was spoiling everything again. Sodding Hitler with his bleeding bombs. Putting him out of work was bad enough, but now the war had cost him his girlfriend. He went into the pictures on Lavender Hill. It was a miserable film with Sylvia Sydney. Every film with Sylvia Sydney was miserable. She had a face made for misery. She could cry real tears at will, and there wasn't even a Laurel and Hardy to cheer it up. Just more news of how our soldiers enjoyed being shot at and splattered in mud. Poor buggers. They might as well make a joke of it.

Maybe he could find out where Hodder's had gone. A firm like that wouldn't just pack up, would they? They would set up somewhere else. But where?

He went home, trailing across Clapham Common with his hands deep in his trouser pockets. There were kids flying kites. Kites were all right. They didn't drop things on you, just floated in the air like butterflies.

His mum had got kippers for tea. He liked the smell of kippers. His new copy of the *Gem* had arrived: Tom Merry and the rest hadn't caught up with the war yet. Would they be unmasking spies, catching parachutists, or would they pretend that the war wasn't happening? His dad came down in his vest and trousers. He shaved in the scullery with his cut-throat razor. You weren't suppose to say anything while he was doing it in case he cut his throat. His dad rarely said anything these days, and his mum had never had much to say at any time. Jimmy sat down and started scraping the kipper.

'What you going to do?' said his mum, not stretching herself.

'What about?' he said, thinking she might have read his mind about his abortive trip to Battersea.

'About getting a job,' she said. 'No taste in nothing.' It was one of her miserable collection of sayings. What she meant was find a job quick as you can't live here without making a contribution.

'I don't know what's going to happen yet, do I?' he said defensively.

His mother munched away while his dad ate his kipper, with bread and strawberry jam.

Suddenly his mother said, 'What d'you mean?' But it was so long after that Jimmy had lost the connection. His mind was wandering into Woolworth's, where he saw Helen on the cosmetics counter, her light hair shining under the electric light, slipping him a sly glance while she served a customer. He smiled at the thought.

'What you laughing at?' said his mother. 'No fun being out of work.'

There was a long silence, then his dad said: 'Need some copy boys at the *Telegraph*.'

The next day Jimmy went to the Labour Exchange. There was a queue right out into the street. He bought a packet of five Player's Weights. He had never smoked before, but he felt he'd like to try, but after the first draw nearly choked him, he gave up. Anyway, there was no joy at the Labour Exchange. He wasn't old enough to draw the dole. They hadn't got any information about Green's. He decided to walk around there; he might see Maurice or somebody. The last time he saw Maurice the poor old bugger looked done for, but he might have got over it by now. As his mother often said, 'No use crying over spilt milk.'

But Green's was still the same mess. Workmen had cleared the site. It looked as though everything that was left had sunk into the basement, the place where they used to go when the siren sounded. There was a blonde woman there, looking upset. What was she upset about? Nothing to do with her. He heard her ask one of the workmen about Green's. 'That's it,' he said. 'What's left of it.' The woman wandered off, looking sad and lost.

Miss Tcherny had given Maurice their addresses, so if he wanted to get in touch he could. Would he send his money? It wasn't his fault that he didn't work the full week. Was it worth going around to the *Telegraph*? Nothing to lose.

Maurice, left in a wilderness of broken buildings, started walking. There was no sign of civilization, not even on the horizon. It was certain that buses did not come along these roads any more. It was difficult to find the boundaries of the road. Here and there were reminders of a previous life: a sheet-metal sign for Sharp's

Toffee and Bovril hung at crazy angles from a blasted wall, while one for Ovaltine lay flat on its back. Maurice was looking for some sense of direction. There must be some sign, some indication of where the rest of London had got to.

As he walked he heard a scuffle behind him. He turned around, but he couldn't see anything. He turned back. There. There it was again. It was the Ovaltine sign, shifting slightly, and yet there was no wind. He bent down to lift it, to prop it up against something, but before he could grasp it the sign moved, seemingly of its own accord, and a head popped out from underneath. It was a dirty, scruffy head, with a clown's white face and one bloodshot eye. 'You all right, mate?' it said.

'Eh?' said Maurice, startled.

The mouth opened to show a dentist's nightmare of jagged black teeth, with gaps in between. 'There's not much room, but you can come down if you like.' The invitation was accompanied by a quirky wink.

'What are you doing down there?' said Maurice.

'We live here,' said the odd-looking man. 'They don't come over here any more. There's nothing left to bomb.' He cackled insanely. 'Safe as houses we are, ain't we, Mum?'

Maurice peered into the hole. There were steps down. Might have been a basement or a cellar. At the bottom there was a bundle of what appeared to be old clothes. It was the body of an old woman but practically shapeless, with a grey head lolling forwards on to the chest, slumped on the steps. The body didn't move. There was a stillness about the lumpish figure that seemed unnatural.

'Is that your mother?' Maurice said. 'Is she all right?'

'Right as rain,' said the odd man, looking up at Maurice. 'You got a fag?'

'How long have you been down there?' Maurice said.

'We came down here about three nights ago. I said to her, "They won't be bombing down there any more. They've done it. Done it to death."'

By this time Maurice had grave misgivings about the man and his silent mother. 'Ask her if she wants anything. Ask her.'

The man levered himself out of the hole. He was short, wearing a collarless shirt and nondescript trousers. He had a couple of day's growth of whiskers, and Maurice thought he looked like a comic's stooge in a music-hall act.

'Here,' said the comical little man. 'What's your game?'

'Game?'

'Coming round here interfering with respectable people. Sling your hook.' His indignation rang hollow. The bloodshot eye looked wild.

'I'm concerned about your mother. She shouldn't be down there on those steps.'

'You leave her alone. She's dead, ain't she? She can't fool me. I know her too well. Died as soon as we got here. Couldn't stand it. All that noise. Bang bloody bang all bloody night. Flesh and blood can't stand it, mister.' There was a tear in his eye. His thin body shook with rage.

'What have we done, eh? What's it to do with us? I don't know any Germans. Why should they do this? Tell me that. Go on.'

'There's no sense in it,' said Maurice.

'You bet your life, mister. There's no sense in it. Bloody hell. They can have a bloody war if they wants, but why drag us into it?'

Suddenly Maurice felt unutterably weary. He realized that he had been on the go since mid-morning. The ridiculous episode with the brassy woman and her mad husband, then getting stuck in the middle of nowhere, and now this demented creature with his dead mother. He needed to get home. To have a bath and a change of clothes.

'Which way is the main road?' he said.

'That's a question,' said the silly old devil, puckering his face like a circus clown registering surprise.

'I need to get home,' said Maurice. 'As soon as I get somewhere I'll make sure somebody comes for you and your mother.'

'She's dead,' said the mad little man. 'No use to man or beast.'

'But she'll have to be buried,' Maurice said.

The little man was clearly out of his mind. He pointed vaguely in several directions. So Maurice set off, feeling out on his feet. He knew that if he walked directly away from the river that he must stumble on a proper road in the end. Eventually, he saw a fire engine. It was standing, on its own, with the crew sitting on the running-boards or laying on the flat body of the appliance. The crew were clearly exhausted. They had probably been fighting fires all night and most of the day. Maurice approached them, thankfully.

'Where am I?' said Maurice.

The fireman pointed him in the right direction. 'There's a poor old man over there who's gone crazy. He's got his mother with him and she's passed away.' The fireman received this information with a show of indifference. Just another tragedy in days and nights of such incidents. One of them started coughing and retching until he went red in the face and then blue. None of his comrades took any notice. There was an air of hopelessness about the unit. Maurice staggered on. He felt that if he stopped and sat down that he would fall asleep. It seemed ages before he saw a moving vehicle. It was a beer dray. The sight was like something from a lost world. He watched it and heard the clomp of the horses' hooves, relishing the sign of normality in a world that had gone mad.

He didn't much care how he got home. He got on the first bus and found himself in Hackney. He caught another bus to Camberwell and another to Brixton. From there he knew he could get to Clapham Common and the Northern Line.

He fell asleep on the Tube and had to be woken up at Morden. It was twilight when he got back to street level. He briefly contemplated taking a taxi as there was a quarter of an hour to wait for a bus, but Clare might see it and then there would be a row about his extravagance. So he waited, and was glad that he had. He climbed on to the top deck and was able to contemplate the landscape as town turned into suburb on the way to turning into country.

There were thousands of little houses, with neat gardens back and front, with sharply cut lawns and garden sheds, flower beds, privet borders, dividing one garden from the next, rows of rose bushes and kitchen gardens, laid out military style. There were miles of red roofs, stretching into the sunset. It was comfortable, secure and settled. Contrasted with the devastation of the East

End it was like another country, another world. This was England, the solid mass of the middle class, the England he knew. These houses, with their mock-Tudor façades, looked as if they had always been there. He knew that they were, in fact, only five years old, and they didn't represent the English middle classes, rather slightly-more-affluent-than-most working class. Anybody who could muster up a fifty-pound deposit and pay five pounds a month for the mortgage could have moved into one of these houses only five years ago. It needed a second wage, but there were bus drivers with daughters with secretarial skills and train drivers with wives who liked to work. The strange thing was that as soon as these people lifted themselves out of Clapham, Peckham or Battersea they saw themselves as gentry, aspiring to a stage of respectability that they would have scorned as pretentious in their previous abode.

And yet, this was the heart of England, a uniform landscape: no council housing, no blocks of flats, no tall buildings, no scrubland; everything clean and ordered and safe. There were no military installations, no factories, even. There were railway lines, but they only led to even calmer and more picturesque towns and miles of open country. This was the land of village fêtes, bell ringing and allotments, of conkers and maypoles, cricket and bowls, Boot's library books, pubs like old royal palaces and carol singers at Christmas. Was this what it was about? Preserving this way of life for those who had only just acquired it?

Maurice reached home in a calmer frame of mind. People's lives had been destroyed. He had lost his warehouse. It was important to him, but how important in the greater scheme of things? He was alive. He hadn't been driven mad like the man he had seen with his dead mother. Somehow he had to rebuild the business, start somewhere else.

When he got into the hallway he sensed that something was wrong. Clare greeted him, which was unusual, as she usually did not even register his presence at all. It wasn't effusive; she merely brushed his cheek with hers but stared at him as though she was, somehow, on his side. When he went into the sitting-room he saw at once the reason for the change of attitude. On the sofa was someone whom he hadn't seen for a while and had been glad for that. It was the mountainous form of his sister Bella. She wore a pleated plaid skirt, a Paisley blouse and a knitted waistcoat. Another Wodehouse aunt of a more formidable variety? No, perhaps one of Somerset Maugham's emotionally retarded spinsters. Bella wasted no time in getting to the point of her visit.

'I hope you're satisfied,' she said, her eyes sparking with spite. 'You wouldn't sell, would you? You knew that was what I wanted – Bernard, too – but no. You wanted to go on playing at being a librarian. Now look what's happened. There's nothing to sell.'

15

Bernard was having a trying evening. The actress who called herself Gloria persisted in treating him as an oaf. She had said that it wasn't her real name – probably Nellie or Alice – but she behaved as though she had royal connections and he was one of the serfs. After all, she'd picked him up, and he was paying for everything. This place, somewhere off the Edgware Road, wasn't as expensive as Claridge's, but at the rate she was knocking it back it would be a fair bill at the end. They'd had a good dinner, some fish with white wine. He didn't like white wine, but when he ordered red she practically went into hysterics.

'Really?' she had said. 'What next?'

'I can have what I like,' he said gruffly. 'I'm paying, aren't I?'

She was furious. Two red spots appeared on her cheeks. 'There's no need to be quite so coarse,' she said. When she'd had a couple of glasses things got a bit easier and her accent began to slip. She gossiped about Evelyn Laye and Sonnie Hale and their duel with Jessie Matthews. In fact, she was full of gossip, and Bernard soon became bored with her endless tittle-tattle.

'Where do you live?' he broke in brutally.

'Don't worry, darling,' she flashed at him. 'You'll get your pound of flesh.'

He'd had a busy time. Ringing around the publishers, putting in orders, ringing his clients to tell them his new address and phone number, ringing to secure the services of Miss Tcherny, although that was not fixed up yet. He had managed to do all this while the Gloria bitch was getting herself ready to go out to dinner. He was looking forward to getting her into bed – bring her down a peg or two, that would. He was as good as anybody at that game.

Gloria, it was clear, wanted to go on drinking. She kept looking at all the bottles behind the bar, selecting a fresh novelty: 'That pretty green one, darling.'

Bernard could see that this would lead to her being unconscious before the action started. 'We'll take a bottle with us,' he said.

'Why?' said Gloria. 'Are we going already?'

He got her outside and soon found a taxi. 'What's the address?'

'Oh. It's Prince of Wales Gardens,' she said. 'Over Battersea Bridge. Are you sure you want to go all that way?'

'I've got to see you home,' he said. Where else, for Christ's sake? If he took her to Ealing she might fall in love with his house, and anyway he didn't want her to know where he lived. So they went along in the taxi, and on the way the lady began to get amorous.

'Are you married?' she murmured. 'It doesn't matter. Just interested.' He didn't reply, and she said, 'I see.'

'You don't see anything,' he said fiercely. 'I've had a bloody awful day. My business has become a bomb site. I've been trying to regroup, and it's not been easy. I don't know whether I'm on my head or my arse.'

'Of course, darling. I understand.'

They reached the outside of a building that bowed its way around a corner, with a Regency façade, which, in its rakish aspect, looked promising. It was a building that, over at least a century of existence, could be housing a thousand secrets.

Gloria produced a torch from her handbag. 'You'll have to follow me,' she whispered. 'There's no black-out in the hall.' They sneaked up the staircase like a pair of cat burglars, and along a corridor to her flat. When they got inside, she switched a light on. It was shaded so he couldn't see beyond the pool of light. When his eyes became accustomed to the dim surroundings he took in the general ambience of the place, which was plush and faintly oriental, with framed playbills on the walls for *Hay Fever* and *A Bill of Divorcement*. This wasn't exactly a flat for daily living; it was a flat for late-night gatherings, after-show conferences, when groups of actors posed with cocktail glasses, picking each others' performances to pieces in clouds of Turkish-cigarette smoke while dance music played on the wireless. During the day, this place would be dead, but at night it could be electric.

Gloria switched the light on in the windowless kitchen. There were spirit bottles in the kitchen cabinet. She poured two whiskies.

'Somebody gave me this,' she said, offering him a glass with a lopsided smile. An actress, he thought. Not a natural bone in her body. Always doing a turn. What was underneath? Where did she really come from?

'Do you want to, er, wash, darling? That's the bathroom.'

He experienced a thumping in his head. He had felt this once before, when he was with that tart Bunty. She didn't take a blind bit of notice of anything he said, and he got into a red rage with her. There was a hard, steel band around his skull, and it was getting tighter. He ought to lie down, try to relax. He found a sofa and sprawled on it.

'Is that going to be all right for you, darling?' she said archly.

'Just a minute,' he said. 'I need to collect myself.' The band around his head was squeezing ever harder. If it got any worse he would scream. He heard the air-raid siren start up its wail.

'What do you do?' he said. 'Go downstairs?'

'No,' said Gloria softly. 'I just go to bed. What do you do?' She was standing at the edge of the pool of light. He noticed that she had put on a dressing-gown. He put out a hand and she came towards him. She knelt in front of him and put her head on his lap.

'This is awful,' she said.

'What is?' he said.

'You see, I quite like you, but the fact is that I'm awfully short of the readies.'

'What?'

'It's best to be clear before we start, isn't it? Saves any unpleasantness afterwards. I'm sorry, but there's no work, you see.' She stood up and opened the dressing-gown. She was quite thin, he noticed, and very white, a sort of porcelain figure, very smooth, very delicate. The request for money took him by surprise. He'd often paid before, but somehow he hadn't expected it, not at this stage. Maybe a touch afterwards, but a commercial proposition from someone whom he had thought of as above such crudities shook him.

'How much?' he said thickly.

'Oh, darling, no need to be sordid. I'll leave that to you. I am sure you'll be suitably generous. Now then, do you want to go into the bed or are you happy on the sofa?'

Bernard's mind raced up crafty nooks and crevices. This Gloria wasn't as clever as she thought. Many of the women he had been with had wanted the money in advance. After all, when it was over how could you guarantee that the client would pay up? Gloria was acting cool, acting the posh prostitute, but she couldn't have had much experience.

'It's all right here,' he said. She slipped off the dressing-gown and sat beside him. He had never seen such a piece of cool cheek before. It was wild and daring but somehow civilized; his desires were taken as a matter of course, as they would be in many places in the world. There was nothing to be ashamed of in pure animal instincts. It was only natural, and everybody knew it.

'Won't you get cold?'

'That's up to you, darling,' she said. He stood up and began to loosen his trousers. 'You're not tattooed or anything, are you? I can't stand tattoos.'

'No,' he said. 'Are you?'

She laughed a tinkly laugh. 'Have you got a . . . ?'

'Yes, I've got one. Do you want to see it?'

'Don't be silly, darling. You know what I mean.'

She spread her body on the sofa with her legs apart, but her head was on one side, looking away, as though she didn't want to see what was going to happen to the rest of her. Bernard looked at her spreadeagled body with a feeling of immense satisfaction. The haughty bitch was going to get what was coming to her. When it came down to it, she was no better than a woman he could have picked up in the street. He positioned himself and then lunged at her, pushing into her up to the hilt.

'Oh my God,' she gasped. 'You didn't put a thing on.' Her head waved from side to side and her body went stiff, as if she was defending herself by retraction. 'Please,' she said. 'I can't risk it.'

'Shut up,' he said and put more strength into his thrusting.

'Get off,' she screamed.

He put his hand over her mouth. She was stiff with fright. 'Think you're better than me?' he said. 'You're nothing but a common tart.'

In the struggle he thought he must have blacked out. For one moment he thought he had died. She was wriggling energetically, her eyes signalling anger and fright, her hands at his face, her fingernails reaching for his eyes. At the same time the skull-crushing band around his head was becoming unbearably tight. He knew he was going to faint. He was fighting this horde of naked women. They all talked with cut-glass accents. They were enjoying his terror, humiliating him, laughing at him. It was a conspiracy of snobbery. Suddenly the steel band snapped. It had done its worst, but he had managed to hold on. His head ached, but it had been released from the torture. He looked down. The naked figure of Gloria was lying very still. Her tongue was hanging out of her mouth like she had vomited it up from her stomach. Her eyes were staring at him, despising him, even in death she was still putting him in his place.

He sat there, holding his head. It was horrible, the way these women made him feel. And now this one was dead, and it was all her fault. She shouldn't have been so aloof. She had made it clear that she despised him, taunted him with her offhand manner, made him feel inferior, and asked him for money as well, before anything had even happened. He hadn't intended to do her any harm. He just wanted to stop her shouting and looking at him like he was so far beneath her. He certainly had not intended to strangle her.

He took the dressing-gown and covered her body and her face, covered the staring, scornful eyes. Had anyone seen him come in? It had been dark. They had used a torch. He had the feeling that this was a very discreet block of flats in which everybody kept themselves to themselves. He straightened himself up and looked at his face in a mirror in the bathroom. The bitch had scratched his cheek. What time was it? He looked at his watch and was surprised to see that it was only ten o'clock.

He moved quietly out into the corridor with her torch. He tried to remember the way they had come. There were stairs. There weren't any lights under the doors in the corridor, and it was very quiet. People who lived in this sort of set-up might have gone away somewhere safer. People who could afford it had all gone into the country. Even the poverty-stricken East Enders had swamped the hop fields of Kent, where they spent their annual summer holidays, sleeping out in the open. There were reports of half the population of Plymouth living on Dartmoor. The Yorkshire Dales were full of campers from Manchester and Leeds. There were rumbles of gunfire in the distance, but it seemed a very long way away.

He got into the deserted street. It was unlikely that there were any taxis running during the alert – in any case, he didn't want to be picked up anywhere near the block of flats, but walking to Ealing was out of the question. He got to the bridge and looked over towards London. There were flashes in the sky. There was a ding-dong going on down river. And then, quite suddenly, he saw a black shape in the sky and heard a tremendous hum as a bomb fell near to the bridge. Of course, the bridge – any bridge – would be a target. A column of water shot up, sploshing over the road and pavement.

Christ, that was close. He decided to get to the other side and started running but was soon out of breath. He got to the crown of the bridge and stopped. The plane that had dropped the bomb had swooped around and was coming back. He dropped to his knees and covered his face with his hands, but the plane passed harmlessly overhead. He looked across the bridge. There was no one in sight. He staggered on, holding on to the railings. He could hear the water lapping around the base. He got to the other side, exhausted, and slumped on to the pavement.

A rickety lorry came along and stopped. The driver got out. 'You all right, mate?'

He looked up. 'Yes. Sure. I'm all right. A bomb fell into the river.'

'Yeah, I heard it. Shakes you up a bit, don't it?' It was a ragged figure, with a cap and scarf, a white pinched face.

'Which way are you going?'

'I don't rightly know,' said the man. 'Never been over this way before. I'm supposed to pick up some stuff from Shepherd's Bush. Never heard of it. Have you?'

Bernard hauled himself up. 'Yes. I can show you.' Shepherd's Bush was on his way home. After that there was the interminable stretch of the Uxbridge Road, but it would get him well on the way. The best bit of luck he'd had all day.

The driver was from Poplar. 'It's bloody chronic over there. There's more houses down than up. Those people ain't got nothing. The bloody hospitals are bursting.'

'What are you after, in Shepherd's Bush?'

'Blankets. It's some Territorial place. A drill hall. I want to get back tonight if I can.'

'Is it your lorry?'

'It is. I use it for rag and bone. Winkles and shrimps on a Sunday. Celery. But this is better. I'm on hire all the time now.' He laughed. 'I'll be able to retire when this is all over.'

Bernard stared out of the window. God knows how the driver could see where he was going. Was that Edith Grove? 'Stop a minute,' he said. 'Let me get my bearings.' He stared out at the rows of Victorian houses. 'Yes. Through here. Keep going on this road. You'll eventually get to the Bush.'

The lorry groaned and shook, Bernard with his head out of the window, trying to navigate. The journey into West London seemed to take for ever. They found a coffee stall still operating outside Earl's Court, and they stopped a while for Bernard to check the direction.

'Blimey,' said the driver. 'Haven't had much over here, have they? We've had a right packet where I come from.'

It was one o'clock when they got to Shepherd's Bush. Bernard asked the driver about running on to West Ealing.

'Ain't got the petrol, mate. Only enough to get back.' So Bernard found himself on Shepherd's Bush Green in the early morning. It was cold and damp, but at least he was well away from the flats and those staring eyes. He sat down under a tree. The ground was hard and knobbly, but he suddenly felt at peace and soon fell asleep. He was in a posh flat somewhere and this woman was mad for it. He kept telling her 'No' and pushing her away. He gave her an almighty shove, and she fell and banged her head on a marble mantelpiece. She was dead, and she said it was his fault. Then he became aware of a slight sticky sensation on his cheek. It was the sort of dry lick you get from a cat sucking with its tongue. He put his hand up and encountered a small nose. He opened his eyes. It was getting light. How long had he been there, sleeping out in the open like a tramp? The small face had a beret on. It was very close and the tongue had been on his cheek. It was a young girl. He couldn't tell how young. Two eyes promising a grubby sensuality were looking at him in an appealing, meaningful way.

'Hello, mister,' said the girl, licking her lips. 'Do you want a –'

'No, I don't,' he said. He'd never been so sure of anything in his life.

Rosa Tcherny thought that Charlie looked ridiculous in her father's clothes. The trousers pulled up tightly under his crotch, the coat sleeves flapped, the shirt collar was two sizes too large. He looked as though he was a part of a variety knockabout act, like he'd left the Army and joined a circus. She thought that he would go as soon as he was dressed, and she made a brown-paper parcel of his uniform and another of his boots, but he sort of hung about, smiling vacantly, looking lost.

'My mother will be in soon,' she said, 'and my father.'

'I know,' he said. 'I was thinking that I ought to wait until it's dark – if you don't mind.' He smiled a nervous smile. He was crazy to have got himself into this predicament, but Rosa couldn't help feeling sorry for the poor fool.

'You'll have to go in the end,' she said pointedly.

'Oh yes, I know.'

'Have you had anything to eat?' Rosa asked. Even a condemned man was entitled to a hearty breakfast.

'Yes,' he said. 'I don't want anything.'

'You don't think it would be better to give yourself up now? The longer you leave it, the worse it will be.'

'I know,' he said. He was trapped by his own foolishness. Whatever indignities the Army dished out, it must have been better to endure them than to run. 'I don't know what to do,' he said helplessly.

Rosa heard a key in the front door lock.

Charlie looked scared. He went white. 'Please,' he said. 'Please.'

Rosa gestured to him to go upstairs, and he scattered away like a frightened rabbit. Her mother came in, looking tired. She worked in shifts, sorting salvage.

'How was it today?'

'Oh, all right,' said her mother. 'I don't mind the work. It's just that I feel so grubby. You never know where some of those things have come from.'

'No. I suppose not.'

'What about you? Any news?'

'I had a call from one of my old bosses. He says he's going to start up again on his own. Run the business from his home.'

'Well, that'll be all right then, won't it?'

'I don't know,' said Rosa. 'He's the black sheep of the family. A bit of a pig. It would've been better if the other one had called.'

Her mother had sat down. She looked tired. 'I'll make some tea,' Rosa said.

'I'll go up for a bath first,' said Mrs Tcherny. 'And I'm having more than four inches.'

'I'll go up and run it for you,' Rosa said quickly. She went upstairs. She didn't know whether Charlie would be in the bathroom. He wasn't. He was on the landing, looking fearful. She shot him a warning look but saw that he was staring over her shoulder, down the stairs. Her mother was in the hall, looking up.

'Who's that?' she called.

Rosa turned. It was all up. Charlie was simply no good at subterfuge. The enemy would easily find him in a haystack. 'It's Charlie,' she said. 'He called in.'

'Good evening, Mrs Tcherny,' said Charlie and smiled his boyish smile.

It seemed as though this was a play in which all the actors had forgotten their lines. Mrs Tcherny felt that there was something odd about the situation because Rosa and Charlie looked so guilty. Surely they hadn't been at it again? Well, that was how it was when you were young. Couldn't get enough. Frederic had been like that when they were in Vienna. She had thought at the time that it might have been the influence of the city of romantic liaisons, but now she knew that urgency in youths was universal.

'You can come down, Charlie. It's all right.'

Charlie came down the stairs wearing his usual sheepish grin. He was a nice enough young man, but he was so shy that it was painful. There was something rather odd about his appearance.

As though he had shrunk inside his clothes. Everything he had on was flapping around him.

'Are you on leave?' she said.

'Yes,' he replied, licking his lips nervously.

'I hope they're giving you enough to eat,' she said. 'You've lost weight.'

'For God's sake, Mother,' Rosa exploded. 'He's got Dad's clothes on. He's on the run.' The boy looked scared. His shoulders began to shake.

'On the run?' said Mrs Tcherny. 'Do you mean he's deserted?' There was a long silence. Rosa looked impatient; Charlie looked scared. 'But why?' said Mrs Tcherny. 'What has happened?'

'He just couldn't take it,' said Rosa in a voice that mixed contempt with pity.

'Oh my God,' said Mrs Tcherny. 'He can't stay here.'

'I've told him that,' said Rosa. 'He wanted to get his Army things off, so he wouldn't be so conspicuous, although I think he looks more conspicuous as he is.'

Mrs Tcherny found herself shouting: 'Go down to the police station and give yourself up.'

Charlie sat on the stairs, a picture of dejection. 'I'd better go,' he said. He stood up and walked to the door, his oversized shoes flapping.

'You'll get locked up, looking like that,' Rosa said. 'Look, I'll ring our doctor and tell him you've had a nervous collapse or something, a breakdown.'

'That won't work,' said Mrs Tcherny. 'They'd all be at it.'

'Look at him,' Rosa shouted. 'He's a bundle of nerves.'

The doctor was out on his calls, but he would get the message when he came back.

'Who's going to pay him?' said Mrs Tcherny. 'They charge half a crown just for calling round.'

'I'll pay him,' said Rosa. 'For pity's sake, they might put him in hospital or something. You can see what he's like.'

Whether Charlie had finally broken or was rehearsing for his role as a mental patient was hard to determine. He sat on the chair in the hall, murmuring things that made little sense.

'Get your proper clothes on,' said Rosa. 'You look a fool like that.' So Rosa brought his Army uniform, to which Charlie reacted with horror, but he was persuaded to put it on, and Mr Tcherny on his arrival was told the whole story. He shook his head.

'The world has gone mad. You did the right thing,' he said to Rosa. 'We can't take the risk of harbouring him.' He looked at Charlie. 'Is this the Army that is protecting us? He'd do himself more harm than he would the enemy. This war is turning into a farce. They should have acted sooner. Everybody could see what this Hitler was like. Our people were set to scrub the streets in Vienna. Hitler has let loose the base side of human nature. When I think of Vienna, what do I think of? Strauss, Freud, the palaces, the Danube? No. I think of Jews scrubbing the streets while jeering gangs of louts kick their backsides.'

It was dark before the doctor came. He was old and tired, in a crumpled suit that only just reached over his waistline. He looked like the pompous, small-town doctor seen in numerous films about country life in rural England, delivering babies by hand while riotously drunk. When he heard the story he called the police. Then he talked to Charlie, and Charlie gave him daft answers, acting now from a strong sense of self-preservation.

'The lad has had a nervous breakdown,' the doctor said. 'Not much I can do about it. He'll have to be handed over to the authorities. And good luck to him.'

Two policemen arrived at the house. 'Come on, son,' said one. 'Nobody is going to hurt you.' It was clear that Charlie didn't believe this story, for he struggled and shouted as they took him away. 'Come on now,' said the policeman. 'No need to take on like that.'

The doctor collected his fee and made out a receipt. 'Battle fatigue. They forget that the human frame can only stand so much. By the time this is over half the population will be barmy. Good night.'

16

THERE were crisp March days. Muffled-up Londoners trudged to work in the frosty mornings as swans swam sedately on the Serpentine, and London seemed its timeless self. But there were black, frightening nights, when it seemed things would never be right again.

The news was profoundly gloomy on all fronts. At sea as well the U-boat reigned supreme, and only a purblind optimist like Churchill could think that Britain might survive. France was occupied by the Germans. The flower of British manhood had been blighted and pushed back across the Channel in a massive retreat that the government had somehow turned into a victory. London, and other major cities – Southampton, Dover, Plymouth – were under continuous bombardment. The underfed, underground population were scurrying around like rats in what seemed like a black expressionist drama of Continental origin.

There was always the threat of an invasion. The people knew that the bombing was only the prelude to an occupation. All along the south coast anti-aircraft guns pumped shells into the sky, more in a spirit of defiance than in the hope of a hit. Rumours of parachute drops of hundreds of Germans sent battered and nervous people into a frenzy. They knew that the enemy were not human, did not live by civilized values, were ruthless and fanatical, had been driven mad by Hitler's propaganda machine and were beyond all reason. They had a military machine manned by robots; we had a half-trained amateur army, short of weapons, ammunition and resolution. They were polished and efficient; we were a disorganized rabble, Fred Karno's Army, sloppy and slapdash.

The newspapers tried to keep up a brave face, but the readers could read between the lines. That day the lead story in the *Star*, *Evening News* and *Standard* was identical – 'Actress Found Dead'. They knew what their readers wanted. It was a good story, after all. The dead woman had been found naked, and you couldn't ask for more than that. She had last been seen at Claridge's Hotel. The head porter said that she left with a man he had never seen before. She seemed perfectly fine. After all, it wasn't the first time she had left with a man. But this was different. This man was not a regular. Nobody in the hotel knew him. He was a complete stranger.

Bert Penrose read about it in hospital in the *Evening News*. There weren't many details, except the plays she had been in and her bit-parts in films. She hadn't been in the front rank of film stars, but someone you saw now and again and soon forgot. She had been a handsome woman and had worked pretty steadily in West End plays: *Autumn Crocus*, *Whiteoaks*, *The Ringer*, sung in Ivor Novello spectaculars. Gloria Grainger – real name Enid Stubbs – had been married once, to a fellow actor, but divorced after two years. He had married again to a wealthy aristocrat and had, by a spectacular piece of foolhardiness, won a medal in the Dunkirk fiasco. Without actually saying it, the papers gave the impression of an unhappy woman, drifting from one man to the next, down on her luck and completely devastated by the closure of London theatres.

Bloody hard luck, thought Bert, and what a waste. It didn't say whether the murderer had done anything to her. He'd have to wait until the Sunday papers to know that. These women, they drove men mad: teased them, taunted them, made half-promises and then retreated. They paraded themselves, all done up. They asked for it.

Bert had settled in at the hospital. They had given him a pair of crutches, and he had started to get about the ward. There was a solo school, and he hung about on the fringes hoping for a chance to play. They were only playing for pennies and ha'pennies, but they hid the money under a towel. If he got in, he would soon up the stakes.

There were grounds that he could see through the window, lawns and tall trees and stumpy statuary, where men looking cheerful and relieved relaxed in the sun, smoking and joking. They were all servicemen, walking around in their loose, pale-blue suits, white shirts and red ties. Some of them had bandages around their heads, some had arms in slings, some plastered legs. It was like a twilight world. They had seen terrible things, been frightened to death and hurt, but now they were in this gentle country garden. If they had been killed this was what they might have imagined heaven would be like. Bert hoped that they would give him a blue suit when he got out of his dressing-gown and pyjamas. He fancied himself as a wounded soldier. If they dressed him in anything else he would feel like the black sheep of the damaged family.

It had been funny finding a stump where his leg should be. Would he be entitled to any compensation, would he get a war pension or something? He hadn't been in the Services, but he'd suffered the same as them. One thing he was sure of, he wasn't going to sit in the street with a tray of matchboxes, like he'd seen some legless blokes who copped it in the last war. A disgrace that was. One-armed mouth-organ players, clanking their medals, with begging cups hanging around their necks.

Edie kept coming, day after day, but she didn't bring any joy. She brought *Titbits* and *Answers* and *John Bull*, but she didn't bring any joy. Of course, she couldn't get anything to bring: no chocolate, no toffees, no fags because they wouldn't let him smoke, no beer. You couldn't even get the old hospital standby, grapes, and there were kids who had never seen a banana. It was purgatory, really, and they expected him to be grateful. Mind you, there were some lovely girls – they were, on the whole, a bit upper class, but they smiled at him, called him Bert, fluffed up his pillows while he sniffed at their powdered bodies, which, mixed with their natural body odour, would be enough to set the bloody Pope off. And they knew, these saucy minxes, they knew what he was thinking, imagining. They were all at it, making him excited and then looking offended. It was a game that women played, and men were the victims.

Oh Gawd, there was Edie again. He couldn't tell her not to come, but he wished she would leave him alone for a bit. Besides, what was it costing, getting out to Epsom every day? 'Hello, love,' he said.

Edie looked shagged out, but she tried to smile. She didn't seem to care what she looked like nowadays. All her clothes were rumpled, her shoes scuffed, her hair as if she had just got out of bed.

'How are we to day?' she said.

'I'm all right,' he said. 'Browned off, of course.'

'Any news? Have you seen the doctor?'

'No, but I'm having a fitness instructor to show me how to work the crutches.'

Edie's eyes filled with tears. 'I think Tim upstairs has got the sack'

'What? From the water board?'

'He went off in one of their vans, without permission.'

'How did they find out?'

'He ran out of petrol. Him and Bunty had to get a taxi from Bow.'

'Blimey, that must have cost them a packet.' Small talk was all he got from Edie. And yet he knew he was going to need her. Who else was going to care tuppence for a one-legged man? She was a good sort, big-hearted. He couldn't help it if he didn't fancy her any more, not like some of these nurses.

The immediate task was to get better on the crutches. How was he going to manage in their basement quarters? If he couldn't get out he would be living in a dungeon. The potential limitations of his life were a depressing prospect. How would they manage? Edie would have to get a job, which meant that he would be alone all day. He might as well stay where he was. At least he could see the light and the gardens and there were people about. Once he was home nobody would know he was there.

'When do they think you'll be ready to come out?' Edie said innocently.

Bert shrugged. 'God knows. They don't tell you much here. I think I'll have to be better at getting about than I am now. But, listen, you don't have to come out here every day. You must spend half your life travelling.'

'It is a bit of a way,' said Edie.

'Well, give it a miss now and again. I won't fret.'

He was relieved when Edie went. It was a struggle of a conversation. She meant well. She'd been a brick really. He lay back and closed his eyes. There she was again, that Indian temple dancer who slithered like a snake on heat. He reached out towards her, but she evaporated. She never stayed around long enough for him to try his luck. Christ, what was he going to do?

He was going to need lifting on and off. Maybe the strength he wasn't using would transfer to his prick. No. Some hope of anything good coming out of this.

Mrs Bennet was turning out her medicine cabinet. There was the liquid paraffin that Tom used to swig and rub into his hair, Carter's Little Liver Pills, Clark's blood mixture, Aspros, a bandage, scissors and tweezers that Tom got with Ardath cigarette coupons when he hadn't got enough to get anything decent. There was a tin of mysterious pellets called Iron Jelloids – God knows what they were for. Tom had always reckoned that you should try this stuff before you called the doctor. Maybe if he'd called the doctor sooner he might still have been around. Not that he would have liked it, any more than she did.

The nightly party didn't last long. It had been quite exciting when they crowded into Edie's basement, but now Edie didn't get back from Epsom until late in the evening, and she was tired out, and Mrs Bennet felt that everybody else in the house preferred to chance it in their beds rather than endure a social with an old woman.

There was that stuff that Tom got from that herbalist. It looked like pieces of tree bark floating in water. Suffered with his stomach, Tom did. She didn't think any of this stuff was any use now. It had been around too long. It had probably lost its strength by now. She made a resolution and swept the whole lot into her apron and carried it out to the dustbin.

There was that pain again. It was sharp and it took her breath away, but it didn't last long. She sat down. Bert used to bring home the papers: the *People* and the *News of the World*. Always something interesting to read in those papers. Made you realize what was going on. The murders and stuff, even in wartime.

What were they going to do now that Bert had lost a leg? If Edie got a job would they ask her to look out for Bert during the day? Mrs Bennet quite liked Bert. You could have a lark with him. Better than that uppity couple on the top floor. That Betty could do something useful instead of moping about all day, and, as for her husband, he seemed to think the King was his uncle.

It was getting dark, and the racket would be starting up again. They said that there was an anti-aircraft gun on a coach on the railway lines and that it ran up and down, firing at the bombers. There had been some tremendous bangs during the night. When would it be possible to get a night's sleep? She thought they might have knocked off on Sundays, but the heathens kept at it just the same.

She had made up a bed under the stairs. Someone had said that it was the safest part of the house. Then she wondered whether Bunty was in. She hadn't heard anything for ages. That husband of hers had a nasty temper.

She scraped up the stairs, humming to herself. She knocked at Bunty's door. 'Hello. Anybody in?'

'What do you want?' said Tim's voice sharply.

'It's all right. I just thought I'd better know who's in.'

Tim opened the door. He looked wild. 'We're all right,' he said.

Mrs Bennet peered into the room. They only had a table light on. There was Bunty, humped on the sofa in a terrific sulk and Tim looking sorry for himself. They'd had another tiff. They were having them all the time. There were screwed-up bits of paper all over the floor. When it was something important Tim wrote down what he wanted to say for Bunty to read. But she'd never seen Bunty looking so stony. Bunty was a naturally bouncy, bubbly person. They must have had a serious disagreement.

'Wondered if you would like to come downstairs?' Bunty stared at the wall and Tim didn't say anything. 'Just wondered,' said Mrs Bennet, as she left.

Tim was worried about Bunty's attitude towards him. Since the incident when he attacked the man she had turned from jolly and bubbly into a cold fury. It was like living with a caged animal. Bunty couldn't tell him what she thought, but she conveyed her feelings graphically enough. He had rung her mother and told her that Bunty was acting like a spoilt child, that he was trying to protect her, and this was all the thanks he got for it. Bunty's mother said she would come over in the morning. It was through his wish to protect his wife from this wild man who knocked her about that he had lost his job. Not that it mattered.

There were hundreds of jobs going, but he had liked the status of his peaked cap, his official bicycle and the turnkey. He could easily get a job in the fire brigade; they were crying out for men, but then he would be out all night in the thick of it. Most of the firemen he had seen looked as if they were living in a nightmare.

He stood over Bunty and pleaded with his eyes. She had never been out with him for so long before. It seemed as if their union had crossed an invisible barrier, that whatever he said or did things would never be the same again.

Behind the serene façade of Claridge's there was an air of polite panic. The management weren't too sure about the effect the publicity regarding Gloria Grainger's murder was generating. The news that the hotel had been the last place she was seen alive had already brought in some curious customers, and that was welcome, but would the notoriety drive the regulars away? This was a place for discreet liaisons and polite meetings that might lead to something more. The report that the actress left with somebody whom nobody knew suggested the place was used for purposes with which the management did not wish to be associated.

And there were the practical problems that came with a police investigation. They had insisted that all the glasses used on the night were not to be washed. Normally they would have been washed and polished the next morning, but there had been a hiccup in the washing-up department, as the dish-washer hadn't shown up for days. The police thought that there were bound to be fingerprints, which, when and if they had a suspect, would be important. They had said that it was all right to wash the dinner things and cutlery, but without the washer-up that wasn't easy. He'd just vanished, without notice.

At first the hotel felt that it was under siege. There were police everywhere, peering under beds, into cupboards, and drawing diagrams of the position of the tables and chairs used by Miss Grainger and her unknown escort. There were uniformed policemen outside and plain-clothes men inside stopping the staff from getting on with their work by asking strings of fatuous questions. Then there was the press, lurking around with suggestive glances, battered trilbys pushed back as seen in Hollywood films, treating every utterance made by management and staff like it was an outright lie.

And just when they thought the fuss might have died down the papers produced a sketch on the mysterious escort's features as remembered by the hall porter, and everybody was looking at everybody else in the place as if they might be Lobby Lud, the holiday man, who, when challenged, produced a reward of a crisp white five-pound note.

Miss Grainger's fellow actors said what a lovely person she had been and such fun to work with. Her ex-husband was found, but he was strangely non-committal about the affair. It was going to be a nine-day wonder.

Bernard bought all the Sunday papers and read them with an increasing sense of bemusement. He didn't know what had happened. He had switched off, just for a second, and she went limp. One thing was certain, he wouldn't be going back to Claridge's again or anywhere near. The drawing that was supposed to be him wasn't very good. Thousands of men could have fit the description, and with all the bombing and general disorder of life, it was unlikely that the police would spend too much time looking for him.

Besides, he was busy setting up his new enterprise. Miss Tcherny was coming over. He was hoping that she would take over all the office work, leaving him to go on the road getting orders. When she arrived Miss Tcherny seemed curiously distant, as though she had something other than work on her mind. It was clear that there wouldn't be much to do at the beginning, and she wasn't too keen at being stuck all day in the wilds of West Ealing in a garage with no heating. Bernard explained that things would take off when he got going. In the end Miss Tcherny said she would try it for a week. It was further than she wanted to travel. He readily offered to pay the difference in her fares and let her off early, so she got home at the same time. He wanted her there in the mornings to start receiving the stock and answer the telephone when he was out. He was getting a carpenter to put up some shelves. He ended up by taking her out to lunch. It was a dreary meal in a local pub, with potatoes and carrots heaped on the plate to disguise the paucity of meat, but she had a snowball and told him about her boyfriend who had just been called up, and how he hated being in the Army. She asked him about Maurice, and he had to confess that he hadn't seen his brother since the disaster.

'It must have been a shock to him,' said Miss Tcherny and told of meeting Maurice in the street and how distressed he had been.

'He'll have to get over it,' said Bernard. 'We're not the only firm that copped it. Most of the publishing industry was wiped out in two nights. But not all,' he said thoughtfully. 'The people I deal with are mostly all right.'

He walked with her to the station. He quite liked Miss Tcherny, he decided. They would get on well.

Miss Tcherny sat on the train back to Paddington and reviewed the situation. It was a bit more money, and easier hours, but the time she would spend travelling would even it out. She didn't like Bernard. There was something shifty about his manner. Mr Maurice was straightforward. He might have been a bit of an old duffer, but she trusted him. You couldn't imagine him doing anything underhand. Not so with Bernard. And this business that he had concocted out of the ruins was just skimming off the cream. The solid background of Green's was the wide diversity of the stock, of the ability to fulfil all orders, however obscure. What Bernard had in mind was a get-rich-quick scheme, dealing with a selection of books that offered a quick turnover.

But these musings occupied second place to the misery she felt about Charlie. His contorted face when the policemen dragged him away, his general unsuitability for military life and his unsuitability for life in general as it was lived today. Charlie had lived in a cocoon of cotton-wool happiness that he had constructed from his general insecurity. The war had caught him out. If it hadn't been for the war Charlie would have bumbled on until the end of his days without having to face up to any of life's realities at all. Jews were always aware of life, of its frightening twists and shocks. They felt themselves lucky if they could get through a day without a catastrophe. Where was Charlie now? Would they keep him at the police station or hand him over to the military authorities? And would he see a doctor, about his nerves, his hysteria, or would he just be punished for being absent without leave? She couldn't get his tragic, comic face out of her mind. He was like a hurt child who had just had a slap from a beloved parent. Could she make some enquiry? Should she contact his parents? She didn't want it to appear that she was in any way connected to Charlie, but she couldn't help being concerned. The night they had spent together was not going to be a bond for the rest of their lives: she had thought of it as a kindness, not a commitment.

That evening she discussed it with her parents. 'Nothing you can do,' said her father. 'In these days you have to let matters take their course. If you start questioning things you can end up in trouble. These are sensitive times. There is no room for compassion. Everything is black or white. Germans bad; English good. What is it they say? The only good German is a dead one. After the war they will have to settle, but now if you were to start to ask what has happened to that poor lad you might get accused of tempting him to desert his post.'

'That's right,' said her mother. 'It doesn't do to stick your neck out. We're not living in a sane world at the moment. When peace comes we shall see how silly we have all been.'

They sat in silence, a silence of acceptance of the injustice and insanity of life in wartime, but with the background knowledge of their position in their adopted country. They were Austrians, not Germans, and the authorities had cleared their residence in Britain. They were registered as British, but any step out of line might lead to complications.

'What about your new job?' her mother asked.

'I don't know,' said Rosa. 'I said I'd give it a trial. He's an odd sort of man. I don't trust him.'

'When was trust a condition of employment?' said her father.

'I was hoping that the other brother would contact me,' said Rosa. 'He's got my address and number.'

'In the meantime,' said her mother, 'the devil you know.'

'Oh, he's a devil all right,' said Rosa. 'I know that.'

Charlie hadn't been kept long at the police station. Two burly red-caps came and bundled him into an Army lorry. He was driven to a barracks somewhere near the Thames, with flagstone floors and the all-pervading smell of sour milk laced with carbolic. And when he got inside they kept shouting at him to stand still, to double up, to march forwards and stop, turn right, then left. He tried to comply, but he never seemed to get it; his mind was always behind the command. They put him in a cell. An officer came to see him who talked to him gently. The officer, a captain, seemed sympathetic and was a relief from the clattering boots of the redcaps, who shouted all the time as though they were calling to him from the top of a mountain.

What had caused him to run off like that? Charlie hadn't any explanation. He didn't like the Army. 'None of us like it,' said the captain. 'It's what we have to do. You see what the swine are doing? Killing women and children. No regard at all for human life.'

Charlie nodded dumbly. The captain's expression hardened, and his manner changed abruptly. Charlie was shocked, feeling somehow that he had been fooled by the captain's soft approach. 'You know what's the matter with you, soldier? You're in a blue funk. That's all.'

And then another officer came, a doctor. He asked if there was any insanity in Charlie's family; did he have headaches, did he have fits, could he read what was on that card? He sounded his chest and took his pulse and told him to get a good night's sleep – and, strangely enough, he did.

The next morning a very young, almost apologetic, officer with a shy smile and short fair hair and blue eyes came and explained that he would be speaking up for him at his court-martial. Could he offer any explanation for his sudden flight? Was he worried about anything at home? Anything to do with his parents; had he got a girl into trouble? When Charlie refuted all these suggestions the young officer looked worried. 'I think we'll have to plead temporary insanity,' he said.

And Charlie wondered: was there a chance that he wasn't quite right in the head? All the other chaps at the camp had seemed to cope with their new way of life, so why couldn't he? It had been such a shock, the shouting and the coarseness of their commands. Was coarseness a sign of manliness? Even the simple instructions on how to clean a rifle with a four-by-two piece of flannel looped into a string pull-through was described as 'a cow's cunt stuffed with bluebells'. And the idiotic orders about lining up his clothes and stuff as though it was in a shop window in Regent Street – there was no sense in any of it. Was the purpose to make him fighting mad? But then, if everybody else accepted these insane proceedings as normal, where did that leave him? The only man out of step must be mad, mustn't he? Maybe if he'd stuck it out things might have returned to normal eventually. On the other hand, if he had got used to this rough view of life he might never be sane again.

They had taken his name and address with the promise that his parents would be informed. Would his mother and father be ashamed of him? Would his case be reported in the papers? What could happen to him as a result of the court-martial? Well, it couldn't be much worse than this cell with its squalid child-sized toilet, with slop food and water and someone peering in at him every few minutes. He could go mad in this place. That would suit them: 'We didn't do anything. The boy was pots for rags, a screw loose.'

And Rosa. It was clear that she was sorry for him but also impatient at his foolishness. She was sensible. She would have known how to cope with a difficult situation. She wouldn't have run away.

There was a bed that you had to pull out to its full length. It creaked like a ghost in the Tower of London. There were three squares of mattress, called biscuits, and two blankets. He arranged them the best he could. They said that if you ate soap you foamed at the mouth. He had to do something to prove that he wasn't all there. Give them a show.

Jimmy was pleased when his money arrived from Green's in the shape of a postal order. There was a note that said 'Will write later'. He presumed that it was from old Maurice. He wasn't a bad old stick. Did that mean that he was still working for them? He showed his dad.

'They have to give you two weeks' notice,' he said, 'or pay you two weeks' money.'

'Yes, but the place isn't there any more.'

'That's not your fault,' said his dad. Jimmy thought this was a one-sided view of events – after all, it wasn't old Maurice's fault either – but as his dad's reasoning came out on his side he was prepared to accept it.

So he was on holiday, but what could he do? There was Ginger Rogers and Fred Astaire on at the pictures, which was all right, as long as they didn't keep on doing that singing and dancing all the time. He treated himself to some better fags. State Express were twice the price of Player's Weights, and they smoked a lot better. So he had some money in his pocket and time to spend it, but these benefits did not lift his spirits. The disappearance of Helen had left a hole in his life. What did the pictures matter if you hadn't got anyone to go with? What did anything matter? His dad had been allocated an allotment on Clapham Common. It was right up by Clapham South station. He helped his dad start digging it over, and they had finished up with a huge pile of bricks. It looked like the government expected everybody to grow their own food. Dad had become quite interested in growing vegetables and had bought Mr Middleton's book about it. Mr Middleton was the old buffer who talked about digging for victory on the wireless. He made it sound easy and good fun. He wanted to get over to Clapham South and see the pile of bricks: it would need some hardy old spuds to force their way up from under all that rubble.

Jimmy was conscious that he was marking time until he could get some news about Helen. If old Maurice was starting up again, there was a fair chance that Hodder's would start up, too. After all, there had to be books, and old Maurice was all for keeping things going. He used to get cross when they were late getting to the post, which he seemed to think, in some mysterious way, was helping the enemy. And yet old Maurice was completely dazed when he and Miss Tcherny had seen him in the street. Didn't seem to know what day it was. Miss Tcherny had taken him to the Underground.

He kept thinking he saw Helen. Her straight copper-coloured hair, her grave, perky face, her plump button nose, her honest eyes and her delicious lips. Dreaming about her came to him with the force of reality. He dreamt about her at night and day-dreamt during the day. He saw her passing by in buses, buying things in shops, staring at him from across the road. She haunted his entire life. Was he imagining that she was as nice as he thought? Could anyone be that perfect, that exciting, that lovable? He tried to think of who she was like: not Sylvia Sydney or Norma Shearer; Ann Sheridan, possibly, but Helen's eyes hadn't got that knowledge of what men were thinking. What about the English stars? Most of them talked as though they'd just had lessons in speaking, but there was Patricia Roc, who had challenging eyes, full lips and an air of independence, which she maintained until she submitted to the fade-out kiss.

He had been misled about girls. They never featured in the *Gem* or *Magnet*. The boys of St Jim's and Greyfriars didn't even have sisters. It was said that Billy Bunter had a sister called Bessie, who was as fat and horrible as he was. But nice girls, ordinary girls, girls you could take out and kiss, they were all alien to the public-school crowd. What was the matter with them?

In the end, Maurice was glad that Bella had emerged and tracked him down. She had never cared much about the business, had always wanted to convert her share into cash, and now she was right to be annoyed that the opportunity had gone. But, after she had lashed out at him, she had settled down and started to make some practical suggestions. 'A business isn't just the premises,' she said. 'It's a name, a reputation. That is still intact. You have your contacts –' Maurice intervened to say that all the records had been lost in the fire and dust. 'Yes, but you know them,' said Bella. 'You know the names. The addresses you can get from the telephone book. You can soon reconstruct you clientele. But it will have to be seen that you are still functioning. Get in touch with your old clients, assure them that service will continue as before, then you will still have a business, and then we shall have something we can sell. Look at you. You're worn out. Just get it up and running. I'll do the rest.'

It was heartening to hear Bella talk in this fashion. The idea of reconstructing Green's had not been in his mind. But Bella was right. They shouldn't just cave in. It had taken fifty years to build the business to its level of eminence in the trade. Before him, his father has started the warehouse in a small shop premises in Blackfriars. It was a pillar of the book business, not something to be given up lightly.

'But where?' he said.

'You'll have to use this address to start with, while we scout around and find somewhere central.'

Suddenly he felt as if something might rise from the ashes. They would never be able to replace the old stock, but they could start now and make sure they had everything current. Despite the war new books were being published, and, of course, there would be an outpouring of books about the war in due course. It would only be a limited service at first, but it could expand.

'What about the staff,' Bella said, 'have they been paid?'

'No,' he said.

'Well, pay them. You've got their addresses?'

'Some of them.'

After Bella had gone Maurice felt elated. Even Vice-Admiral Clare had been impressed by Bella's decisiveness. Maurice thought he would ring around some of the publishers and proclaim the resurrection of Green's. The first place he rang, the warehouse manager seemed surprised.

'Just thought I'd let you know that we are starting up again.'

'I know,' said the manager.

'And to give you our temporary address.'

'I've got it,' said the manager. 'I'm sending some stuff off today. It's West Ealing, isn't it?'

17

BETTY felt she was being left behind by events. Stephen had got his promotion to store manager. As staff members were called up there was a game of musical chairs to plug the gaps. The manager at Stephen's branch had been sent to a larger store, and Stephen was the youngest ever to have been appointed a manager in the whole company. Of course, if it hadn't been for the war he would have had a long time waiting in the wings, as it were. They said he was only on probation, but Betty was sure that he would make a go of it. The trouble was that she felt even more at a disadvantage. She had nothing to do all day. Stephen wouldn't hear of her working in a shop. With his new position he didn't want his colleagues knowing that his wife was a shop assistant in another store, but her situation made life so boring.

The extra money provided by Stephen's advancement gave them the opportunity to move out of number seventy-seven to somewhere better. She longed for a better kitchen, for a sitting-room that did not also double as a bedroom. Stephen needed a wardrobe for his clothes, and she needed a dressing-table with a mirror. Stephen insisted on her wearing a beret when they went out because her hair was still part blonde, although the dark roots were beginning to take over. Why had she ever allowed Bunty to persuade her to dye it? She wasn't prepared to keep dyeing it, not like Bunty, who was always walking about with a towel around her head like a turban.

Something was going on with Bunty and Tim. Tim had left his job at the water board and was driving a delivery van for the big department store in the high street. Tim didn't look at all happy, and Bunty had lost all her bounce. Bunty didn't invite her in any more and often glared at her on the stairs like she had done something wrong. Of course, you couldn't ask her, so you had to swallow it. Betty wasn't sure whether Bunty even went out any more.

The first thing was to convince Stephen that they should find better accommodation. After all, he couldn't invite his work people around to a one-room flat with a shared toilet. She pored over the letting columns in the local paper. There were places in Norwood, Norbury and Streatham with two bedrooms and own bathroom at double the rent they were paying currently. There were cheaper places in Balham, which, she had heard, was quite nice. The trouble was that when Stephen came home he was whacked out. He sat in a chair looking limp and went to bed early. He coughed a lot at night and sweated so badly that she was forced to open the window.

Stephen was cautious about committing himself to paying more rent. 'Something will turn up,' he said, which meant that he didn't want her to go looking for it. Since the new job he had gone pale and thin. Sometimes she urged him to take a day off – he really needed a holiday – but Stephen seemed terrified to take time off.

Betty decided to take a look around Balham way. There were several flats available, all with two bedrooms, kitchen and bathroom, with gardens as well. As she got to the ground floor she saw Mrs Bennet in her makeshift bed under the stairs. Poor old dear. She crept close. The old woman had her mouth open. She was dead to the world. Had probably been awake all night and now was catching up.

Balham seemed to be trying to break out of a stern sense of God-fearing respectability. The high street had curved terraces of imposing shops that supplied general household goods and clothes and shoes, which were of some quality but suffered from the description 'hard-wearing'. It was an epithet that would not be seen in, say, Streatham. Streatham, with its Locarno, theatre and slightly raffish ice rink, was properly smart. Smart was right for Streatham, and hard-wearing was right for Balham. Balham was bounded by the straggly Tooting Bec Common and Wandsworth Common, the latter of which seemed ultra-respectable, even though it was in the shadow of the prison. Balham bristled with its respectability. There seemed to be more tabernacles, Salvation Army halls and churches for all kinds of denominations and varieties of religion than elsewhere. It housed the headquarters of the Rechabites, a national organization of total abstainers, and each chapel had its subsidiary organization of Bands of Hope, Boys' Brigades and Girl Guide troupes. Indeed, the Hyde Estate had been built by a teetotaller who had made no provision at all for a public house on the site and would not even allow an off-licence to trade there. There was an outside market, but it was only used by the really poor, as the respectable people of Balham preferred the extortion of little shops with their lick-spittle proprietors, who, as likely as not, were the vergers of the church or chapel – although looking at the faces of Balham men you might have concluded that there were more vergers than churches.

Balham people tended their gardens, never had wild parties, kept themselves to themselves. If you wanted fun you could go to bosky Brixton with its theatrical boarding-houses, its rough pubs and markets and prostitutes. If a prostitute showed her face in Balham it was likely she'd be stoned. There was a cinema – not one of the new, black, flashy Astorias, with their ornate interiors designed to represent paradise, but a drab Victorian place that may have once been a theatre and which, from its general appearance, you might have thought was still showing silent films.

Maybe it was because of its strait-laced appearance that flats were cheaper to rent.

Betty started at Clapham South and walked down Balham Hill. There was a pile of bricks where the Hippodrome had been, possibly the only godless establishment in the area. For the rest, it was lace curtains and aspidistras, dark suits and the hush of a perpetual funeral. The Southern Railway station allowed the respectable to be ferried to respectable jobs in the centre of London, returning in the evening with the air of men who had spent the day doing God's work.

Betty found a flat she had seen advertised in the paper. It was above a piano shop, which also sold brass-band instruments and music as well as prams. It had a card in the window stating 'Terms available'. She went into the shop and was charmed by the shining pianos, the smell of furniture polish. A dapperly dressed, sallow-complexioned man of about thirty, with dark, wavy hair, smiled expectantly, but his smile faded when she enquired about the flat. He said that the flat was nothing to do with him, that the letting was in the hands of an estate agent.

She had tea in the ABC, then found the estate agent's office. A deposit of five pounds could secure the flat. Would she like to see it? The flustery little man with a stiff collar and dark-blue tie took the keys off the rack, and they walked back to the music shop. She liked the idea of being over such a respectable business; as they went by a piano tuner was at work on one of the uprights. It sounded nice the way he plonked the keys and tightened the notes.

The flat was beyond her dreams. It was light, spacious, had a bathroom and a good-sized kitchen with a gas oven and adequate china and utensils. It was very bright and clean. The sitting-room had a modern three-piece suite in an autumn-leaf design. The bedroom was a fair size, too, with windows that overlooked the high street, an oak wardrobe and – her heart leapt – a mahogany dressing-table with a mirror. You felt that you were somebody up here. She could imagine making tea in the kitchen and drinking it peering out of the windows to the traffic below. She must bring Stephen.

She hurried home, full of her discovery of their future in the elegant flat, with no neighbours up or down. It was a wonder that they had stuck together in that poky flat. When she got to the top of the street she saw a taxi draw up outside number seventy-seven. Stephen got out and paid the driver. She ran down the street to greet him. Stephen looked confused.

'Come in,' she said. 'I've got some good news.' He stared at her as though he was unable to take in what she was telling him. 'Posh,' she said. 'Coming home in a taxi.' She hoped that a lot of the neighbours had seen it.

'I was taken ill at work,' Stephen said. 'I had to get home.'

They went up the steps and into the hall. Mrs Bennet was still in her bed under the stairs.

'Is she all right?' Stephen said.

'She just worn out, poor old lady,' Betty said. 'She was there when I went out.'

Stephen stared at Mrs Bennet. He touched her hand and

drew it back sharply as though he'd been stung by a wasp. 'She's dead,' he said.

Betty looked at the recumbent body, the mouth open, as it was before she left for Balham; the unseeing eyes were just slits, not really closed.

'Oh my God,' she said. Neither of them had seen a dead body before.

'Let's get her inside,' Stephen said. They lifted her. Stephen took the head and trunk and Betty held the legs. It was difficult because Mrs Bennet's knees were practically under her chin and they couldn't straighten them. There was scarcely any weight. Mrs Bennet felt like a bag of bones. It was a surprise that she didn't rattle.

They dragged her into her sitting-room. It smelt of dust and urine. It was untidy, with dirty cups and plates on the floor. A many-coloured crocheted blanket was spread out like a rug. Cobwebs hung on the curtains.

'Better get her on to the bed,' said Stephen. They dragged her into the bedroom and on to the lumpy bed with its iron frame with brass knobs. It was like lifting a baby. They spread her on the bed, a little ball of old bones, and then looked at each other, horrified at what they had done.

'Has she got any relatives?'

'Her husband died years ago,' said Betty, 'but she had a son.'

There were piles of paper on the tables, on chairs and some on the floor. Betty started going through the papers, not really knowing why except that they might yield some clue to a relative, a friend. Stephen stayed in the bedroom, looking in the bedroom cupboard, festooned with old clothes. There was only a small window in the bedroom, and Mrs Bennet was, Stephen was pleased to note, in the shadow.

Betty, in the sitting-room, heard Stephen gasp. Then he said, in an odd low voice, 'Betty. Come in here.' She went in. He was standing by the window, looking very calm and serious. There was a dry cracked note in his voice.

'Close the door,' he said. She closed the door, wondering why Stephen suddenly seemed so masterful. He was like a man who had suddenly come to a serious decision.

'Is there anyone else in the house?'

Tim would be at work. Edie would be at Epsom, visiting Bert. 'I don't think so. Only Bunty, but she won't have heard anything.'

Stephen turned back to the cupboard. He put his hand in the pocket of one of Mrs Bennet's old coats and pulled out an old envelope. He opened it and took out a handful of one-pound and ten-shilling notes. 'Look,' he said.

'I expect she was saving it,' Betty said.

'Of course she was,' said Stephen. 'Heaps of it. There's some in every pocket.'

Betty glanced at Mrs Bennet, quite still on the bed. And yet, could she just be ill, in a trance or something? Was she going to wake up and say, 'Here, you two. What are you doing with my money?'

Stephen's eyes had taken on a furtive look. 'I didn't go to work today.'

'Oh? Why?'

'I went to the hospital. I've got to go to a sanatorium.'

'Why?'

'My chest, for God's sake. Otherwise I'd be in the Army.' Betty had the feeling that this was an important moment. What was going to happen now would influence their whole lives. 'The point is that you'll be on your own . . . for a while.'

'You will get better?'

'Yes, but not too soon, I hope. I don't want to get shipped off to France when they start up again. This money could see us through.' He was whispering, almost as if he thought that the dead woman could hear. 'Find a bag.' It was an urgent command. Stephen had taken charge of this situation. She found a cloth shopping bag in the kitchen. 'Hold it open.' Then, with the speed and skill of a pickpocket, Stephen emptied the pockets. Bundles of notes in paper bags or in wads with elastic bands tumbled into the bag until it was nearly full. Betty was fearful but fascinated. She kept glancing at Mrs Bennet, but the old lady seemed completely inert.

'Come on,' said Stephen. 'Let's get out of here.' He closed the cupboard door. They were holding their breath as they got out into the corridor. They ran into Bunty on the landing coming out of the toilet. Bunty just looked at them belligerently and flounced back into her room. When they got to their room Stephen counted the notes. Three hundred and twenty pounds. A fortune.

'There,' said Stephen. 'That should see us right for a while.'

'But it's not our money,' Betty said, innocently.

'It won't do her any good now,' Stephen said briskly, 'but it'll see us out of a hole. I bet that if the old dear knew she'd be pleased. D'you know, I think we could afford to move from here. Best thing to get away. As far as we can.' Now was Betty's chance to tell him about the flat in Balham.

'It sounds ideal,' he said. 'When can we go?'

'You have to pay a deposit. It's five pounds.'

'Five pounds,' he laughed. 'We could pay fifty pounds.'

They packed up their things in a suitcase. Their possessions were pitifully small.

'Don't we have to give notice?'

'Who to?' Stephen seemed to have grown in stature since the find. 'Now listen, Betty. We have to be very careful. We can't put this money in a bank account.'

'No,' she said. Bank accounts were out of her orbit.

'We must keep it and just use it as we need to. It'll last a long time. I might be away for six months.'

'Six months?' she said, panicking.

'But it'll be all right. You'll be able to come and see me. It's just that I need fresh air and rest and no worries. Can't you see? What has happened is a godsend. It's as though someone up there was looking after us. It's almost a miracle.'

They walked down to the taxi rank. Betty had to carry the suitcase as Stephen was too weak, although he managed to carry the bag. They took a taxi to Balham and arrived just as the estate agent was closing. He seemed surprised and fussed at their sudden arrival. Stephen signed an agreement, and they were given the keys.

Stephen was delighted with the flat. 'I'd like to live here. I really would.'

'But you can,' she said, puzzled.

'Not yet,' he reminded her. 'I've got to go into isolation for a while. I've got to go tomorrow.'

Betty suddenly realized that there was nothing to eat. They had brought half a packet of tea and some sugar but no milk. She made Stephen lie on the bed while she hurried along the high street, but there were no shops open. She was just going to turn back when she caught the potent whiff of fish and chips. All they had was rock salmon, but they had chips, and she bore them back to the flat as though they were a banquet. Stephen had spread the money out on the bed. He sat there looking at it with immense enjoyment. She laid the table in the window, and they ate the meal as though it might be their last, followed by tea without milk. In fact, it would be their last, at least for a while, and she wanted Stephen to have happy memories of the flat.

After eating Stephen placed the money in the drawer of the dressing-table with an expression of pride mixed with reverence. She had never seen so much money in one place. It looked like the inside of a till.

'You must look after this,' he said. 'Don't buy anything big. Just take what you need. Never have more than five pounds on you when you go out.' He covered the money with newspaper and closed the drawer. 'Put that bag in the dustbin,' he said, looking very serious.

That night Stephen slept soundly. It may have been the new surroundings, the money or the realization that he was ill and needed treatment, but he didn't cough at all. Betty didn't sleep so well. Mrs Bennet kept waking up, shouting: 'You stole my money!' Betty tried to placate her, but Mrs Bennet just got wilder and wilder. Betty awoke sweating with fear. Good dollops of good fortune were always paid for in the end.

She need not have worried. A German bomber, on its way back after dropping its load on the City, found a last bomb that would not dislodge. The pilot banked the plane and the bomb finally rolled into place. It was a direct hit on number seventy-seven. Bunty and Tim were in bed. In spite of herself, Bunty was beginning to submit to Tim's caresses. When it came to it Bunty couldn't help herself. She was still cross with him, but that wasn't going to stop her having her fun. They were buried and so was Edie underneath. The body of Mrs Bennet was never found.

Maurice was furious with Bernard. He spoke to Bella on the phone. His sister wasn't surprised. 'He always was an opportunist,' she said.

'But he's assumed the control of the business.'

'You'll have to see the solicitors,' Bella replied. 'He can't do that.'

'It looks as though he's done it. It'll take ages to go through the courts. No, I'm going over to see him.'

Meanwhile Bernard was revelling in his new-found freedom. He had made a speculative run and was surprised at the orders he gathered. Some of the shops were willing to let him send anything he thought suitable: 'You know what we want. Just send it. It'll be all right.' Even though it was effectively a new business he had to use the Green's connection to get the discount. Later he would register a new name and deal directly with the publishers as a new client. Miss Tcherny came every morning. She soon processed the orders, and he packed the stuff for the carriers. They charged extra for coming out to Ealing, but he would still show a healthy profit.

He liked Miss Tcherny coming in. He got fed up with his own company. The people he had let the upstairs to were a snooty pair. Just came in and out without a word. They paid the rent all right. That was all he was going to get from them. That was why he went out a lot. It was all right for Maurice, comfortably married to Clare. Not that Bernard ever fancied Clare. It would be like going to bed with a battleship. He had nearly got married once, that was when he bought the house, but the cow had cleared off with the best man on the eve of the wedding. He wasn't so much hurt as angry. The wedding had been arranged and the honeymoon paid for in advance. And he had felt such a fool trying to contact people to tell them not to come. And some of them did come, all dressed up to the nines, with fatuous smiles on their fatuous faces, who thought he was joking when he told them the wedding was off.

After that bitter experience Bernard had been cautious. He wanted women, badly – his hungry eyes were everywhere, on the Underground, in bookshops, cinemas, shops – but he wasn't going to be caught out again. He didn't mind paying, so long as the fee was reasonable. That Bunty, for example, she thought she was worth twice what he was prepared to pay and got quite nasty when he flung down a quid, came at him with her eyes blazing, trying to scratch his eyes out. He was prepared to take his time with Miss Tcherny: the occasional drink, a meal, to thank her for coming in with him. Her boyfriend had just been called up, so she was available, so to speak.

He had found a new publisher who did reprints of American books in the pocket-paperbook form. They were all about gangsters and their molls, written in racy American slang, basic English that even a chimp could read. The paper was thick and rough, the printing too heavy, but the lurid covers, usually depicting a hard-faced woman with a pistol, promised more than they delivered. He could get a good deal on this line, provided he could order in bulk. After delivery he had a month to pay, and he reckoned he could shift the lot before the due date. He had never subscribed to the idea that dealing in books was some kind of holy calling. Books were merchandise. You bought them, and sold them at a profit, and that's all there was in it.

Miss Tcherny had finished for the day, but it was only two o'clock. She sat there in her tight jumper, wondering what time she could reasonably ask to leave. Bernard, feeling that things were going well, was smiling and relaxed. Sometimes he saw Miss Tcherny as an efficient employee, sometimes as a pretty girl and sometimes as a temptation. It was when he felt light-hearted that he would dare himself. What could he lose? She could only say no. She wouldn't give up a cushy job so easily. He came up behind her and slipped his arms around her, grabbing her breasts.

'Stop it,' she shouted. 'What do you think you're doing?' It was the time for Bernard to retreat into a shame-faced apology, but Bernard, in this mood, thought that her protests were just playful resistance.

'Come on,' he said. 'You know how I feel about you.'

She twisted herself out of his grasp. 'For God's sake,' she said.

'Get a hold of yourself.' It was the same as before. This woman was shouting at him, belittling him. That actress tart had condescended to speak to him and then asked for money before he'd even made up his mind. These women, they drove him crazy, played games with him. He didn't want to get out of control again. He released Miss Tcherny, who was holding her neck, looking at him as though he was a dangerous madman.

'I'm sorry,' he said. 'I've had a lot on my mind lately.'

'You nearly strangled me,' she said. There was no doubt that the girl was frightened.

'I don't know what happened,' he said, holding his head. 'Look, I'm sorry. I really am. It's setting up this business. It's taken a lot out of me.'

The girl was still looking at him. 'You ought to see someone,' she said. 'A doctor.'

'I just need a holiday,' he said. 'But I can't go away now.'

'I think I must go home,' she said, backing away towards the door.

'Of course,' he said. 'I'll walk you to the station.'

'No,' she said. 'I'll be all right.' She went into the hall. The front doorbell rang. 'Who's that?' she said.

'I don't know.'

'Well, I'll be going,' she said, and opened the door. Maurice was standing there. Miss Tcherny flung herself at Maurice.

'Oh God,' she cried. 'Thank God!'

Maurice was startled at the sudden onslaught. 'Miss Tcherny. What's the matter?'

'It's your brother,' she sobbed. 'He tried to kill me.'

Bernard felt trapped. Reported to big brother again. Trust Maurice to get in on the act. 'It's nothing,' he said. 'Just a bit of horseplay.'

'But what is she doing here?' Maurice demanded.

'I'm just getting the business going again. I thought you'd be pleased.'

'You mean you're trying to steal the business,' Maurice said. 'What have you done to this girl?'

'Oh, you know what it's like. They give you the eye, and then they go all coy if you follow it up.'

Maurice was disturbed. It was clear that Bernard had attacked Miss Tcherny. He had known that Bernard was capable of many unpleasant things, but this was a new and dangerous side to his difficult brother. 'Are you all right, my dear?' he said to Miss Tcherny.

'I am now,' said the girl. 'I ought to go to the police.'

'I think you'll find that the police are quite busy,' said Bernard coolly, but inside part of his brain was gripped in a panic. 'Besides, remember it's only your word against mine.'

Maurice saw that he had to do something decisive. 'You'll get a solicitor's letter in the morning. It requires you to cease trading as Green's.'

'I'm starting up my own company,' Bernard said stiffly.

'But you're using all Green's contacts,' said Maurice. 'And you can't do that. So if I were you I'd wind up this sordid little enterprise, and, in the meantime, I'll take this young woman home.'

Maurice and Miss Tcherny walked along together.

'Now then,' Maurice said. 'I think you'd better tell me all about this.'

That night the bombers came early. It was scarcely dark. Betty was alone in her dream flat, and Stephen was in hospital in Caterham. They had gone on a Greenline bus. Everybody in the place was dressed in white, and they made her put on a white gown and hat while she was there. They said she could go and see him but not yet. They wanted to assess his condition. They would let her know if there was any change. Yes, she could ring at the end of the week. She suddenly realized that, as nice as the flat was, she was going to be alone in it, that she would spend the black nights on her own. But she was well provided for, Stephen had seen to that. There was a concrete shelter in the next side street, and the Underground wasn't far away.

She sat at the window and saw zigzag flashes in the sky. In the distance she could see flames leaping into the sky, red and orange, sometimes purple. Guns were firing quite near by. The building trembled with the vibrations. As she watched she heard a tremendous crash somewhere below. It seemed right beneath the flat. She opened the window, but she couldn't see anything. Then a scurry of wardens and policemen seemed to be gathering below. Cautiously she went downstairs and into the street. The plate-glass window of the shop had crashed into the street. There were big jagged sheets of glass on the pavement and in the road. Rain was lashing in on the pianos and brand-new perambulators. Then the shop manager appeared, looking less suave than he did usually, with his overcoat collar up and his hair messed up, as if he'd just got out of bed. He looked worried. He talked to the policemen and then came over to her. 'Are you all right, my dear?'

'Yes,' she said. 'I heard a crash.'

'Don't worry. I'll get some workmen in the morning. Try to make it tidy. I think the police will remove the glass. What a shocking business. I hope it didn't disturb you too much.'

'I wasn't asleep,' Betty said. 'The noise . . .'

'I know,' said the manager. 'It'll put us out of business for a few days. I'll have to hang on for a bit.'

'Would you like a cup of tea? You can see what's happening from upstairs, and you'll be in the dry.' The manager came up to the flat and introduced himself as Mr Gerston. He sat in the window while she made some tea.

'Is your husband sleeping through all this?' he asked.

'He's away,' said Betty. 'Poor thing. He's in hospital.'

'Nothing serious I hope.'

'It's his chest.'

'Ah. TB?'

'I expect so. He'll be all right. In the end.'

'Of course he will,' said Mr Gerston heartily, as he looked at his hostess speculatively. 'I'm sure he will.'

18

'STAND up!' Charlie sat on his bunk and stared inanely at the stiff figure in front of him. The corporal's neck muscles tightened. He forced his shoulders back and his chest out. 'Don't you fuck about with me, boy. I know your little game, don't I? You're not barmy, are you? But you're bloody mad if you think you can fool me. You're a malingerer. What are you?'

Charlie looked at his tormentor, apparently without seeing him. Charlie knew that this was a deadly game. It would need all his skill and cunning to come out on top. He'd lost track of how long they'd been at it. First the sergeant, then the corporal, shouting, going red, staring at him with angry eyes. His only resistance was passive. If he made an effort to defend himself they would say that he had attacked them.

'Stand up. Come on, lad.'

'Can I go home now?' Charlie said.

'I'll give you bloody home,' the corporal exploded. 'You're not going anywhere.' He grasped Charlie by his tunic and bunched it up, pulling Charlie's face close to his own. Charlie could see the pigmentation on the corporal's skin, the slight sweating on his neck, the short bristles of hair under his nose that had been missed by the razor. 'Oh yes, you're bloody good at it, ain't you? Making out you're not all there. But I know different, don't I?'

'I don't like the clothes,' said Charlie.

'Oh,' said the corporal, reaching the heights of mockery. 'So we don't like the clothes. Would you feel better in a dress and a pair of knickers? Is that it?'

'What?' Charlie said, stupidly.

The remark about clothes had released an automatic stream of irony, and the corporal hadn't finished with it yet. 'Tell you what. We'll get a bleeding tailor in. We'll get some ponce from bleeding Savile Row, get you measured up. Can't have you looking like a bag of shit, can we?'

Charlie stood mute. Not defiant but accepting.

'I've had nearly enough of this,' said the corporal menacingly. 'I'll ask you one more time. Stand up!'

Charlie shambled to his feet. 'It's cold,' he said.

'Cold, are we? That's a real shame. A real bleeding shame. There's a cure for that. Exercise. Now, come on. March! Move those feet.' Charlie looked as though if he moved his feet he might fall down. He was limp. His trousers bagged at the knees, his arms hung uselessly by his sides.

'All right,' said the corporal. 'If that's how you want to play it . . . Make it hard on yourself.' The corporal left the cell, clanging the door shut and turning the lock.

Charlie sat down again. It wasn't a question of keeping up this dumb show of being a useless half-wit. He had no other option. It was his defence. The young captain who was representing him had brought another officer to talk to him, one who had a crown on his shoulder.

'I just went for a walk,' he had told him. 'I wanted to get home. I've never been away before.'

'You did know that you were out of bounds?' said the major, earnestly searching Charlie's face, looking for a key to this puzzle.

'I'll do something else,' said Charlie. 'I'll be an ambulance man. I'll go in the ARP.' He thought he had got them puzzled. If he could just keep it up. And yet, in an odd way, he knew that he wasn't acting. He really was this half-mad incompetent who didn't know the rules. And this half-mad person inside him was looking after him, telling him what to do, judging the reactions of his inquisitors, weighing up all the clues, watching how it was going. This person inside knew that he wasn't mad, but he could be. It was touch and go. If he let go of his act they would have him marching up and down at the double all day and all night. He had to be solid, he had to be convincing, but surely only a madman would have embarked on this course of action. It was a puzzle.

The major looked at him curiously, as though Charlie was a specimen he hadn't come across before. 'You do know what your bayonet is for, don't you?'

Ah. That was referring to the time he was chopping wood in

the barrack room, bits of the bed at that. That corporal who told him to do it had given him a good start as the barmy recruit.

He still thought about Rosa. Had she made any attempt to visit him, to find out how he was getting on? Did she care? His mother and father hadn't been either. Maybe these bastards wouldn't let him have visitors, to make him feel that nobody cared about him. That was all a part of the treatment, to break him down, to make him eat that porridge shit they brought around. Well, it wouldn't work. He was surprised how strong he really was. He had an inner strength. He would see this through until they discharged him as being useless and barmy beyond all hope.

He knew at the back of his mind that they couldn't force him to do anything. They could push and shove, shout and stamp and lose their tempers, but any punishment he would receive was dependent on some co-operation on his part. If he was mad he hadn't done anything wrong. He wasn't responsible for running off because he wasn't all there. Anything he did wasn't down to him. He couldn't be blamed. The orderly who brought him bread and margarine had winked at him and whispered, 'Keep it up, mate. You've got them going.'

They left him for long periods when he had mad dreams of becoming invisible and floating between the bars. Mind you, they had eased off lately. When he first came in the corporal had held his arms behind his back while the sergeant punched him in the stomach until he was sick. They had signals between them, the sergeant and the corporal, warning glances, significant nods. He lay on the floor a long time to alarm them into thinking they might have done him a permanent injury. That was when he saw the signals.

After that they confined themselves to verbal bullying, which Charlie, being a madman, couldn't appreciate. His court-martial was still some time away. His defending officer seemed more hopeful after he had brought that major to see him. Maybe it wasn't temporary insanity after all but something more serious, more excusable. The young captain wasn't much older than Charlie. He was trying to take the job seriously, but you could see that he was out of his depth.

Charlie set off on his task. He was counting all the bricks in the cell. He'd done one wall and scratched the number on the floor with his boot. He had two more full walls to do and the bits each side of the door.

He never knew what time it was. It got dark and it got light, which was all he knew. They had taken his watch away. Maybe that was part of the treatment, just depriving someone of a sense of time. What the fools didn't realize was that what they were doing to him was the easiest way of sending him mad.

Rosa Tcherny was pleased to have run into Maurice. She had never liked the idea of working for Bernard. Maurice treated her with respect. She was full of the attack. 'He was like a madman, almost as though he didn't know what he was doing.'

Maurice was sympathetic but seemed disinclined to delve into the matter. If she went to the police and the matter came up in court Maurice and the family name and the business would all be mentioned. Obviously Maurice didn't want that. Besides, he was talking of starting up again. He had found a railway arch with a wooden office section in Wandsworth Road that had been used as a warehouse for fruit and vegetables but which had now been cleaned out. It wouldn't be a permanent home, but it would do just to get things going again.

'I've written to Jimmy and to Harry, asking them to meet me at the steps of St Paul's on Friday at eleven o'clock. We'll go in that tea room and talk. Can you come too?' She readily agreed. Her old job back. And with a decent old stick, not a leering beast who jumped on you and then tried to throttle you.

Maurice thought that the girl would be placated by the offer of a job. But the fact was that he was alarmed and worried about Bernard. Even as a boy Bernard had had an uncontrollable temper. Bernard had been slower than other boys of his age, and he had always been jealous of Maurice. Bernard was never going to accept second place to anybody for anything. Maurice wished that his father's will hadn't tied them together so permanently. Of course, Bernard had suffered dreadfully when that girl pulled out of the marriage at the last minute. But you couldn't sympathize with him. Any show of fellow feeling for a fellow human being Bernard shrugged off with a snarl. Maurice ought to talk to him. True, it was only Miss Tcherny's word against Bernard's, but Maurice knew which one he believed. The girl had been frightened, that was clear. Was it possible that his brother was a trifle unhinged? If that were the case, what could he, Maurice, do about it? You couldn't accuse someone of being a dangerous lunatic without real proof. He thought of talking it over with Clare but immediately dismissed the notion. Bella perhaps? She had been so decisive about the business.

He got to Paddington just in time to hear the air-raid siren. Some of the would-be passengers immediately scurried to the Underground. Some stood, irresolutely, as though they were hoping that their train would run and take them away from the danger zone. Some stood stoically, almost daring the enemy to do its worst. Maurice had to get to the Underground anyway, so he went down the escalator with the mass of people, all looking grim-faced, frightened yet determined. The platform was the usual mess of underfoot rubbish, papers, crisp packets, bits of sandwiches, orange peel, dirty milk bottles, Tizer bottles and cigarette packets, chewing-gum and phlegm. People were standing at the edge of the platform to be the first to get on the train. Any sudden surge from the back would have tipped someone on to the line. Squatting on the floor, against the wall, were pale-faced women with bundled babies. It was like a crazy Noah's Ark, jam-packed with people instead of animals. Each person seemed determined on their own safety with not even scant consideration of others. This was a scramble for survival.

The train came in and the doors opened. People surged in and those that wanted to get out were pushed back inside, and then had to fight their way out again. Maurice got in right at the end and found his head and neck bent forwards by the curvature of the door when it closed. The train started with its packed human cargo, crushed into intimate contact but all staring ahead, trying to avoid the eyes of their neighbours. How many people in this carriage? A hundred, two hundred? At the first stop Maurice found himself pushed off the train on to the platform as people pressed to get off, and then pushed back in by another surge of people wanting to get on. The only good part about this journey was that he knew he was safe.

When he changed to the Northern Line it was the same thing all over again. But then the train stopped in a tunnel and the lights went out, and there was a slight tremor of collective unease. What a way to live, Maurice thought.

When he got out to the daylight of Morden he felt as though he had just been spared execution. The bus was a civilized experience. Maybe he could devise an overland route to Wandsworth Road? Had the people who had built the Underground ever dreamt that it would descend into such a dehumanizing experience?

When he got home there was a message to call the solicitors.

'Under the terms of the will the business cannot be split up without the agreement of the three shareholders.'

'Good,' said Maurice. 'Will you send my brother a letter to that effect?' Then he was at it. Compiling a list of titles, remembering the publishers, organizing the backlist and other items that he knew they would need, building up a list of his stock on paper: ready reckoners; Hugo's foreign-language phrase books; Whitakers; Wisden's Yearbooks; bloodstock books and the racing calendar; Hansard; and specialist diaries. After an hour he heaved a sigh of satisfaction. He had completely lost himself in his old world, remembering all the titles by Priestley, Wells, Huxley, Waugh, the whole canon of the Peter Rabbit books, Milly Molly Mandy, Alison Uttley, the Arthur Ransome books, *Anne of Green Gables*, Agatha Christie, Chesterton, Wilde – and the special editions with Beardsley illustrations – and such out-of-the-way writers as Garnett, A.G. Macdonell, Storer Clouston, Linklater, even Herbert Jenkins. They all had their followers. How many Jeeves and Wooster books were there? How many Mr Mulliner? It had been a delightful pastime.

When Clare came in looking as if she had just been relieved at the wheel of a frigate, he regarded her fondly. Poor old Bernard. He had never known the boon of being married. Clare and Maurice had never really hit it off – in fact, they had tacitly agreed not to hit it off – but, somehow, they had stayed together, maintained a home and, in the fullness of time, become an old couple. She had found her feet after years of paddling in the shallow end. He could not deny her the pleasure of being in charge of a troupe of half-wits who looked up to her because she was the only one who could strike out with confidence, even when she was steering them in entirely the wrong direction. Clare was a genuine English eccentric, and, oddly enough, that type had become the back-bone of the war effort. It was because they never questioned anything. They knew they were right. They ignored any contrary arguments. It didn't really matter whether they were right or not; they had to be right even when they were wrong. It was this indomitable conviction that drove them stubbornly forward. Churchill had got some of it, this innate belief in the rightness of their view of life and the structure of society, that the majority of the population were better off when they were in the charge of their superiors. The trouble was that most of the 'inferiors' believed in the status quo as well. If they didn't they became a political extremist, which wasn't so funny – probably a Bolshie, with foreign allegiances.

Maurice moved to his armchair to listen to the news at nine o'clock. Clare was still arranging piles of papers in the back-ground and filling in one of her endless rotas, pursing her lips like a child puzzling over a jigsaw. He picked up a newspaper. He had got used to reading between the lines, and it wasn't good news, although Churchill, as usual, said it was. There was a picture of an actress who had been found strangled. A motiveless crime, said the police. Dead in her own flat. Been there for days. Ironically she had been found by her agent, who couldn't get her on the telephone. The agent had some news of a part in a film. He thought of the marks on Miss Tcherny's neck. Surely not. Bernard hadn't got the courage, the conviction, to pull off a murder. And yet he recalled Miss Tcherny's verdict: 'He was like a madman, almost as though he didn't know what he was doing.' He shook his head. It was too fanciful. Bernard might act like a lout, but he was smart enough to keep himself out of trouble. And yet, Bernard was always under the impression that he was being put down in some way, overlooked, slighted. But how would Bernard get intimate with a West End actress? She would soon see him for the oaf that he was. No. It was impossible. Bernard wouldn't put himself in that position.

Maurice folded the paper carefully. 'I'm off to bed,' he said. 'I've got a busy day tomorrow.'

Betty quite enjoyed the bustle and knocking of the workmen down below.

She watched as they unloaded the big pane of glass from the long lorry, and went downstairs to watch them fit it into the window. Mr Gerston was watching, too.

'Not too much damage to the stock,' he said. 'The insurance people are prepared to take it as read, as long as we keep it within bounds. They just haven't got the men to assess every piece of damage.'

She invited him up for a cup of tea, and he began to talk. He had trained as a pianist but realized that he wasn't good enough to make the top grade and so became the manager of a music shop. He still played, to demonstrate the pianos and for his own pleasure. He also gave lessons, mainly to children, but there weren't many children around any more. They had been sent away, as had his own wife and child, spending a prolonged holiday with relatives in Wales. He hadn't sold many pianos lately; people were just not interested in music now. The only sheet music they sold in the shop nowadays was patriotic jingles and sentimental songs about the possibility of couples being reunited after terrible times. Wartime songs had replaced 'the latest pantomime hits' and the yearning, summer songs of the seaside.

Betty was soon as impressed by Mr Gerston as she had been by Maurice Green. Maurice knew about books, but Mr Gerston knew about music. She asked him what kind of music he liked, and he offered to bring a gramophone from the shop and play her some Strauss, which, he judged, would suit her uninformed taste. That night around six he asked her if she would like to accompany him for a quick drink.

'Where?' she said, excited and fearful at the same time. Women had only just started to go into pubs. The war was breaking down inhibitions. Women in uniform thought themselves equal to men.

'It's a place where I used to play,' he said. 'The Glenroy. It's not like a pub. It's more of a hotel. I just thought it'd be nice to unwind.'

What would Stephen think about her stepping out with a man she had only just met? He wouldn't object. As Mr Gerston said, it wasn't exactly a pub, and Mr Gerston himself was very polite, just like Maurice, and she could do with the company.

The Glenroy was trying hard to hold on to its reputation for respectable gentility, if not quite Palm Court. There were barrels of geraniums in the entrance porch and staid Victorian pots holding stern leafy plants with rugged trunks that seemed to forbid any excess drinking or behaviour in their presence. The place was divided into different rooms marked 'Private', 'Saloon' and 'Public'. Mr Gerston steered Betty into the saloon. It was funny, because the bar in the middle served people in either bar, and you could see people in the public, but not in the private, which was secluded on the left. Betty didn't know what to ask for. On the door, bevelled in glass, the gold lettering said 'Wines, Spirits and Beers'.

'What can I get you?' said Mr Gerston, knowing that his guest had no knowledge of the range of drinks on offer. 'What about a sherry?'

Betty looked confused. 'Yes, if you think so.'

'Sweet or dry?'

'I don't mind,' said Betty, 'really.'

They settled by the fire, which was laid but wasn't lit. There were three couples besides themselves: a young WAAF with an RAF officer, who looked strained and thoughtful; an older man, stout, with a short haircut, accompanied by a younger woman who bunched herself up in her coat as though she hoped that nobody would notice she was there; and an odd couple, small and neat, wearing berets tight on their heads, who sat grinning at each other like two elves out on a spree and who only had to look at each other to break into suppressed fits of giggles.

There was noise coming from the public bar, but there were only whispers in the saloon, where looks, for the most part, substituted for speech.

'Have you heard anything about your husband?'

'They say he's comfortable,' Betty said.

'They don't tell you much, do they? Do you mind if I smoke?'

'Not at all,' Betty said primly.

Mr Gerston produced a pink packet of Passing Cloud. When he lit the cigarette there was the delicate whiff of a foreign perfume. It was a new and pleasant experience, sitting in this quiet room with Mr Gerston, sipping sherry and breathing this exotic smell.

'I do envy you,' said Betty. 'Playing the piano.'

Mr Gerston shrugged. 'I'm not very good,' he said. 'I don't keep up the practice. I've let it all go.'

'Oh, you shouldn't,' Betty gushed.

Mr Gerston drew heavily on his cigarette and wafted the smoke away with his hand. 'I know,' he said. 'I know, but there's only so much time in the day.'

Suddenly there was a shout. It came from the public bar, where a face could be seen urgently wanting recognition.

'Bertie,' said the face. It was a red, round face with an even redder nose and a halo of white hair. 'Bertie,' it repeated, getting louder, and the other occupants of the saloon seemed to wince at the intrusion.

'Oh dear,' said Mr Gerston.

'Bertie. Round here.'

'Is it someone you know?'

'I'm afraid it is,' said Mr Gerston. 'My father.'

'Are you going to join him?'

'I think not,' said Mr Gerston loftily. 'I think we'd better go. I'm sorry about this,' he added. 'This is not his usual haunt.' He drank his sherry and indicated that she should do the same. But she just couldn't drink it all down in one go.

'It's all right,' he said. 'Don't choke yourself.'

Suddenly the door swung open and Mr Gerston senior was coming forward with a jovial smile of greeting. 'If mountain won't come to Mohammed . . .' he said thickly. 'How are you, Bertie? Aren't you going to introduce me?'

Mr Gerston looked uncomfortable. 'Mrs May, my father.'

Betty looked up at the Father Christmas face, quite jolly – but the eyes were light blue and not so jolly.

'Good to meet you,' said Mr Gerston's father. 'Mrs, eh Bertie? Oh well. No skin off my nose.'

'We were just going,' said Mr Gerston stiffly.

'We can have a quick 'un, can't we, dear?' said Mr Gerston's father. 'Jerry won't be over for a bit. What's that you're drinking?'

'It's a sherry,' said Betty, 'but I don't think I'd better have another.'

'Nonsense,' cried the old man. 'Here, Bertie,' he said, fishing in his pocket. 'Get them in.'

There was a change in the atmosphere of the saloon bar. The RAF officer was wearing an indulgent smile, the man with the stiff haircut motioned to his companion that they should leave, and the two elves couldn't believe their luck.

'It's a terrible business,' said the old man. 'I was in the last lot, you know. That was a real war. Hand to hand, cold steel and all that. And what thanks did we get? F-bugger all. Land fit for heroes? Bol-baloney. And it wasn't asking a lot. Most of the poor bu-beggars never came back. Pity. They missed the Means Test. Sell that table. You don't need a mangle. Wonder they didn't tell you to sell the wife.'

'Dad,' said Mr Gerston. 'I don't think Mrs May needs to know about your war experiences.'

'No,' said the old man. 'She wants to know about the after-the-war experiences, when we were all living on tuppence ha'penny. You see, they'd spent all the money on blowing people up, and they hadn't got enough left to look after those who were left over. Oh, it's a joke. You think you're making sacrifices for something better, but when it's all over it's a blood-blimming-sight worse.'

The RAF officer was beginning to look uncomfortable; the old man wasn't keeping his voice down to the saloon-bar level, he was still in public-bar mode.

'You take this Churchill. They wouldn't have the silly old bugger in the government before the war. Now they've put him in charge. But it ain't made no difference. He's still a silly old bugger. The reason they put him in charge was that he was the only one that wasn't in with Hitler. They thought that the Germans would go for Russia, which is what they wanted. Kill two birds with one stone. But this Hitler, he ain't no fool. He's going to finish us off first. Then he'll have all our factories, munitions and that to turn on the Russians.'

The Air Force officer had gone white. He stood up. 'That's enough of that defeatist talk,' he said. 'There's people dying for our country, our freedoms.'

'It may be your country,' said the old man, rounding on his accuser, 'but it ain't mine. What about freedom of speech, eh? Is that why you're trying to shut me up?'

The two little elves, who might have been two women or one of each sex, looked at each of the protagonists in turn. The man with the short trim haircut and his mysterious companion had left. The WAAF tugged at the RAF officer's sleeve. 'Sit down, Nigel,' she said. 'He's drunk.'

Mr Gerston's father heard the remark. 'That's as may be, miss, but I'd say the same if I was cold sober. This lot, who's in charge of everything, they don't know what to do any more than you and me. Look at the state of us. Nothing in the shops, eating cats' meat, beer like water, being bombed from arsehole to breakfast time, working flat out like bees in a hive, paying tax up to our armpits. And what for? So that Lord Shitface can go on with his hunting and shooting. The people in this country – load of mugs. Always have been, always will be.'

Betty was shocked and yet fascinated by the old man's tirade.

'That's enough, Dad,' Mr Gerston said.

The old man sighed. 'Yes. I suppose you're right, Bertie. Don't do any good. Freedom of speech. It's all right saying things, but it don't make no difference, do it?'

Mr Gerston was full of apologies on the way back to the flat. 'He gets a drink or two into him and he goes off like a rocket.'

'I didn't agree with what he was saying, but he is interesting.'

'Nobody agrees with what he says,' said Mr Gerston.

'What was that he called you? Bertie?'

'Yes. It's Bertram really. I don't know why they called me that. Must have been to Bertram Mills's Circus, I expect.'

'No,' said Betty loyally. 'I think it suits you.' Betty was feeling slightly less overwhelmed by Mr Gerston after the encounter with his father. 'Bertram,' she said.

'Yes,' he said. 'Betty.'

'It's been very nice,' she said. 'Taken me out of myself. Thank you for taking me. You've no idea how lonesome I get.' She looked at him sideways. He was quite handsome, with his dark complexion and wavy hair, and artistic, too.

Mr Gerston looked down at her sparkling eyes. There was no doubt that the girl was excited, stimulated by what she had seen and heard. She was like a new leaf, slowly opening and taking stock of its surroundings. It would be an experience and an amusement to introduce her to the many things in life that she did not appreciate. At least it was an interest. She put the key in her door and went in, leaving the door open. He took the hint and followed her upstairs. It was a nice roomy flat, but it lacked all those things that gave a home character. Of course, she'd only just moved in, but somehow he didn't think that her presence would make any impression. She was like a blank sheet of paper, waiting for someone to make a mark on it. It was an intriguing prospect.

She made a pot of tea, and he smoked one of his cigarettes.

'They do smell posh,' she said.

'Turkish,' he said. 'Well, a mixture.'

She looked at him, her mouth open, her shoulders relaxed. She was feeling somehow different. Was it the drink, the smell of the cigarettes, the bizarre outing? She was in this new flat with a new man, and Stephen was in hospital, a few miles away.

'I think', she said, watching his face for a reaction, 'that I would like to play the piano. Would you teach me?'

He laughed. 'You'd need a piano first.'

'Oh, that would be all right. I could manage it.'

Hello, Gerston thought. A woman with money. And I thought that, with her husband away, she would be up against it. 'Well, I could soon sell you a piano,' he said, 'and I could teach you to play it.'

She smiled a secret smile. She was like a child, he thought. She had a woman's body but an undeveloped brain.

There was a bakelite wireless on a table. He walked over to it. 'Does this work?' he said and switched it on. There was music, delicate music. Mozart.

'Do you like that? Or Henry Hall?'

'I like this,' she said. 'What is it called?'

'*Eine Kleine Nachtmusik*,' he said loftily.

'Ooh, what's that?'

'It's Mozart: *A Little Night Music*.'

'Do you know everything about music?'

'Well, no, but this is a very popular piece.'

Betty licked her lips. She was feeling cosy. She was at home with this man. He didn't look down on her because she didn't know anything about music. And he was smart and polite all the time, despite having that dreadful old father. She spread herself on the sofa, feeling somehow luxurious, expensive.

Gerston recognized the signs. The woman was feeling fruity. She didn't know it, would not acknowledge it, but with care and consideration he could encourage her mood and bring it to a fruitful conclusion. Women behaved like this almost unconsciously and would have been shocked if anyone had told them that they were behaving provocatively.

He knelt down beside her on the floor. It had been a quiet night. No sound of planes, no siren. He'd better get on with it. If that damn thing went off it would disrupt the mood completely. He leant over and kissed her full on the mouth. She moaned a little and clung to him. The music weaved intricate patterns but always proceeding with logic and neatness. It was pure music, untainted by any other consideration. It rose and fell but never quite attained a crescendo, moving surely on like a river of clear bubbly water.

He slipped his hand down the front of her dress and she gasped, not, he thought, from any sense of outrage but with the shock of pleasure. He pulled up her dress and she closed her eyes, not daring to imagine what would happen next. It wasn't so much a seduction as a submission. She was married, but so was he, which didn't so much double the deception as even it out. They were two strangers caught up in a whirlpool of life. Life that could be shortened or ended at any time without warning. If they did one thing to express their existence it could be in a single act of love-making. The one act that defied the war, the mess that life had become, the sheer worry of surviving in a world careering into ultimate catastrophe.

Betty felt fear and pleasure but somehow no shame. She had been placed in an impossible situation. Bertram had been kind to her. He was obviously a man of some education. If she hadn't met Stephen and married him she would have been pleased to have met Bertram. She hadn't known that such men as Maurice and Bertram existed, and she'd had no idea that they would bother with her.

As they climaxed the siren sounded. It was back to the real world again, after a moment of bliss. Back to military bands instead of Mozart, to thinking about rations and gas masks and how long this bloody war was going to last.

Bertram eased himself off Betty's exposed body.

'I haven't drawn the curtains,' she said.

'We don't need the light on,' he said. 'We can just lie here and nobody will ever find us.'

'Who?' she said, puzzled. And he winced. She was a plain and simple girl all right. Not subject to flights of fancy. Play the piano? Never.

19

Rosa stared at herself in the mirror. Her neck was still red and blue. When Bernard had grabbed her she thought it might have been the end. She had felt herself blacking out. And the way he had looked, with a sort of mad mist in his eyes, it was probably fair to say that he didn't know what he was doing. A rage had lifted him out of his senses. It is true that she had never liked him, and why she agreed to help him in his sordid little enterprise she couldn't think. It was the fear of not having a job and not wanting to be forced to take one of the routine jobs that were going, mainly in factories. At Green's she had led a civilized existence – and it wasn't anything to do with the war effort. Why was everybody so keen to make bombs, parachutes, Army clothing, guns or get into uniform? The bloody war had distorted values, caused a kind of mass hysteria. By keeping together in factories, canteens, shelters, desperately singing and laughing in boisterous groups, people bolstered their confidence, all whistling in the dark together. As far as Rosa could see the next move would be occupation. It had happened in France, Belgium, Holland, Poland, Czechoslovakia, Austria. Why did these British think it couldn't happen to them? They thought that foreign countries weren't proper countries, and all foreigners were crazy anyway. And if Hitler arrived, what would happen to them, the Jews? Would the natural-born British people lift a finger to protect them, if their own lives were put in danger as a consequence? Had they in Austria, or anywhere else? Would Hitler let Mosley out of detention and put him in charge? That was a laugh. When Mosley was detained under some regulation about potential traitors people had written to the papers protesting. Not Mosley's supporters but Englishmen protesting about the erosion of free speech. These English! They had it coming to them.

She put some cold cream on the bruises on her neck, but it just looked blue and greasy so she wiped it off. She found a small scarf that covered it. She didn't want any embarrassing questions.

Her mother had found some kippers for tea. She had boiled them, as there was no fat. The little bit of fat allowed in the rations was used to roast a small joint for Sunday. There was margarine, but Rosa preferred dry bread to that tasteless oily spread. Only last year they used to have lashings of butter with everything. The government said that the diet was not only adequate but healthy. The Ministry of Food was always publishing little pamphlets telling how you could make a nourishing meal from potato peelings and dried egg and nutmeg.

She poked at the kipper. It didn't even smell of fish, let alone kipper.

'What's the matter with your neck?' her mother said.

Rosa knew her mother's instinct for spotting a weakness. 'Nothing,' she said. 'I found this scarf in the drawer and I decided to wear it.'

Her mother said nothing, but Rosa could see that she wasn't convinced.

Her father came in and sat at the table. Rosa's mother put his plate, with the juiciest kipper, in front of him.

'Excuse me,' he said. 'Is this for the cat?'

'Look,' said his wife, red and harassed, 'everything's gone. We've used up the rations. It was all I could get.'

They ate it silence.

Then Mr Tcherny said, 'I'm going to make some jam.'

'Oh,' said Mrs Tcherny. 'And where are you going to get the fruit from?'

'Someone at work has an allotment.'

'And the sugar?'

'Black market. Where else?' He said this in a matter-of-fact way, which was in line with his downbeat view that everything in the state of Britain – and everywhere else for that matter – was rotten.

'Do you think that's right?' said Rosa.

'And why not?' said Mr Tcherny.

'Because some people can't afford to get things on the black market.'

'Some people can afford things black market, some can't. There's always been people who can't afford things,' said her father. 'It's the way of the world.' He looked at her sharply. 'What's the matter with your neck?'

'Nothing,' said Rosa.

'She won't say,' said her mother.

'For God's sake,' said Rosa. 'Just because I've taken a fancy to wear a scarf.'

Her father looked surprised at this outburst. 'Well, if there's nothing wrong with your neck you won't mind us having a look.' And before she could react he had leant over and deftly plucked way the scarf and held it in his hand like a conjuror at the end of a trick.

'How did you do that?' her mother said. 'What's happened to you?'

'It's nothing,' said Rosa. 'Don't make a fuss.'

'You decided to strangle yourself?' said her father. 'And gave up half-way?'

Rosa sat silent. What should she say? 'It's nothing to do with you,' she said finally.

But Mr Tcherny was beginning to enjoy the role of chief interrogator. 'Did you hear that, Lena? Our daughter decides to try to strangle herself and thinks that it is nothing to do with us? Have you been seeing that mad boy again? The one that was taken away?'

'Who?'

'Charlie. Have you forgotten him so quickly?'

'No. I don't know what happened to him.'

'He was a poor creature,' said Rosa's mother. 'I felt sorry for him.'

'Yes,' said Rosa, glad of the diversion. 'I suppose I ought to ask his parents.'

'Don't get involved,' said Mr Tcherny. 'Sleeping dogs, as they say.'

Mrs Tcherny removed the plates and returned with some rice pudding.

'Oh well,' said Rosa's father. 'The Chinese have lived on it for thousands of years. By the way, how did you get that bruise on your neck?'

Rosa felt trapped. If she didn't tell them something they

would keep at it until things got nasty. 'We were playing about at work,' she said lamely.

'Of course,' said Mr Tcherny. 'Seeing who couldn't strangle the other first? Old English pastime. Morris-dancing, folk-singing, the hokey-cokey and strangling each other.'

'Oh, shut up,' Rosa shouted. 'If you must know, the man I work with went a bit mad. I'm not going back any more. I've given in my notice. I think I might get my proper job back now, with the other brother, Maurice, who's quite all right.'

Mr Tcherny was rolling a cigarette. It was a complicated business with a little machine, paper and a filter tip. He prided himself on the outcome, making it as near to a manufactured cigarette as possible. He lit the cigarette and smoked with satisfaction.

'This man', he said, 'who tried to strangle you. Is he mad?'

Rosa looked down. The whole business would have to come out. 'I think he might be,' she said. 'He seemed to be in a fit, like he didn't know he was doing it.'

Mrs Tcherny looked worried. 'Do you think he might do it again?'

'I don't know,' said Rosa. 'But I won't be there if he does.'

Mr Tcherny drew heavily on his home-made cigarette. 'Rosa,' he said quietly. 'Do you realize what you've said? You don't mind if he strangles someone as long as it's not you?'

'I didn't mean it like that,' Rosa mumbled.

'Well, that's what it sounded like to me,' said her mother.

'Look,' said Rosa. 'It's all over. I'm all right. Now let's forget all about it.'

Mr Tcherny stood up. 'I don't think we can. It sounds as though you've encountered a dangerous lunatic. And I think you have a duty to do something about it. If we were to hear of some other girl who's been strangled, I, for one, would never forgive myself.'

As Bernard had warned, the police had their hands full, but, as she was there, with her father as well, they had to take her statement. The statement was written by hand, by a sweating policeman who seemed as if he was not only unfamiliar with writing but with most of the English language. They took Bernard's name and address and said they would look into it. It was nearly dark when they left. Rosa's father took her into a pub and bought her a brandy.

'Messy business,' he said, 'but you had no option.'

It was a noisy pub, with servicemen and servicewomen on leave and determined to let everyone know it. The civilian population bought drinks for them as if they were glad they weren't one of them. Everybody knew that there were bloody times ahead, either at home or abroad. The Germans had caught Britain on the hop. The British didn't think that the enemy would turn so nasty so soon. In the tradition of fair play they expected that they would get fair warning. That's what had upset them more than anything. It was only eight o'clock, but there were sailors and soldiers reeling about, bumping into people, and flushed ATS with their collars open and ties askew. They were more drunk on excitement than beer, which was hardly strong enough to cause any insobriety. Outside the door were the redcaps, ready to sweep the worst cases up into a van.

Bernard had taken himself up to town. God knows what he was going to do now. He needed to think about this but not now. He needed a rest from thinking. All his plans had come to nothing. And the worst thing was that Maurice had arrived just as he'd got into an awkward spot with that girl. What got into him these days? Was it anger, frustration, lust? It was all those things, but they had been with him for a long time without previously bursting out into uncontrollable destructive impulses.

He slipped into the Windmill, a tiny little theatre at the back of Piccadilly Circus. It was the only place going for live entertainment. It was called *Revaudeville*, a little show that lasted about ninety minutes, which, after a performance and a short interval, started all over again, day and night, continuously. There was a piano and drums, comics and singers, two old men dressed up as women called Biddie and Fanny, but, most importantly, chorus girls, some of whom danced in a sketchy sort of way and others who were completely static and appeared to be nude, just staring ahead as though they didn't know anyone was watching. They appeared in practically every scene, with a bass singer whose shirt was open to show his body glistening with grease and who appeared variously as a desperate pirate, a lovelorn gypsy, a light-hearted romantic matelot and a swarthy Frenchman with memories of 'Gay Paree'. As a show it was a shambles, and the performers knew it – especially the comedians, who knew that they might as well be putting on shows for the deaf – but it was received with rapt attention by the audience that sat in darkness and seemed to be nailed to their seats and to have taken a vow of silence.

As the show finished Bernard crept closer to the front row. It was soon dark again and the nudes would be on, Britannia and La Belle France and the little Dutch girl, all with outstanding breasts, baring them with patriotic zeal for the men who might be dead next week without ever seeing a woman in all her naked glory.

After the second show Bernard felt stiff. There was little room between the rows. His long legs were cramped and aching. Reluctant as he was he knew he would have to move. As soon as he got up someone sidled into his seat. He moved to the exit, noticing the faces, from the brazen to the shamefaced. It seemed that nobody was enjoying themselves.

He walked further, to the shops, usually filled with foreign food but now looking sad with depleted stocks, and found one of his clients. The bookshop window was full of titles supplied by him: *No Pockets in a Shroud*, *The History of the Rod*, *Brother and Sister*, *The Rainbow*. It was a good selection, better than bloody Arnold Bennet. Maybe if he talked to Maurice he might get his old patch back. Maybe he shouldn't have tried to branch out on his own.

Somehow, without consciously making a beeline for it, he found himself outside the Hostess Club. He poked his head in the door. The place seemed quiet, deserted. He went into the bar. There were a few drinkers but no piano player or drummer. It was unnaturally quiet, more like a funeral parlour than a place for high jinks. He went to the bar.

'Quiet, ain't it?' he said to the barman.

'They've gone to the funeral,' the barman said.

'Funeral?'

'Bunty,' said the barman. 'You know. The blonde one. Deaf and dumb she was but always out for a good time. Bloody good sort she was.'

Bunty; it was an odd sort of name, maybe from a children's book, but somehow it suited her. Yes, she had been a good sort in her way. She'd put up with some of his nonsense. She was always bubbly and eager to please. He hadn't known she was deaf and dumb. That explained a few things.

'What happened to her?'

'A bomb.' The barman graphically described a bomb falling with two fingers shooting downwards and a low whistle. 'Smack. A direct hit.'

Bernard felt sick. This was a woman he had been with quite recently. He remembered the day he had brought Maurice, and he took Bunty upstairs, just to show Maurice how it was done. Of course, it was too much like real life for Maurice. It would have been all right if he had read about it in some French book.

Bernard found that he couldn't stay in the place. It had lost its sense of excitement. The war had caught up with it, neutralized it, rendered it ordinary and sad. Bunty's death might well be the death of the place. He could never go there again. He came out, experiencing a cold shiver, but outside didn't seem much better. The area devoted to gaiety seemed to have gone into mourning. People with set faces mooned about. A blight had settled on Soho. Maybe it would never be the same again. Blast the war. Stopping everybody's pleasure, making everything dull.

He made his way to Tottenham Court Road. He could get to Ealing Broadway and then catch a bus to his home. The time had come for a penitent telephone call to his brother. He got off the bus and walked towards his house. There was a policeman standing outside, chatting to a postman. What was this about? He stopped and turned back. Too late. The postman was pointing at him. The policeman was coming towards him. He felt that he ought to run but dismissed the idea as the action of a guilty man. He went ahead.

'Mr Green? Mr Bernard Green?'

'Yes,' Bernard replied, smiling a smile that strained credulity.

'It's nothing to worry about, sir. We'd just like you to come down to the station.'

'Oh,' he said. 'What about?'

'It's only a street away, sir.'

'Yes, I know,' he said. 'In Uxbridge Road.'

'That's right, sir. Can you get into the car?'

The car sped through the ordinary streets, terraces and some larger detached houses. The little front gardens seemed plain and drab. It was an area inhabited by hard-working artisans who lived plain, ordinary lives. He had seen them with their plain, ordinary wives, armholed to the shops, with baskets and bags and with not an ounce of joy between them. What would they think if they knew what he had been up to?

They put him in a small office, a cheerless room, nothing to read, nothing to see. There was just a table with a chair on either side. After what seemed like an age a chap in civilian clothes came in and sat down opposite him. He had a foxy face. He looked at Bernard and smiled as if he was just going to eat Red Riding Hood. The man was reading through some notes. Bernard couldn't tell anything from his expression. The man rubbed the side of his face. He had a world-weary air, as though he would never understand why people did the things they did.

'Mr Green,' he said finally. 'Mr Bernard Green . . . Would you mind giving me your address?'

Bernard swallowed hard. That damned Tcherny girl must have reported him. He'd lost his temper with her, but she hadn't come to any harm. He gave his address, his age, his business. It all seemed quite normal, like a visit to a new bank. Then suddenly it turned very serious.

'Did you know an actress called Gloria Grainger?'

My God, they'd put two and two together in double-quick time. 'No,' he said slowly. 'I don't think so.'

A expression of distaste and annoyance arrived on his questioner's face. 'Are you sure, sir?' he said, as if he knew Bernard was lying and so wasting his time.

'Think so,' said Bernard.

'Right,' said the man. 'I'm afraid you'll have to stay with us for a while. We'll be setting up an identity parade.'

Bert Penrose had been told that he would be fitted with an artificial leg. He would be sent to a centre in Richmond to be measured up. He was pleased to hear of some progress in his affairs, as he'd been feeling down lately, just sitting around, whiling time away, his life slipping through his fingers. Edie didn't come any more. He'd never really welcomed her visits, but she was somebody he knew and who knew him, which made him feel as if he belonged somewhere, had somebody. Without Edie's visits he became anonymous, just someone who was around. It was probably his own fault. He hadn't been very nice to her. Her white anxious face had got on his nerves. He couldn't help the way he was. She had been all right, had Edie. When they first met she was a pretty little thing, very shy and blushed easily, and he had enjoyed saying those things to her that turned her pretty cheeks red. The trouble was that he'd never had much of a job. He left school at fourteen with no exams behind him. He was only fit for manual labour. In the circumstances he hadn't done badly. He didn't know anybody, had no influence, just his final report when he left school, signed by the headmaster, saying he was honest, intelligent and industrious. He had drifted into the hotel business by answering an advertisement in the *Telegraph*. He had never been out of work, and now he felt useless. He'd be stuck in this place making poppies for Armistice Day or maybe sitting behind a cloakroom counter. He was never going to flower into a hall porter now. He thought about getting some paper and envelopes and writing to Edie, but, no, she'd turn up. That was one thing about Edie: however nasty, however critical, whatever he said, she always came back for more. She knew she was stuck with him – and, he supposed, he was stuck with her. All these fantasies he had about Bunty and other bits of stuff he'd seen about were never going to amount to anything now. In a way he was lucky he had Edie, despite her being nothing to write home about.

There were women, with home-knitted jumpers, straight skirts and set, kind faces, who came around with books and magazines or just to talk. They were all right. They smiled all the time like they had some secret key to happiness, but they weren't telling him. He could ask one of them to go and see Edie. Maybe she'd just given up on him. He hadn't been very nice to her when she came. Told her not to come so often. And now she didn't come at all. He'd managed to get into the solo school, but the silly buggers really didn't know how to play. Somebody had taught him how to play chess, and now he could beat anyone on the ward. He'd always been quick to pick things up.

Sometimes an 'old vic' came around, a fat old bugger with two chins over his dog collar who looked as if he drank holy water. He'd asked Bert if he had any plans for the future, and Bert just made a wry face. 'Oh, don't think it's all over,' the vicar had said. 'God still has a purpose for you.' In the end he'd had to tell him to piss off as he was getting on his nerves.

The food was all right but not very exciting. When he thought of the stuff he used to nick from the hotels, slices of duck and cream pastries that Edie used to wolf down, looking guilty, like a child. Once he got a whole cold tongue, calf's liver that went down like strawberries, pâté and a bloody goose down his trousers; now they kept asking him about his ration card. Edie ought to have brought it in. It looked as if he'd stopped smoking, mainly because he couldn't get any fags. It had been agony for a week, but now he had got used to it, although it left a void in his life. He had started carving things out of bits of Perspex. He did a ring first, which he gave to one of the nurses, and the other nurses ribbed her about it, but now he was making little pistols and daggers and trying his hand at a Spitfire. It might develop into something if he did them for Christmas crackers.

He could get himself to the toilet now and had developed a technique for getting in and out of the bath, although it had been better when the nurses did it, but they wouldn't always be there, and he couldn't see any particular thrill in Edie soaping him down. He wondered how they were getting on at number seventy-seven. Bunty, and Mrs Bennet, cantankerous old cow, and that snooty couple on the top floor. Oh Christ, there was that bloody old vic again, looking more miserable than ever.

'Bert,' he said. He'd never called him Bert before. 'I'm afraid I am the bearer of bad tidings.' Hell. Had he found out that there was no God after all? 'There was an indiscriminate raid last night. Bombs were just dropped without thought or reason. One of them was a direct hit on your house.'

'Number seventy-seven?'

'Yes. Unfortunately all the occupants were in their beds. They could have gone to the shelter, but they decided to take their chances. Your wife was one of the victims. I am most dreadfully sorry. The Lord will smite those who offend him.'

'Eh?' said Bert. 'Edie? Gone?'

'I'm afraid so,' said the vicar and started muttering prayers.

'Sod that!' Bert said angrily. 'That's not going to bring her back. You and your bloody church make me sick. What can you do, eh? Just stand there and let people get killed? Hasn't your God got any control over anything? He's supposed to be powerful, made the earth and everything in five days or something. Why doesn't he look after it?' He heard himself sobbing. 'Edie. What had she done, eh? Why sort her out?'

'I know how you must feel,' said the vicar. 'And I wish I had some answers. I know that in times like these we begin to question our faith.'

'Sorry, vicar,' said Bert. 'It's not your fault. But . . . it don't make sense, do it?'

'It is hard to see a pattern in all this,' said the vicar sorrowfully. 'It's not God who is killing people. It's men, who have turned away from Him.'

Bert Penrose was a heap of dejection. A man with a comical Charlie Chaplin moustache, a raving sexual appetite, now disabled, relying on his wife to pull him through and now finding that this prop had disappeared.

'What am I going to do now?' he said.

Bernard shuffled into line with the other men. There must have been ten of them. Talk about the long and the short and the tall. There were all sizes. Hardly any of them looked a bit like him. They were tall and thin, short and fat, smart and ragged. Some were wearing suits, some overalls. They all looked wary, as though they wished they hadn't been drawn into this pantomime. Nobody spoke. He was shoved into the line by a policeman, who then walked up and down like he was inspecting them. The bulbous man next to Bernard smelt of beer and farted loudly. Nobody laughed. It wasn't that sort of occasion. Bernard wondered who they were going to bring in. Surely not the Tcherny girl? That would be disastrous. Surely he was entitled to a solicitor. He had tried to ring Maurice but had got no answer. Not that Maurice would have been much help.

There was a shuffling outside, and the door opened. The plain-clothes man who had interviewed him led in a tall grey-haired man who looked vaguely familiar. The man looked distinguished, almost aristocratic, but there was something not quite right, as if he were playing a part, like an actor in country-house comedies or courtroom dramas. The detective led him along the row of men, who all stood stock still with stolid expressions of piety and respectability on their faces. There was a slight strain in the air, however; something important was going on here. When the man came to Bernard he gave Bernard a long, hard look. It suddenly came to him, in a flash of horror, that this distinguished-looking man in a long Melton overcoat was, in fact, the hall porter at Claridge's, the very man who had tipped him off about the gin and tonic parading as lemonade. He had seen Bernard in the bar with the actress; probably saw them leave together. Bernard settled his face into a stern scowl. The head porter had made his decision. He stepped forward and touched Bernard on the arm.

'You sure, sir?' said the detective.

The hall porter nodded. He didn't bother to go any further down the line.

'Thank you, gentlemen,' said the detective, and the men filed out. Bernard was left until last and was accompanied out by a policeman. Then it was back to the little room again. This time the questioning was not so polite.

'So you didn't know this lady, but you left together from Claridge's, after talking and drinking with her for around thirty minutes.'

'I felt sorry for her,' said Bernard. 'She was out of work.'

'But you said you didn't know her.'

'I didn't want to cause her any trouble. You know, with these well-known people scandal soon gets around.'

'And where did you go when you left the hotel?'

'Look,' said Bernard, 'this is a bit embarrassing. The fact is that she asked me for money. She was flat broke. I gave her a fiver and put her in a taxi. Please don't blow it about. It won't do her career much good, will it?'

'I don't think it'll do it any harm, sir. She's dead.'

'Dead? Good Lord. How? Was it an accident? A bomb?'

'No, sir. She seems to have been strangled in her own flat.'

Bernard was shocked. 'Really? Well, I'm blowed.'

The detective looked at him quizzically, as though he was evaluating his performance. 'How can we verify your account of putting Miss Grainger in a taxi?'

'I don't know,' said Bernard, scratching his head with bewilderment. 'That's what happened. All I can say.'

'I don't think it will be enough,' said the detective quietly. 'You see, there is evidence of a similar attack on a Miss Rosa Tcherny at your house in West Ealing.'

'Oh that. That was just larking about. Women like it, you know. The rough stuff.'

'Do they?' said the detective. 'Or is it you that likes the rough stuff?'

'Look,' said Bernard earnestly. 'I'm no angel, but strangling people, that's not my line. I could have had it off with her, but . . . The fact is, close up, I didn't fancy her.'

20

ROSA arrived early at St Paul's. It was strange that it was still standing in the midst of the general devastation. It stood proudly, surrounded by blasted buildings, water pumps and shattered shops. The other outpost that had survived was the Old Bailey, less than a quarter of a mile away. If these two pillars of the Establishment had gone it would have, in some way, been significant. The fact that the symbols of religion and law were still intact was reassuring.

It was a bright day towards the end of March, and the pigeons, to whom one day was the same as any other, scavenged in the churchyard for discarded sandwiches, bits of stale cake and biscuit crumbs. There were lots of people on the steps, as it was a popular meeting point. There was always a policeman around and people giving out religious tracts. There were also plenty of older men, looking dazed but defiant, wearing their Great War medals as though they were lucky charms against anything that might happen in the present. Rosa couldn't help wondering what had happened to Bernard. He was a thoroughly unpleasant man, but she didn't want to be responsible for him being arrested or something. If that happened she would have to go to court, and if that happened Bernard was bound to say that she led him on, then she would be in the papers as a scarlet woman, a tease who led men to the point of excitement and then screamed at the last minute. She wondered what Maurice would think of it all. He wouldn't want Green's mixed up in a scandal. If it had been up to her she would have let it go, but she knew that her parents were right to insist that she reported the incident.

There was a religious nut with a placard: 'Be sure your sins will find you out.' Rosa shivered. Would there be anything in the papers? She walked down the steps and bought the *Evening News* from a newsboy. She skimmed through it. No sign of Bernard. 'A new lead on dead actress' was the headline.

She thought of going into the ABC when she saw Jimmy

arrive on his bicycle. He looked flushed as he heaved it against the low wall and propped it up. She was surprised at how pleased she was to see him. She had missed his sulky face, his cocky manner that scarcely concealed the vulnerability of a young boy in an adult world. She walked down the steps.

'Hello, Jimmy.'

He seemed surprised to see her. 'I had a letter from Mr Maurice. He said I was to meet him here.'

'I know,' she said. 'I had one, too. Hope it's good news, eh?'

They sat together on the steps. Buses puffed around the base on their way into the City. Smart men in stockbrokers' suits walked by with cardboard gas-mask containers around their necks, which made them look faintly ridiculous.

'What have you been doing?' she asked Jimmy.

'Nothing,' he said. 'Do you think they're going to start up again, miss?'

'I hope so,' she said. 'I liked working there. Didn't you?'

Jimmy considered the question seriously. 'Yes. I suppose so,' he said reluctantly. 'I miss all those books. Didn't read them, but I liked looking at them. You know there was something in it, getting them in for people who wanted them.'

Just then they saw Maurice approaching, looking quite jaunty, with his bowler hat and umbrella.

'Sorry if I kept you waiting. Have you seen Harry around?'

Maurice ushered them into the teashop. There were some fairy cakes and bath buns. Maurice ordered the tea.

'Used to order a plate of mixed fancies,' he said. 'You know, éclairs, madeleines, cream horns and those coconut things with a cherry on top.' Maurice was in good spirits, nothing like the broken man they had seen only just a few weeks ago in this very shop. 'We've found a premises in Wandsworth Road. Most of the publishers have moved out of town. There won't be much collecting, Jimmy, but there'll be plenty for you to do. It won't be much like the old place. It'll take time to build up the stock, but I think we can tick over until this business is finished. There'll be a surge in reading after the war. People will want to get back to civilized life, put all this war nonsense behind them.'

Rosa looked doubtful. Maurice was looking forward to an end

to the war that was not yet in sight. Jimmy wasn't too pleased either. No collecting meant that he would be inside all day, no meandering trips around London, no sneaky half-hours with bread and dripping, no chance of cheeky glances with the girls on trade counters.

Maurice gave them the address of the new place, and Jimmy realized that it was the other side of the river. It was drab over there. Just shops and houses. No interesting buildings, no bustle, no art galleries to while away an hour, no theatres with photos outside, no buskers for the matinée performance, no hot chestnuts, no life at all. Compared with being in the centre of things, Wandsworth Road was a dump.

Maurice was explaining to Miss Tcherny about getting in touch with all their old customers, and Jimmy's mind had already left the scene. He was watching out for his bicycle, which they hadn't let him bring inside. It was propped up in the doorway. He went outside, just to stand by it. It was unlikely that anyone would pinch it. It was a junior size, not big enough for a man to ride off with. He glanced over to the steps. There were always people on the steps. They were a magnet. Maybe people felt safe there. Then he spotted a young girl with reddish hair. It wasn't ginger, it was copper-coloured and straight and hung down the sides of a pale, pouty little face, with delicious lips and a button nose. At first he couldn't believe it. It was another one of his daily fantasies, those illusions where he saw this Helen on every bus, every shop window and in a white nightdress in his dreams. He picked up his bicycle and wheeled it across the road, expecting the vision to evaporate before he reached it.

But, no, she was still there. He went up to her. 'Where have you been?' he said accusingly.

Helen sort of blushed and looked away. 'Reigate,' she said.

'I know that,' he said. 'You might have told me.'

'I didn't know myself,' she said. 'My mum got worried, about the raids.'

He couldn't be cross with her for long. He was already experiencing a warm glow of relief that he had found her. 'What are you doing here?'

'I've got to meet my old boss,' she said. 'About starting up somewhere else.'

'Me too,' said Jimmy. 'But I've finished. I'll wait for you.'

'All right,' she said, looking at him in a wondering kind of way.

'Then we can go to the pictures,' he said.

'All right,' she said meekly.

Rosa felt that she had to tell Maurice about her visit to the police station.

'Oh dear,' Maurice said, obviously dismayed.

'My parents said I ought to tell somebody, in case it happened again.'

'Of course,' said Maurice slowly. 'I can't blame them for that. I don't know what's happening to Bernard. I should have kept more of an eye on him. He was badly let down with his wedding. The girl more or less left him at the altar. He's not been really right since.'

'I was really frightened,' said Rosa.

Jimmy waited while Helen took her turn in the teashop. She came out looking thoughtful.

'All right?' said Jimmy.

'I don't know,' she frowned. 'They're moving to Hemel Hempstead.'

'Where's that?'

'It's out in the country somewhere. About thirty miles from London.'

'And are you going to go out there every day?'

'No. I'll have to live there, won't I?'

Jimmy's world, so recently recovered, was shattered once again. Everything seemed to be conspiring against him having a nice romance with Helen. 'Well, that's no good,' he said. 'Can't you get another job? Somewhere nearer?'

She looked earnestly at him. 'I don't want to go away,' she said simply.

'Well then,' he said decisively and marched her off, holding her with one hand and his bicycle with the other. He had an argument to get his bicycle on the bus, but eventually he was allowed to stand it up under the stairs. He took Helen to his house so that he could leave the bicycle there. There was no one in, so they were soon kissing like mad, she as eager as he. When they stopped for breath he gave her a glass of cream soda and showed her how to get all the bubbles out by putting a shilling into the glass, which made a fizz and left the drink flat.

Then they went to the Astoria, two sixpenny seats. It was still afternoon. There was an Our Gang short and a Popeye and a musical called *New Moon*, set in a strange part of America called Louisiana and was practically all singing. Jeanette MacDonald and Nelson Eddy sung solidly at each other and sometimes together, hardly stopping for breath. Not that Jimmy and Helen cared much what was going on. King Kong could have got into the stalls, a train crash could have spilt off the screen, wild animals could have been loose; none of these events would have broken through their romantic haze.

'Can you come out tomorrow?' he asked.

'Where to?'

'What's it matter? We could walk on the common or something.'

'All right,' she said contentedly.

They took the tram and rattled along, holding hands.

'I've got to go to Wandsworth Road,' he told her. 'I don't think I'll stick it.'

'I think I'll try to get something else,' she said. 'I don't fancy Hemel Hempstead.'

'I should think not,' he said stoutly.

The next day, a Saturday, they met on Clapham Common, which seemed to be crowded with young couples of a similar age and intention. They wandered slowly to the bandstand and then into the sparse wood, near the pond, and kissed in the dark patches, and he put his arm around her and drew her to him so he could feel her body close to his, smell her hair. The war was still on. God knows what was going to happen next. The whole town could be reduced to a brick shambles. People who had lived blameless lives could be killed, but, at this moment, everything was tender and precious. They were cut off from the world and all its troubles, cocooned in their own happiness. They had transformed a neglected piece of scrubland into a magical wood, the Forest of Arden no less. The real world was still alive, working its chemical and biological tricks on unsuspecting young people, who would have this moment of enchantment before life, in all its grimness, pushed their faces in the mud.

Detective-Inspector Thomas knew that he was up against it with Mr Bernard Green. Attempts had been made to find the taxi that was supposed to have picked up Gloria Grainger near Claridge's Hotel but with no result. He didn't believe a word that Green had told him. He could smell his guilt, but proving it was another matter. In interview, with quite aggressive questioning – because Thomas knew that his best hope was getting a confession – this Green character had appeared quite unperturbed, and despite all the tricks Thomas had sprung on him he'd stuck to his story. After putting the actress into the taxi Green himself had gone home by Underground. Thomas had checked that the trains had been running, hoping that a disruption in the service might have broken the alibi. Green had got out at Ealing Broadway and walked the rest.

Of course, nobody saw him. It was late at night. Everybody was indoors or in their shelters. Thomas knew that he was short of a concrete fact, which meant that he would have to let the suspect go. There could be a strategy in that, however. If Green then disappeared, it would prove his guilt. But somehow Thomas didn't think that this cool customer would do anything incriminating.

Bernard, brooding in his cell, thought he had managed pretty well up to now. To be honest, he really didn't remember doing anything to that woman. He remembered going with her to her flat and he remembered her being dead, but he didn't remember how it happened. It was as if he checked out of consciousness for a few minutes and some other wild creature took possession of his body. Frightening how easily it could happen.

Then Detective-Inspector Thomas got the call he was hoping for. A taxi driver, Bob Simmons, rang in. He'd taken a break in Chorley Wood with his family to get away frm the bombing and catch up on some sleep. He remembered picking up Gloria Grainger outside Claridge's Hotel. He'd picked her up there before, always with a different bloke. She had someone in tow that night. Would he remember him? He was doubtful. It was dark. Thomas scratched his face. They didn't call him 'Doubting Thomas' for nothing. Was it enough? Green was seen with the actress leaving the hotel. He was, in fact, the last person to see her alive. Without a confession it was circumstantial, but, yes, it was good enough to arrest him. He motioned to his sergeant, who collected a constable on the way to Bernard's cell.

Bernard looked up. 'Can I go now?'

The detective-inspector had put on his deadly face. 'Bernard Green, I am arresting you for the murder of –'

'Wait a minute,' said Bernard angrily. 'I told you, I put her in a taxi –'

'Yes,' said Thomas, 'but you neglected to tell me that you got in with her.'

Bernard's face was contorted into a snarl. He could feel the rage welling up inside him. He knew that he would lose control if he couldn't suppress it. 'You bastard!' he shouted and started towards the policeman, his face a mask of black rage. The constable grabbed him from behind, his broad arm across Bernard's throat.

'I have to inform you that you are not obliged to say anything . . .' Detective-Inspector Thomas monotoned.

Bernard had transformed into a snarling animal. The sergeant had to help the constable to hold on to him. 'Don't you sod me about,' Bernard was shouting. 'She asked for it. Wanted me to pay for it. Right at the last minute.'

'. . . but if you do say anything, it may be used in evidence against you. I think you've said enough,' Thomas added drily.

Betty didn't know whether she was full of shame or delight. Bertie had taken her by surprise, but she knew that she hadn't put up any resistance. The fact was that she had thoroughly enjoyed the experience. She knew that it wasn't fair on Stephen. He couldn't help being in the hospital, but if he had been at home nothing would have happened. Now that she was on her own she took what company was at hand. She liked Bertie. She liked his faintly artistic, black, curly hair. He knew about music and other things, the things that had always been missing from her life. She wondered what she would say when she saw him again. The piano shop was still closed, but he seemed to come every day.

And he came again the very next morning and rang her bell. He looked worried. Was he not sure of his reception perhaps? He came upstairs. He looked dejected.

'Is something wrong?' she said.

'The owner has decided to close the shop,' he replied. 'Without all the damage the place wasn't doing any business. Who's going to buy a piano when it might be blown up next week?'

'I think it's a lovely shop,' she said.

'It may be,' said Bertie, frowning, 'but not at the moment. The only things we can sell are sheet music and a few records. And that's not enough for a business of its size. You ought to see the books.'

They had moved easily into a new phase. His troubles were her troubles. After only one night of intimacy they had somehow become a couple. This was different from her life with Stephen, who never talked anything over with her and made her feel stupid when she asked a question.

'Never mind,' Bertie said. 'Not your problem. I'll have to find something else.'

'Of course it's my problem,' she said. 'We're friends, aren't we?'

He looked up and grinned. 'I certainly hope so,' he said, and she fell into her old trick of blushing.

'Why don't you start something on your own?'

'I haven't got the money. Pianos are very expensive instruments.'

'Never mind pianos,' she said. 'You're not selling any. Why don't you take a small shop and sell the music and records?'

Bertram looked at her, astounded. Maybe she wasn't so woolly-headed after all.

'I'd still need the rent and the stock.'

'Yes, but it's not like buying a piano, is it?'

'No,' he said. 'Buying pianos is a big investment, especially when nobody wants them.'

They drank tea, and Bertie spoke of small shops in an arcade near the market. It was the rough end of town, but those were the kind of people who bought sheet music and records.

'I'll go to the bank,' he said. 'See if I can raise the wind.'

'No need for that,' she said coolly.

'Why? Have you come into a fortune?'

'No, but I've got enough to start you off. Mind you, I'd have to come in with you. Be a partner.'

He was amazed. 'Well, I don't know,' he said. 'Whatever next?'

Betty smiled. Someone was taking her seriously. 'Drink your tea,' she said. 'We'll go and look.'

Charlie thought he'd counted all the bricks in his cell, and yet he couldn't be certain that he hadn't missed some. So this time he would write down the number of each wall separately. He'd found a bit of old slate so he could scratch the numbers down. He was working on this when a redcap sergeant came in with an officer with red braid on his shoulders. He was an old man with worried eyes.

'Attention!' shouted the sergeant.

'Just a minute,' Charlie said, 'I've just got to finish this', and he carried on counting.

'What are you doing?' the officer asked in a mild sort of tone.

'Counting the bricks,' said Charlie. 'I think I missed some last time.'

'Really,' said the officer. 'Can I ask for what purpose you are counting the bricks?'

'I don't know,' said Charlie. 'I'm not all right, am I?'

'Stand up, man, when you're addressing an officer,' the sergeant shouted.

'I am standing up,' Charlie said. 'I'm not sitting down, am I?'

The officer seemed immersed in thought. 'Court-martial?' he said.

'Oh yes,' said the sergeant, and then added loudly, 'sir!'

The officer looked at Charlie. 'Waste of time,' he said. He stared at Charlie, still busy with his counting. 'How would you like to work in the kitchen?'

'I don't know,' said Charlie. 'Might be all right.'

The sergeant looked as though he was about to explode. 'He was absent without leave, sir,' and the way he said 'sir' sounded like a threat.

A look of weary distaste appeared on the officer's face. 'I know all that, sergeant,' said the officer. 'I'm just trying to make the best use of the manpower we've got.'

After hopping about for a while Bert Penrose got the balance of his wonky leg. He needed the crutches, of course, but the fact of only having one real leg didn't stop him getting about. Then things began to move. A charity found him a ground-floor flat near Clapham Junction, and he moved in there, which was all right, what with the bustle of the market near by. And then he heard that the staff at Claridge's had had a whip-round and that the management had put in something on top, which pushed up the total to two hundred and forty pounds. The charity sent an adviser to see Bert, who suggested that he might start a flower stall outside the station. He liked the idea of being out and about, and took a brief delight in arranging the stall.

But there was a snag. You couldn't get many flowers. Flowers had been registered as non-essential goods, and that meant they couldn't be carried as freight on the railway. This restriction had led to a bizarre situation, where flower growers from as far afield as Cornwall took day returns and arrived in London with large damp suitcases and trunks full of roses and chrysanthemums, touting them around the flower shops like spivs selling black-market stuff.

In a funny way, Bert quite enjoyed the battle for survival. It was the only thing that kept him going. The truth of it was that he was finished. An awful blackness had entered his mind. When he saw the crowds scuttling into the shelters at the moan of the siren he viewed the unseemly panic with a kind of grim amusement. If they dropped another bomb on him it would only be finishing off what they had started. They'd had his leg and Edie, left him as a one-legged wonder, on his own to do his own shopping, cooking and not in a fit state to enjoy life as a man. What woman was going to look at him any more? And the worst of it was that he had stopped looking at them. He was there all right, with his little stall, and some people took pity on him, bought flowers they didn't want, let him keep the change, but he was dead inside, couldn't respond to kindness, was surly when confronted by a friendly face. People had begun to notice that he was a miserable old bugger. One, a red-faced plump woman whom they called Maisie, told him so to his face. The next time she saw him she went further.

'What are you going to do? Cheer up or cut your throat?'

The directness shocked him. He began to protest. 'I've lost me leg,' he said.

Maisie looked him directly in the eye. She knew she was using shock tactics, but she thought it might be worth the risk. 'Well, don't look at me. I ain't got it.'

Bert was stunned. It wasn't a joke, was it? Losing a leg was a serious business. It was for him. 'And that's not all . . .' He meant that he had lost Edie as well, but the woman wouldn't leave it like that.

'You mean you've lost the middle one as well.'

The reference to his cock tweaked something in his subconscious mind. So he was alive after all. 'Yeah,' he leered. 'That's all right, don't you worry.'

The Maisie woman winked. 'Glad to hear it,' she said.

And Bert smiled a twisted smile. He gave the woman a bunch of pink roses that had just arrived that morning from Kent. 'Here,' he said. 'Have those on me.'

'Well, thank you, kind sir,' Maisie said, and did a mock curtsy. 'Tell you what,' she said. 'If you get down to Clapham Common about six I'll stand you a half in the Plough.'

Bert's shoulders relaxed, for at just that moment he felt all right again. 'You're on.'

21

Helen got a job with Geoffrey Bles, which wasn't a big firm in the publishing world, and she said she hadn't got much to do. Jimmy, who was now in Wandsworth Road, knew that they could never now meet up in their lunchtimes. But they continued to see each other and went to the pictures at weekends, each feeling that this was pleasant enough but somehow not really satisfactory. It was Helen who broke the cycle. She had a married sister, who had a little baby called Fred, after his dad who was in the Navy. Fred senior was home on leave, and he and his wife Sheila wanted to go out together one evening, and Helen had got the job of looking after Fred junior while they were out. Helen said that Jimmy could come and sit with her. They would have a place to be which was private, and they could sit and talk. Jimmy was happy to fall in with these plans. After all, the parents couldn't leave a baby all on its own, what with air raids going on, and they needed some time out together, as husband Fred would be off to God knows where and they might not see each other again for months.

Jimmy arrived at the little house in Clapham Old Town. Sheila was an older version of Helen, the same silky copper hair, the fresh, pale face, the little nose. Fred was in his sailor's uniform. He was tall and bony, flat-faced with wavy hair. He kept bending his knees and hoisting his trousers up, and he walked with a roll as though he was still aboard ship. He kept winking at Jimmy as if they were in a secret conspiracy that they knew the women wouldn't understand.

'All right then, Jim?' he said and winked like a ventriloquist's dummy.

Jimmy found all this puzzling. And he found baby Fred a bit of an oddity. He had never been at close quarters with a baby. Fred junior seemed preoccupied with blowing bubbles which burst in his face and made him cry.

'He's all right,' said Sheila. 'He's been fed. Just put him down in a minute and he'll sleep.'

The mother and father were dressed up like they were going to get their photograph taken. Helen took the baby and they all said goodbye as though they were going on a long journey.

'We won't be late,' Sheila said. 'We're going to the Majestic, and then Fred will want a drink.'

Fred looked serious. 'You'll be all right. If Moaning Minnie starts, go under the stairs. Safest place.'

They went out. Jimmy looked at Helen. This was a new situation. Just the two of them alone – well, there was the baby, but he wasn't likely to say anything. Anyway, he was soon asleep in his pram, which Helen said was the best place in case they had to wheel him under the stairs.

A dreadful quiet followed, in which Jimmy wondered what was going to happen. Now they were free to act natural he was a bit worried. They couldn't go on kissing for about three hours, could they? Even kissing had its limits. He sat close to Helen on the settee and put his arm around her. She responded by going limp in his arms like he'd stabbed her with a poisoned dart. He kissed her, and her mouth was open. She seemed to have given herself up to him entirely, a sort of human parcel for which he was responsible. They kissed and kissed and got hot and sticky. They broke away, gasping.

'Phew,' he said. 'Hot in here.' He moved to the end of the sofa. Helen was staring at the floor.

'I suppose', she said haltingly, 'that you want to see me.' Jimmy felt uneasy. What did she mean? 'Well, look away. I'll tell you when.'

He looked at a series of grey castles on the wallpaper, listening to slight scurrying movements behind him.

'All right,' came a small voice. 'You can look now.'

He turned his head and was stunned to see that she had taken all her clothes off. 'Blimey,' he said and felt the onset of a moment of panic. Christ Almighty. He hadn't been prepared for this. Naked women never came into the sphere of the *Gem* or *Magnet*. Some of the fellows had sisters who played hockey, but they never appeared as anything but another version of boys. He didn't know how to deal with this new manifestation of their relationship.

'You can touch me if you like,' Helen said in a slightly severe manner, 'but don't go mad.'

He stared at her. She wasn't very big. Her little breasts were like rosebuds on the point of bursting into flower, her limbs slim and very white, a ginger triangle between her thighs. She was looking at him, waiting for some reaction, some encouragement, some acceptance. After all, she had taken the first step. It was his turn now. He moved closer to her. He could feel something strange happening to him, something in his trousers that had never happened before, at least not in front of another person. His cock had taken on a life of its own, outside his control. This was grown-up stuff. Should they, at their age, being playing these kind of games?

'Helen,' he said.

'What?'

'I don't know what to say. I've never seen anyone before . . . like that.'

She smiled a smug smile. She was on top of this situation. Despite the fact of them being the same age she felt at least two years older than him. The poor boy was embarrassed, and didn't she love embarrassing him.

'Your turn,' she said, and the poor boy went red. He was all right cuddling in the back row, kissing in dark corners, but when it came down to it he was a bit slow.

Relief came for Jimmy when Fred junior started making a choking sound. Helen picked the baby up and stroked his back, jogging him up and down. When he stopped choking he started crying, and then there was the spectacle of Helen, stark naked, walking up and down the room with the squawking baby. After a while the baby subsided and Helen put him back in the pram.

'Well,' she said, 'you've had your sixpenny's-worth,' and she started to put her clothes back on.

After that they sat in silence. Neither of them seemed to know what to say. It was clear that there had been a definite shift in their relationship. Helen had been willing to make a tentative step into the adult world, while Jimmy had hung on to his childhood. They both knew that things between them could never be the same again. When Sheila and Fred returned, Jimmy and Helen were sitting at opposite ends of the sofa as if they had had a row.

'Wasn't any trouble, was he?'

'No,' said Helen. 'He was very good.'

Jimmy walked her home to Battersea. It was quiet that night. Nothing threatening in the sky, but momentous movements on the ground between the two young people. When they said good night, he kissed her, but there was no warmth in her lips. They didn't make any arrangements to meet up again, and they never did.

Betty was pleased with the way that life was shaping up in Balham. Bertie had found a shop near the market, and she had given the money for the first month's rent and enough to buy the stock. For the moment Bertie was giving his services free. She still had to make the Greenline trips to Caterham to visit Stephen. As time went on Stephen began to look thinner and paler, and she found she was unable to engage him in conversation. And there was a funny smell about him, maybe caused by the stuff they were giving him. The poor dear looked weak and exhausted all the time. She didn't tell him about the new shop or about Bertie, as she didn't want to worry him, although Bertie came with her on a Wednesday when it was half-day closing, waiting in the grounds until she came out. She found Bertie was quite good company. He didn't get on with his wife, who was always wanting things they couldn't afford. They had lots of rows because the wife attributed their low state of affluence to Bertie's lack of ambition and get-up-and-go.

In fact, Bertie did have ambition, ambition for their joint venture, which had started to go quite well. The business partnership meant that Betty and Bertie were drawn together. They discussed future plans. Bertie was surprised that this seemingly dumb girl, who would never appreciate the finer things in life, had an acute business brain. She saw things in black and white, which were the colours of accountancy. Bertie installed a piano in the shop and began playing some of the sheet music, which attracted a crowd of dreamy housewives, who bought the music as though they were taking home a piece of Bertie. In these drab days, any piece of glamour was a tonic. Betty suggested that he started giving regular performances, at two o'clock and four, and the crowd in the shop was spilling into the street at the appointed hours.

The breakthrough came when one of the music publishers came around to ask if Bertie would play all their songs and ignore all the others. Bertie was given an offer of increased commission on sales, but Betty insisted that he was paid extra as a performer. 'It's taken you years to learn to play like that,' she said.

But all the time the shop was doing well Stephen was sinking further. It pained Betty to see him. She cut down the number of visits to once a week, and each time she was shocked to see how he had deteriorated in that short time. One of the nurses had shaken her head as she came out of the ward as if it was all over bar the burying, so when Stephen died Betty wasn't too surprised. To her he had died when he first went into the place. She had prepared herself for the inevitable, built a new life before the old one was properly ended. She knew now that she had married too soon, too young. She had had no experience of the world, had no idea of her potential, no idea that people like Bertie were around who could offer true companionship on a more equal basis.

It was a quiet funeral. Stephen's parents couldn't come down because the journey might be too much for them on the slow-moving, overcrowded trains. A couple of chaps from Stephen's firm attended, but it was a ramshackle affair. A short service and tea and cakes in a local bookshop. She was glad when it was all over and she was left with Bertie, especially when he said he was going to leave his wife. He called it 'a trial separation', but Betty knew in her shrewd way that the break would be final.

So in 1939 the City of London and its environs had looked much as J.B. Priestley left it in *Angel Pavement* when it was published in 1930. Dank, with often the whiff of the Thames in its mist, stern Victorian buildings, brooding tabernacles of finance and insurance with liveried footman and smartly bobbed shorthand typists, comfortable teashops, tree-lined squares, with parcels moved by horses and carts, honking buses with no cover on the upper decks where men in smart suits pulled a fitted tarpaulin over their knees when it rained. It was a sound, serious place with its particular customs and charms. But by the end of 1940 it was a cowed, shabby place, with its business arrangements in total chaos, with scars and gaps in its fabric, awkward holes in its roads, battered and shattered beyond repair, with its citizens bewildered, roaming the streets without purpose, trying to affect an air of normality, knowing that things would never be normal again.

And amidst this upheaval the people of London tried to go about their business, turning a blind eye, cheering themselves with the thought that they were the only survivors of a collective madness.

After a spectacular trial, avidly reported, Bernard was sentenced to death for murder. Maurice failed to revive the business, and after a time Green's closed down, Maurice and Bella filing for post-war compensation.

Charlie spent the rest of his war not knowing whether he was mad or not. He was categorized as the lowest order in the Army's scale of usefulness. So he scraped zinc pots with sand, peeled mountains of potatoes, cleaned fatty ovens.

Rosa Tcherny went to Wandsworth Road for a short while, but she didn't stay at Green's when she found that she was pregnant with Charlie's baby.